"Frank DiBianca knows his way around a sci
packed novel will have the reader racing
Lana, and Dan's roommate, Chumbo, to fol
hapless but lovable Daniel Butler, who's disappeared at the hands of
the enigma, Eos. I thoroughly enjoyed the race."

—Sherri Stewart, editor and author of *A Song for Her Enemies*

"Frank DiBianca, a new author with a fabulous first book intertwines
mystery, romance, and leading-edge technology in *Laser Trap*. Well-
developed characters with an attention-grabbing plot. A nonstop
page-turner."

—Susan Reichert, editor-in-chief (ret.) of *Southern Writers
Magazine* and author *of God's Prayer Power*

"Frank DiBianca's debut novel, *Laser Trap*, is a laser beam of
enjoyment starting on page one and carrying the reader through
to the last page—an end that comes well before the reader is ready
to leave the world DiBianca has created. Using a skilled hand, he
introduces a cast of flawed, one-of-a-kind characters to walk us
through the implications of such a dangerous discovery, drawing
the reader deep into the devastating realm of what-if possibilities.
With plenty of sweet romance and a dog named Angel, this story
is wrapped in a message of redemption and hope that will have
readers eagerly awaiting his next book."

—Lori Altebaumer, author of *A Firm Place to Stand*

"Those who appreciate stories with a strong science-based plot that
captures the lucrative and cutthroat business of being first to market
with a new intellectual property will find plenty to like in *Laser
Trap*. But this is also a story of friendships, budding romances, self-
reflection, and godly faith that withstands testing, as well as faith
that is sending out its first fragile shoots. The story's tension comes
from characters with strong moral certitude juxtaposed against
others who will abandon their ethics and even their humanity to
ensure a big payout."

—Judy Karge, author of *A Light in the Dark: Reflections on Proverbs*

"The debut novel, *Laser Trap*, by Frank DiBianca, might surprise many, and be forewarned, more will likely follow. He skillfully weaves a medical, technological, business thriller with a non-syrupy romance that has a unique twist. The mix of clever word plays with scientific terminology provides a captivating story that will engage your mind. *Laser Trap* provides a fine read, one well worth your time."

—Tim Riter, author of *Outdoor Paths, Sacred Trails: Poems of a Traveling Man* and *God, a Motorcycle, and the Open Road*

"Graduate student Dan Butler has a lot going for him, but he has a problem. Dan chokes every time he tries to talk with a young woman. Not good for a guy who's looking for the love of his life. Dan's crippling shyness soon becomes the least of his worries when an organization targets him to hijack his laser research for nefarious purposes. *Laser Trap* takes readers on a high-stakes ride with plenty of suspense, friendship, and even love along the way. Highly recommended!"

—L. K. Simonds, author of *Stork Bite*

"*Laser Trap* is an intriguing read for anyone who enjoys mystery and romance with a little espionage thrown in. Frank has managed to incorporate mechanical engineering in a way to trap one into wanting to discover why there is such an interest in lasers."

—Brenda W. Morris, author of *Snap Shots from the Past*

LASER
TRAP

LASER TRAP

Frank DiBianca

Birmingham, Alabama

Laser Trap

Iron Stream Fiction
An imprint of Iron Stream Media
100 Missionary Ridge
Birmingham, AL 35242
IronStreamMedia.com

Library of Congress Control Number: 2022933934

Cover design by Jonathan Lewis / Jonlin Creative

ISBN: 978-1-64526-368-5 (paperback)
ISBN: 978-1-64526-369-2 (e-book)

1 2 3 4 5—26 25 24 23 22

BOOK ONE

Chapter 1

Friday, August 16

What's wrong with that man?" J. J. "Eos" Puller growled to himself as he neared the parking lot on Alabama Avenue. He was frustrated and angry about being jerked away from his tour of university research seminars by his boss. And with under twenty-four hours' notice, no less. Luckily, he'd finished his business at UNC-Chapel Hill, attending a public seminar on laser research before he left. Since he couldn't get a flight reservation, he'd had to make the four-hour drive to their meeting place, a hiking trail in Fort Circle Park, in the DC area.

He parked his rental car and walked to the specified meeting point inside the park. After rounding a turn in the trail, he spotted Darrel "Sirius" Holden sitting on a log by the side of the hiking path, smoking a cigar.

Sirius looked up at the sound of Eos's footsteps and greeted him with a slight twist of his hand. "How was the trip, J. J.?"

"Not bad, Si, if you like driving alone for four hours in heavy traffic on I-85," Eos answered, as he parked himself on the log and ran a tired hand through his dark hair. "Now that we're absolutely isolated, maybe the CEO of StarWay Labs will condescend to tell his indentured servant about the meeting he had with the boys from the far side?"

3

Sirius reached inside his jacket and retrieved a metal flask. He handed it to Eos, who took a long swallow. "First, I want to hear what you found out in Chapel Hill, and then I'll update you on some big breakthroughs in the Vibricity Project," Sirius said. He took the flask back and drained it.

Eos turned his body to face his boss directly. "I heard a colloquium at UNC on laser physics by a professor . . . W. W. Kensington. He's studying the optical properties of doped yttrium oxide at temperatures near absolute zero."

"How many dopants?"

"Only one."

"Dr. Powers is pretty clear we need three."

"I know, I know," Eos said. "After the talk was over, I went up front and asked Kensington if he'd be interested in studying three, or at least two dopants. He said no. Too many possible combinations, and company-funded research wouldn't help his career. The university wants federal grant money. So do the other universities I've been to so far."

Sirius groaned and shook his head. "Where else are you going?"

"I plan to head to the West Coast next week for three stops. Two universities and a federally funded lab. Then I'll fly to Virginia the following week to catch a laser seminar at Quincy University. They have a small project that uses laser beams in yttrium oxide. And get this—they use two dopants! Close to what Powers wants. Should be interesting."

A young man and woman jogged around the bend, and Sirius diverted the conversation to football until the pair had passed.

"Look, J. J., you have to come up with something soon. Halsey Powers, our physics genius, has been on the money twice already. Do you know her biggest hit, the Xanadu 3-D digital device, has earned over 15 percent of the cumulative twenty-year income of StarWay Labs?

"We had to borrow a bunch of patented electronic elements and some patented software, but who cares? The owners will never know. Halsey designed it for Asia Group Three, and they paid us forty million for it. We added a huge premium for the risk we were taking for the illegal components, and AGT paid it without a hiccup. We never found out what they use it for."

"Right. We shoot bullets in the air. Where they land—not our affair."

Sirius frowned. "All right, Shakespeare, let's get back to Halsey and her Vibricity Project. That's why you're going to all these seminars."

"No kidding. I've heard most of her seminars at the lab over the past two years. She keeps telling us that crystals like yttrium oxide doped with three elements can create these vibricity zones that store energy. Right? And, if you run a laser beam through the crystal, the zones create more light, making the power of the beam increase big-time. Right?"

"That's what she says." Sirius rubbed his hands together. "We've discussed all the, shall we say, benefits that arise."

"Yeah," Eos interjected. "Blasting out tunnels, cutting metals, clearing trees and obstructions for road-building, laser-induced nuclear fusion. And dozens of other things that can help people."

"I'm interested in money," Sirius exclaimed. "Big money, not people. We need lasers with *huge* power!" Sirius punched an arm skyward. "For things like military weapons. Antiballistic missile systems, anti-tank weapons, antipersonnel, destroying enemy buildings, you name it. Trillions spent on that. Another blockbuster—digging deeper oil wells. Crude oil production is another multitrillion dollar operation.

"Look, J. J., business is business. If we can pull off this vibricity stuff, it will be our biggest coup ever."

"OK, I get it. But we have two nasty problems. One: Powers still doesn't know how big the power increase is, and two: which elements make good dopants. Why have we been working on this for two years if she's only eked out a speck of beam energy increase?"

"That's why we're meeting like spooks in the woods," Sirius snorted. "Halsey just made some theoretical breakthroughs in her vibricity model. Now she says the power increase can be up to a thousand times bigger, maybe ten thousand or more. She believes at least two of the best dopants should be lanthanide elements. There are only fourteen of these metals, so that reduces the number of possible combinations."

"That's fantastic, Si!"

"Now wait till you hear this. When I told some of our prospective overseas customers about this, even without divulging which elements, their mouths fell open. Vibricity lasers are going to give them access to power beyond anything they've seen before, and they're ready to pay fantastic amounts. The highest offer so far is a hundred million dollars, if we meet their specs.

"I'm counting on you, J. J., to find something. If you do, we'll do whatever we need to get our hands on it. We go straight for the jugular vein!" Sirius stood and stomped on his cigar for emphasis. "That's it for now."

Sirius put his hand on Eos's shoulder as he gave him a devilish smile. "And to say thanks for the long drive, I'm going to take you to dinner. I know a French restaurant in DC with food and wine that will melt that frown right off your face."

Chapter 2

Even the best foundation makeup wouldn't cover everything. "Stop feeling sorry for yourself!" Lana Madison stared at herself in the bathroom mirror and sighed. *So what if all my color hasn't come back yet? But what a job you did making my scars disappear, Daddy.* She studied her face and neck in the mirror and looked down at her hands. As opposed to her head and neck, the makeup didn't erase the pink areas on her hands. They were constant reminders of Jimmy's death and the guilt she still bore.

Lana replaced the bottle of foundation makeup on the vanity and picked up her concealer. She dabbed some on the remaining discolored areas of her body. *Thank God I had my arm over my eyes.* After finishing her daily routine, she moved into her apartment's walk-in closet and scanned the clothes in the table tennis–sized room.

What to wear? Slacks or a skirt? Lana looked away from her clothes. "Will I meet any decent guys at the masked icebreaker?" she murmured. "Or just the usual body-hunters? Will I ever find someone who loves me for who I am?" She coughed. "And to top it all off, I'm still getting over laryngitis."

OK. Back to the clothes. Lana picked out a sky-blue turtleneck that matched her eyes and pulled it on, then picked out a pair of navy slacks. After dressing, she twirled. *Good to go.*

But where was her life going? Mom had been dropping hints about her lack of socializing. Wasn't she allowed to find the man of *her* choice and *when* she chose to? Right now, getting a good start on her graduate program was more important than men. But what if she failed in her research endeavors?

Lana glanced at her watch again and took a deep breath. She grabbed her mask and headed for the door.

No faces. I can do this! Daniel Butler breathed an audible sigh of relief. But his damp underarms and parched mouth undercut his resolve. He sucked on a peppermint. *Relax, man. Lord, please get me over this inhibition with women. The masks will definitely help.*

Several hundred people wearing gray, full-face masks filled Quincy University Hall. From where Dan stood, everyone's face looked identical.

Dan folded his hands and lowered his head. *Lord, You know how many years I've been praying about this. Help me find her. Not because I deserve it, but because You are good.*

Today was Campus Awareness Day. He'd signed up for this Mask and Meet event where people were paired by computer. Participants had filled out an online form, specifying personal and partner information and the desired number of twenty-minute meetings.

Dan took a deep breath and pulled out the printed sheet showing the ID letter and contact point for his first meetup. Her letter was *V. Table* 67.

He found the right table and a young woman wearing a *V*.

Wavy, dark-blonde hair. Good figure. Maybe five-seven or -eight—perfect height. That light blue pullover and dark blue slacks look great on her too.

Dan pointed to his ID badge with a big *T* on it. He held out one of his cards with his identifier, *T314,* on it.

"Hi, V. I'm T. Don't you love getting so personal?"

She laughed, her voice breaking, and handed him her card labeled *V159.* "Hi, T. It's nice to *almost* meet you. Shall we walk around outside? It'd be a lot quieter. Or we could catch a little *TV*?"

Dan chuckled at her play on their code names. "I'm gonna enjoy this."

They stepped out together into the warm August day and into a crowd of like-minded pairs pouring out onto the walkways around University Hall.

I'll bet you're either coming down with, or getting over, something," Dan said. "You sound a little *hoarsey*."

V tipped her head. "Are you saying my voice isn't *stable?*"

"Neigh. Neigh."

V gave Dan a little shoulder bump.

"Why don't we get away from the traffic?" she suggested. "But let's remember to turn around in . . . eight minutes."

"Wow. My M-and-M partner is a math whiz. No calculator. Impressive."

V snickered. "Be careful, Mr. T, or we may get back sooner."

"I'll be good. Y'think everybody follows all the rules they gave us? No names. No identifiers or contact information." He turned and gazed at her mask.

"Well, I love suspense, don't you?" V's soft voice soothed Dan, and he relaxed.

"I think you're right about that. But it's better to know who you're talking to." Already feeling protective toward her, he moved between V and the curb.

"A real gentleman." V sighed. "Back to the rules. You know the code numbers, so you can contact a partner online. I guess they don't want to be responsible for personal information. Email addresses. Phone numbers."

Dan turned and leaned toward V. "Can't blame them for that, can we? Wow. Isn't it awesome to live in the Piedmont? I love the hills and valleys. Inhale that late summer fragrance."

V moved closer to Dan. "I did. And I like your Polo aftershave."

"Thanks. V, I'm usually not this poetic, but—" *Should I say it? If I blush, she can't see it.* "Your scent reminds me of a Georgia peach orchard blooming in the spring."

"That's very sweet, T. Ooh, my favorite—'sweet tea.' And peach, no less. We're in the groove today," V said with a lilt in her voice. As they walked past a man riding a mower, she asked, "Smell that grass? I read that the odor of injured plants is a defense mechanism."

"Against what?"

"Against what's eating the plant. So, when a caterpillar starts munching away, its saliva makes the plant give off odors. The odors attract bugs that eat the caterpillars. How cool is that?"

"Wow. Plants are smarter than bugs," Dan replied. "I'll tell my roommate. He's a biologist. A zoology student to be precise. By the way, I asked for grad students. Are you one?"

"Yes, my first year after my MS, but we're not supposed to be more detailed than that. How about you?"

"It's my fourth, but I still have a way to go to finish my—oops. Almost forgot the rules."

"You mentioned Georgia. Is that your home, or are you from Virginia?" V asked.

"Yep, I'm from here, but I stayed with an uncle in Savannah for a few months. I graduated from UVA six years ago."

"I was a Wahoo too," V said. "We're from Cedarwood Falls. It's halfway between Quincy and Charlottesville. A thirty-minute drive from here."

Their conversation turned to outside interests. His about hiking and hers, volunteerism.

"What else should we talk about?" V asked.

"I'll answer your question with another one. Why are we here? The whole world."

"I asked Mom that when I was seven. I'll never forget. She said, 'God made me to know Him, to love Him, and to serve Him in this world and to be happy with Him forever in the next'."

"Your mom is my kind of lady," Dan replied.

V glanced at her watch. "Uh-oh, looks like our time is up, and there's University Hall."

"That was wonderful," she said, moving still closer to him. "Did I give you my card?"

Dan grinned and pulled her card out of his pocket and held it up. "You did, and here it is. But I sure would like to see the person behind the mask." His sigh was soft and wistful.

V touched his arm and waved. He stared at her dwindling form until she reentered the hall.

Three tiresome meetings later, Dan left the building, stopping to check his partners' ID cards.

Four meetings—three duds. V had it all. Smart, classy, easy on my nerves. He pulled the cards out of his pocket. He was short two partner cards and still had two of his own.

No V! Ugh, I gave her card and B's to the other two girls. What was her contact number? He banged his forehead with his fist. *Idiot!*

Dan rushed back to the almost empty hall. *Gone.* He grabbed his head and groaned.

Chapter 3

Saturday, August 17

Mother, please tell me what's going on." Lana laid her coat and purse on a chair in the den of her parents' home in Cedarwood Falls, where she'd arrived several minutes earlier. "You said you were having some friends over for dinner. You didn't mention the Van Burens. Especially Harrison. You know what happened in school. How he wouldn't take no for an answer." *How he gave me the deepest wound of my youth, next to my loss of Jimmy!*

"There's no problem, sweetheart. After all, he's an adult now. Besides, Constance asked me if they could bring Harrison along, and I agreed. What was I supposed to tell her?" Ann Martina Madison brushed away lint from Lana's shoulder.

"*Her*? What were you supposed to tell *me*?" Lana pulled away, heat rising in her face.

"Let's get back to our guests, dear. Good heavens, you scooted me out of the living room almost as soon as you arrived. Can we talk about this after the Van Burens leave?"

The Madison women returned to the living room, where Lana's dad, Dr. James Madison, the mayor of Cedarwood Falls, and his family were chatting.

Constance Van Buren, a Cedarwood Falls town commissioner, leaned forward. "Well, Lana, you look marvelous. It's been ages since we've seen you. I'm sure you still remember Harrison from your school days here."

"Thank you, Mrs. Van Buren. It's so nice to see you and the mayor again. And yes, I still remember Harrison quite well." She turned toward the young man and smiled politely.

After the usual chitchat over appetizers, the party moved to the dining room. The seating arrangement for dinner was well thought out. Ann and James sat at the ends of the table. Constance and Theodore Van Buren occupied one side of the table, and the two younger people took the empty seats on the other side.

While their parents discussed the latest happenings in Cedarwood Falls, Lana and Harrison sat in silence. All she could think about was the Mask and Meet. *Will T contact me? He pulled out my card.* His image confronted her wherever she moved her eyes. *So tall. Thick black hair. Those piercing blue eyes. Powerful build.*

Clara Tinsley, the Madisons' cook and housekeeper, wheeled in the steaming food and placed it on the dining room table.

"Wow, Clara, this looks and smells scrumptious. Thank you so much," Lana said, rubbing her hands together and smiling.

"You always were the kind one, Miss Lana. I hope y'all enjoy everything now."

Dad said the blessing. Short but sincere, as usual. They all said amen, except Harrison.

Lana stopped toying with her silverware, put her napkin on her lap, and looked at Harrison. "It's been a while, hasn't it? What've you been doing for the past six years since we graduated from good old Cedarwood High?"

"I got my BA in business administration and traveled for two years teaching English. I just started as an assistant-in-training to the president of the Cedarwood Falls First National Bank. My mother said you were studying biomechanical engineering at Quincy U. What's that?"

Lana winced. "It's actually called biomedical engineering. We use engineering and math to solve problems in human health."

"For example?"

"Well, like designing implantable insulin pumps, heart and brain monitors, artificial joints, CT scanners. Things like that. I'm doing my graduate research on artificial skin."

"Oh." Harrison reached for a roll and the butter, then the water pitcher.

Lana squeezed her lips. *Yeah, you really look interested in my research.*

"Lana, you're all work and no play," Harrison said. "You need some R and R."

Why does he care about that? I'll stick to the weather.

After everyone finished eating, Clara cleared the table for dessert. Mom stood and tapped her glass with her dessert fork.

"Let's have some fun," Mom said. "Dr. Feingold, James's former colleague in plastic surgery, asked us to test a board game his daughter developed. It's called I Think I Know."

Lana tightened. *Uh-oh. Mom's cooking something up. Better get out of here.*

"Mom, this has been a wonderful dinner, and I enjoyed spending time with the Van Burens, but I need to finish studying for an exam." Lana pushed her chair back.

"Oh, come on, dear. It's only seven thirty. Will you stay if we just play until eight o'clock? Six people make the perfect group size to test the game, and I'd hate to disappoint Susan Feingold." Mom would've made a fairground huckster seem shy.

Hearing no more objections, her mother turned and picked up the game box from her magnificent dark-cherry buffet. She placed the game board at the center of the table and put three pawn-shaped pieces of different colors on the start space of the square track. In the center of the board, she set a box of game cards with a hinged lid.

"To speed things up, we'll play as three teams with one marker for each team. The senior Van Burens get the red piece; the senior Madisons, white; and the young folks are blue. We'll go clockwise around the table, starting with Theo."

Mrs. Van Buren waved her hand. "There are no dice. How do you know where to move?"

"Good question, Constance," answered Mom and put her hand on her friend's. "At your turn, you take a card from the card box, and it tells you how far to move, depending on your answer. If you know the answer, you say, 'I think I know.' But don't worry if you forget that. If you're not sure, you pass. Be careful, because if you guess wrong, you have to move backward two squares. First team around the board wins. Everybody ready?"

The mayor took out a card and read it aloud. "Which is the largest ocean in the world? Ooh, could it be the Pacific Ocean?" Turning over the card, he added, "How about that!" and with a smirk tossed the card on the table. According to the number on the card, he moved the red Van Buren piece forward two squares.

Mrs. Van Buren took the next card and read, "Who was the fourth president of the United States?" She winked at Mom and guessed, "John Quincy Adams." But the correct answer on the underside of the card was James Madison, so she had to move the red piece backward two squares to the start space.

Mr. Van Buren looked at her and folded his hands. "Tough question, wasn't it?" Everyone burst out in laughter as he nodded at their hosts. Even Mrs. Van Buren gave a little snicker.

"Well, dear," he said, "whenever we play as a team, we always end up where we started, don't we?"

Dad put down his glass of tonic water and chuckled. Everyone else kept quiet.

The commissioner turned toward her husband with a light snigger. "Well, dear, that's because *your* question was *so difficult.*"

Everybody hooted and Mom even clapped.

The game moved along. Several rounds later, the blue marker was five squares ahead of the other two, and Harrison had just read a question.

Lana looked at the board and frowned. *The mothers are deliberately giving wrong answers. Why do they want us to win?* The large black letters on the box top proclaimed I THINK I KNOW. Lana muttered, "Yeah. I do, too, and I don't like it."

"Sorry, did you say something, Lana?" Harrison asked, turning to her. "Or were you going to answer my game question?"

"No, just thinking out loud."

When the grandfather clock chimed on the hour, Lana and Harrison were still three squares ahead, despite Lana purposely missing two easy questions.

Mom stood and tapped her glass. "Time's up. I have a prize for the lucky winners." She reached into the game box and handed Harrison an envelope.

When he opened it, his faced brightened. "Cool. A gift certificate for two at the Quincy Heights Panorama Restaurant. Lana and I have a lot of catching up to do, don't we?"

Lana turned to Harrison. "We sure do," she answered flatly.

Mom sat again and the chatter resumed, but Lana was no longer ready to leave. *Gotta stay and have it out with Mom. Ooh!*

Harrison wore a weird smile. "Did you hear the one about the pregnant woman who—"

"I think I left the freezer door open," interrupted his father. "We better get home."

Following some brief closing pleasantries, the Madisons walked their guests to the foyer. After the front door closed, Lana herded her mom straight to the den while Dad retreated to his study. Mom dropped into a lounge chair, but Lana remained standing.

"Mother," Lana said, "what did you do to me? Why not books or something?"

"But remember, darling," her mom answered, "I didn't know who was going to win, did I? I wanted a special gift any of the couples—however you want to say it—would enjoy."

Lana huffed in exasperation. "How could you not know, the way you and Mrs. Van Buren kept getting amnesia when your turns came up? I'm not stupid, Mother."

"Lana, the Van Burens of Cedarwood Falls would be the ideal family for you to become part of. Why don't you give Harrison a chance? Get to know him better."

"Harrison? I know him plenty well enough." Lana approached her mom and took her hand. "I want to find a *man* to love and marry someday, not an upper-crust *family* to ally with. How do I get out of this arranged date without causing hurt feelings and a strain in your friendship with the Van Burens? Ooh!"

"Well, dear, if you're so adamant about it, I'm sure you'll think of something." Mom rubbed her jaw. "Why don't you tell him you have a boyfriend?"

"What?" Lana dropped Mom's hand. *Yeah, let's see if my latest prospect comes around.* "You know I won't lie my way out of this. I'll go out with him this *one* time, but only if you *stop* trying to find me a husband. Is that a deal?"

Mom raised her fingers and nodded.

"Oh, and another thing," Lana said. "You'd better tell Susan Feingold she needs to check out Trivial Pursuit. It has a lot in common with I Think I Know. It's funny we're talking about Trivial Pursuit. Isn't that what this dinner was all about?"

Her mother stood and kissed Lana's cheek. "I want you to be happy and comfortable, darling, not starry-eyed in love. You're my only child now." Tears welling in her eyes, she put her hands on Lana's shoulders and gazed at her.

"I know, Mom. I still miss him too." Lana put her arms around her mother. "But I have my own life to live. I'll find Dad on the way out. Good night and thanks for dinner."

She kissed her mother's forehead and hurried out of the den, looking back as she passed through the doorway. "Remember. One date. And don't expect my feelings for Harrison to change."

Chapter 4

Late in the evening, Dan sat with his roommate, Chumbo, in the den of their shared apartment.

"Hey, Chumbo, I've got a question for you. An important one."

"Which is?"

"Were you at the Mask and Meet yesterday?"

"Are you serious? I don't want my women behind any masks when I meet them."

"Well, *I* went. *And* I met someone I really liked. Her code name was V. But I accidentally gave her ID card to one of my other partners. I did everything I could to find her. Went to Student Affairs. They can't give out information about other students. I contacted my two other partners whose cards I still had. One of them said she found a card with a V on it, but she threw it out."

Chumbo frowned and asked, "Isn't there some other way to find her?"

"No. We couldn't share personal information, so there's no way to track her down."

"What do you want *me* to do?" Chumbo spread his arms apart and leaned back.

"I can't believe how much I like this girl. We spent twenty minutes together, and I already have her on a pedestal. I want to do anything I can to find her. Anything. But how can I? I don't know what she looks like or, dang, even what she *sounds* like. She was just getting over laryngitis and croaked like a frog. V could pass me on campus in a bathing suit reciting the Declaration of Independence, and I'd never recognize her. How do I find her?"

"I don't know." Chumbo shrugged. "She's got *your* contact info, right? If she likes you a lot, she'll get in touch. If she doesn't, maybe she's less interested than you think."

"You're right," Dan said. "Meanwhile, I'll try to find someone else. V made me realize I want someone I can get serious about. I must be psychic, because before the M-and-M, I signed up on a dating website. First results due soon. Even though I've been shooting blanks with girls for ten years, I'm gonna find the woman who makes me stop searching."

"That's why you're in grad school?"

"No, although it might not hurt. The main reason I'm here is to learn how to do engineering research. I believe I can make a positive impact on the world."

"Good answer. Now I have another question for you," Chumbo said as he got up. "But hang on a sec."

Chumbo walked down the hall to the kitchen. He came back with a soda for Dan and a beer. Returning to his chair, Chumbo tapped his fingertips together. "Why do you have so much trouble with women?"

Dan's stomach tightened. "Every time I meet a desirable, single woman—attractive, classy, smart, whatever—I freeze. I can't get any words out, or they come out jumbled. I'm *fine* if she doesn't impress me or I can't see her face, like at the M-and-M. Or I think I have no chance with her. Things like that. What makes me panic?"

"You're like the camper who thought he was a tunnel tent. Sometimes a dome tent."

Dan squinted. "What?"

"He finally got diagnosed by a psychiatrist. The doc said he was '*two tents*.'"

Dan kicked Chumbo's leg. When they stopped chuckling, Chumbo asked, "Feel better?"

"A lot better, doc. Maybe you should be a psychiatrist instead of a biology major. Judging by how many dates you've been getting, you could advise patients that have relationship problems."

"Look, my dates don't always work out as well as you think, pal," Chumbo admitted. "One really cute girl I had a couple dates with, a sweetie named Karen Winston, for example. We decided to stop dating a few weeks ago, but we're still friends. I guess she wasn't into my need for . . . affection. She's okay, but too proper for me."

"That's too bad, buddy, but you still gotta help me. I need to do more than chill."

"Lemme ask you something. You got any sisters, Dan?"

"Nope. Just an older brother."

"There you go, dude. I had two younger sisters. Got pretty good at manipulating them to do stuff for me. Also got popular with the ladies in high school and college. I think you need more practice. We can talk more about this if you want."

"I appreciate that a lot." Dan got up and started to leave. He stopped at the door and turned around. "There's something I keep forgetting to ask you, roomeo."

"Which is?"

"How in the world did I end up with a roommate called Chumbo?"

"If it helps any, my birth certificate says Charles Porter Jr., which morphed to Chummy, and in high school to Chumbo."

"So, you were named after your dad?"

"Yeah. He died when I was eight. The God you worship didn't bother to save him." Chumbo added, "Now, since we're gettin' so nosy, I have a question for *you*."

"Which is?" Dan said, mimicking his roommate.

"Why didn't you go for a physics degree? Your mind operates more like a scientist than an engineer."

"I considered it," Dan replied. "But I love designing and analyzing devices. When I found out mechanical engineering also had an engineering physics program, I said yeah! Well, Chum, I gotta head out now. I need to hit the books for an hour or two."

"Hang on another minute. I just got a brainstorm. Let's see, it's not nine yet. Should be OK." Chumbo pulled out his phone.

Uh-oh. Dan walked back to his chair.

Chumbo took his time placing the call. He pinched his chin between his thumb and forefinger. "Hey, Karen. It's me. Chumbo. How've you been?" He pumped his fist at Dan. "I just wanted to buzz in and say hey. Listen, Karen, my roommate and I are sitting here having this deep discussion. Then it hits me—I'll bet he wants to say hey too. Right, Dan?"

Dan frowned.

"He's kinda quiet, but he's smiling. Put you on speaker, OK?" Chumbo tapped his phone.

"Hi, Dan. Your roommate wants to play games. What's the deep discussion about?"

"Nothing really. We were talking about, uh, campers," Dan replied.

"Campers? Are you an outdoorsman?"

"Yeah. I like being in the woods. You?"

"I love it. Especially in the spring and fall when the wildflowers bloom."

"Wow, you two sound like a couple of deer prancin' through the forest. Karen, I think you should meet Dan sometime. He looks like Chris Pratt, and he's on his way to a Nobel Prize in engineering."

Dan rose, gave a parting wave, and headed for the door again. *Quite a compliment. Should I tell him there are no Nobel Prizes in engineering?*

Sunday, August 18

In the early evening, Dan drove to the Ibis Grille. He turned on the radio to drown out his heartbeat. *So, I end up with a date with Karen Winston after my roommate pushes me into calling her.*

Dan parked and entered the Ibis at the appointed time. A hostess seated him at an empty table for two. A few minutes later, she returned, accompanied by a tall, slender, black-haired woman wearing a black sheath and a gray silk scarf. *She's gorgeous. I'm dead. Lord, help me!*

"Hello, Dan," Karen said as she reached their table. "Sorry I'm late. There was an accident on the highway."

Dan stood and pulled out Karen's chair for her. "You're right on time. I'm glad you made it." Then he returned to his seat.

For the next several minutes, he sat across from her, his fists knotted under the table. They ordered, and Dan sat in silence as Karen did almost all the talking in the opening conversation.

Dan stared into her pale gray eyes and was hypnotized by her soft words. *She's so lovely and pleasant. Why can't I relax?*

Thankfully, the waiter brought their dinners, and there was no need to speak for several minutes. Karen began again with a coaxing tone in her voice, like she was trying to pull him out of his inhibition. "What do you do when you're not working in the lab?"

He shook his legs rapid fire under the table. *Come on, answer her.* "Let's see. I like music."

"That's nice. What kind of music?"

Dan muttered a few false starts and then blurted out, "Different kinds. Mostly classical."

Karen gazed at him expectantly. Silent seconds passed like viewers at a funeral. "Classical. Can you enlighten me a little?"

Dan made sounds somewhere between grunts and moans. "Tchaikovsky."

Karen breathed and released the air like a punctured tire. "Do you like fiction? I love Ian McEwan. *Enduring Love* is one of my favorite novels. How about you?"

His face grew hot. A moment later, he spoke. "MacYune? No. Not really." This was followed by more minutes of silence and pea pushing before she asked about the weather and he said, "Yeah, it's been warm lately."

The evening dragged on.

Finally, they stood in the parking lot. He leaned over her open car door. He felt his shoulders sag under the weight of his failure to avoid the disaster now mercifully ending. *Lord, give me the courage to ask her out again.*

Dan was ready to blurt out his invitation when Karen huffed. "My goodness, Dan, do you have any idea what it's like for a girl to spend a whole evening talking to herself? I'm sorry you didn't find me more appealing. Maybe you'll have better luck with someone else."

Before a word rolled off his tongue, she pulled the door closed and drove away.

Later that night, dispirited but not desperate, Dan walked through his neighborhood and ended up in Caraway Park, a few blocks from his apartment. A nearly full moon cast its glow on the path. The cool air invigorated his lungs. Birds chirped their evening chorus, and the squirrels disappeared with the approaching night. Despite his pleasant surroundings, he sighed and looked up at the moon. Life was outmaneuvering him.

He stopped to pick up a fallen limb and with all his might, he heaved it into the trees. It swooshed through the leaves of low hanging branches and landed with a thud. Picking up his pace, Dan's heart beat harder. *What a rotten week. Two fastballs past my stinking swings. How long until strike three?*

A superbright planet eased out from behind a cloud above the faded sunset.

Venus. The goddess of love. How appropriate. You're fired!

When Dan came to a bench, he sat and buried his face in his hands.

Ten years. . . I feel so bad. Please send me some help, Lord. Send me an angel.

He sat motionless with his eyes closed and his face still in his palms. He didn't move, couldn't move, and minutes passed. He felt a need to recite the only two prayers he knew by heart. One from the Jewish Bible and one from the Christian New Testament. Psalm 23 and the Lord's Prayer. He repeated them slowly and with deep fervor, his breath rising and falling. A profound peace settled on him, and his mind seemed to float like a balloon on a summer breeze.

A soft, warm sensation between Dan's ankles snapped him back to alertness. He jerked his eyes open.

What the heck?

A small dog sat in front of him, ardently licking his ankles. It looked up with woeful eyes.

"Who are you?" Dan reached down slowly to let his visitor sniff his hands, then he put them on the dog's head. "Who are you, little pup?"

The dog tilted its head.

"You're cute." He stroked and scratched his new friend. "But you didn't tell me who you are. Are you the angel I prayed for? Is that who you are, puppy?"

Woof. Woof.

"Maybe you are then. You're a fine piece of work, little one. Big brown eyes. Look at that beautiful bushy coat." Dan took the pup's head in his hands and gently moved it from side to side. "What kind of dog are you? No ID collar, pup? Do you have a home?"

Woof.

"Maybe I can give you one. Oh, get real. With my luck, somebody's gonna walk up any minute and claim you."

The pup tried to climb up Dan's legs, so he lifted it to his lap and scratched the happy, moaning creature all over its body.

"You're young, but I bet you're doing better with the ladies than I am. Got any lassies making eyes at you? Wait a minute. Are you a laddie or a lassie?" Dan picked up the black-and-white canine by its shoulders and strained his eyes in the dimming light. "You're a lassie, that's for sure."

The puppy put a paw on Dan's hand and wagged her tail. Then she stiffened and barked. The sound of footsteps approaching the bench from behind sent a chill up Dan's back.

"The park closed at sunset, fella," a city police officer called out, beaming a flashlight in Dan's face. "And dogs need to be on leashes in this area. They can run free in that large, fenced-in area there." He pointed the flashlight beam down the road.

The pup snarled and bared her fangs. Dan put his hand on the dog's neck. "It's OK, sweetie. Shhh. Sorry, I didn't know that, Officer."

"Both regulations are posted at every entrance. Got any ID?"

"Sure." Dan stood, reached into his pocket, and handed him his campus photo ID.

The officer held up the card and aimed his flashlight beam at it and then Dan's face. The puppy started barking again. "OK. Just be careful about the leash and the park closing time."

"Thank you, Officer. It won't happen again."

The police officer turned away. Dan stood and patted his leg. "Wanna come home with me and be my little angel?"

Woof. Woof.

All the way home, Angel stuck to him like a rodeo cowboy to his horse.

Entering his apartment, Dan picked up his puppy and went straight to the front room, where Chumbo was sprawled out on the sofa watching TV. "Look what I found at the park. Isn't she a sweetheart?"

Chumbo clicked off the television and sat up. "What's this, a third roommate? I hope she can cook better than us."

They both burst out laughing. The pup whimpered and yelped. "It's OK, little girl. We'll pipe down," Dan said, as he lowered his new friend onto the floor.

"Where'd you find her?"

"Hold on a minute, Chum, first comes the date."

"Yeah, how did it go tonight?"

"A complete catastrophe."

"You didn't like her?" Chumbo asked, his mouth falling open.

"I liked her too much. My tongue went on vacation. She tried to pull me out of it and ended up leaving mad." Dan chuffed out a sigh. "Same old story. Over and over."

"Look, roomie, these things take time. Especially the way you've been handling women. Now tell me how you found the puppy."

"After my disaster with Karen tonight, I was wandering around the park feeling rotten. I sat on a bench and asked God to send me an angel. Next thing I know, this cute critter is at my feet, and we fall in love. So, you OK with keeping her here?" Dan dropped onto the easy chair.

The puppy moved toward Chumbo, who had his hands out. "No problem, as long as you're gonna take care of her. All right, I'll help out a little. I love animals. After all, I *am* getting an MS in zoology," he said. "You got a name for her yet?"

"I do, animal man. Because of the way she appeared to me, I'm gonna call her Angel."

Chumbo snorted and shook his head in disbelief. "OK, Saint Francis, why don't you zip over to the pet store on Belmar. They're open late. Grab a collar and leash. Puppy food. Some treats. And see if they have any puppy bibles while you're there."

This is what happens when you get a roommate by posting an ad in the cafeteria. "Very funny. Got any idea about her age and breed?" Dan asked.

Chumbo nodded. "Probably eight to ten months old. And she looks like a sheltie."

Dan frowned and Chumbo explained. "A sheltie is a Shetland sheepdog, dude. My cousin Todd has one. They're smart. Friendly. Good herders. His dog stays in his apartment. No problem."

"You think I can leave Angel alone all day?"

"Shelties need attention. Maybe you could leave her with Mrs. Haynes upstairs during the day. She's been alone since her dog died. Bet she'd love the company."

"Interesting idea. I'll talk to her. But now, I think I'll drive over to the pet store. Maybe you can cut up some apple chunks for her while I'm gone. Dogs like apples, don't they?"

Dan left the room and opened the back door of the apartment to go to his car. Angel barked and darted to him. He picked her up and hugging her, took her back to his roommate.

"Will you hold Angel till I leave?" Dan asked.

"Sure thing," Chumbo said as he petted his new playmate's head. "By the way, while you were out, I had an idea about your problem. I think you have a fear of good-looking women. I'll bet there's a name for that." He took out his phone and began tapping it.

"Not exactly a fear. More like an anxiety," Dan retorted and waited for an answer.

"Whatever. Here's what my search program calls it. Caligynephobia." Chumbo grinned and made more strokes on his phone. "Let's check on fear of rejection while we're at it."

"Does giving it a name really help?"

"Maybe. It might help us find medical articles. Stuff like that. Oh, this is interesting. Can't find an official name, but somebody came up with a Greek word for it—how do you pronounce this tongue twister? Aporr—aporripsiphobia. I love it!"

Dan turned to leave. "Keep it up, Chum. By the time I get back, doc, you should have my therapy plan all set up."

Chapter 5

Monday, August 19

S irius's taxi arrived at Paul's Place Grill and Bar in the upper east side of NYC at nine p.m. for his meeting. The US contact for Eastern Europe Group 2 had asked for an urgent meeting with the CEO of StarWay on the East Coast. Sirius was wearing casual clothing, as his counterpart had agreed to do. He didn't like the rushed tone of the message he'd received, but for a hundred million dollars, he could overlook that little detail.

He paid the driver and went into Paul's Place. Two men and a woman were sitting at the bar.

He flashed his driver's license at the bartender. "Hi, I'm Sirius. Paul sends his best. I have the back room reserved from nine to midnight. OK to go in now?"

"Yes, sir. I have your reservation. The room is all set up. Would you like a drink?"

"Chivas, rocks." He laid a hundred-dollar bill on the counter, away from the sight of the other customers.

The bartender quickly pocketed the money. "Thank you, sir. I'll be right in with your drink, sir."

Sirius entered the room. It contained only one large, square wooden table and two wooden chairs with seat and back cushions as he had asked. Almost immediately, the bartender came in with his drink, and the CEO nursed it while he thought. His counterpart's name was hard to pinpoint, being common in Russia, Bulgaria, and Ukraine. His accent didn't help much either. After hearing the recording they made, the electrician said he must have lived in several Eastern European countries.

When his guest arrived, Sirius stood, and they met in the middle of the room.

"I hope your flight was pleasant, Mr. Ivanov."

"Very good, Mr. Sirius, very good."

The barkeep returned to take their orders, after which, he left the room.

Ivanov was the first to speak. "I know you are a busy man, Mr. Sirius, so I won't—as you Americans say—beat around the bush. I have two things I would like to discuss with you, if that is permissible." He plastered a small grin on his face.

"Please."

"Thank you. The first is the subject we spoke about recently. Your interesting discovery of vibricity to make more powerful lasers." He looked up under heavy brows and dropped the smile. "As I understand it, the delivery date is in question." Ivanov stroked his chin whiskers. "Have you made any progress since we spoke?"

Sirius had an answer prepared. Ivanov tilted his head to the side and frowned.

The barkeep returned with their drinks, and the two men maintained an uncomfortable silence until he left.

Ivanov fingered the base of his vodka glass. "Well, Mr. Sirius, I have to inform you that we have recently learned that a Western European laboratory has been conducting research in this area, and my sponsors are becoming impatient. We cannot afford to let the western countries get their hands on this technology. The timeline we originally agreed upon has passed. You need to deliver your end of the bargain, extremely soon, or I may have to reclaim the deposit we gave you."

Sirius cleared his throat. "I am doing as much as I can, but I will assign more scientists and engineers to the Vibricity Project, quickly."

"Good." Ivanov sat back and the smile returned. "I wouldn't want you to disappoint us. My superiors would not be happy."

Sirius stared at Ivanov's black eyes and felt a chill slide down his spine. He shifted uncomfortably in his chair. "What's the other topic?"

"Ah, yes. The other topic." Ivanov took a slow swig of his drink and patted his mouth with the small cocktail napkin. Like he was playing cat and mouse. "I'm not permitted to give you any details until you decide your level of interest. It's a smaller project for which we will pay ten million. Shall I proceed, Mr. Sirius?"

"Please do, Mr. Ivanov." He put his palms on the table.

"An Eastern European scientist, working for a large, shall we say for now, material producer, has discovered a much improved, hmm . . . product. The scientist will be coming to the US in a few days to attend a research conference. Sorry for the pressure, but we just learned of his travel plans. We would like you to invite, ha ha, the scientist, to spend some time at your laboratory—wherever that may be—so he can, hmm . . . give you and us a few details about his discovery. If possible, we would like him to eventually be returned to his homeland. Is that something you might be interested in doing for us?"

"Definitely. Such operations are not, shall we say, unfamiliar to us. I'll start the preparations as soon as I return."

"Good, here are the project and financial details." Ivanov took a folded envelope from his pocket and handed it to Sirius. "I think I can use your cooperation here to forestall my sponsors' impatience a bit."

"That would be greatly appreciated, Mr. Ivanov."

They had another drink. After Ivanov left, Sirius went to the men's room and scrubbed his hands with soap until they stung.

Chapter 6

Tuesday, August 20

After a restless night, Lana got up at dawn and took her usual morning jog in a park near her apartment. *Stop thinking about T. Will he contact me? Get real. It's been four days. Up the pace . . . Will I ever find the right guy? . . . Stop it! Breathe in peace. Breathe out tension.*

Lana tried to concentrate on the trees surrounding her. On the here and now. But her mind refused to cooperate. It took her back eleven years. Three months after the fire. Her first day back in seventh grade.

The building had looked the same but darker. Harsher. Would her friends stare at the ugly red scars on her lower face and hands? Dad had said to call him if there were any problems.

When Lana approached the main door, her friend and classmate Beth came alongside her, and they entered together.

"I'm so thrilled you're back at school, Lana." Beth smiled and hugged Lana's shoulders gently. "If you'd like to get together and go over the material you missed, just let me know, since you're in most of my classes."

"Only two people came to see me. You were one of them. I'll remember that for the rest of my life." Lana squeezed her friend's hand and choked up on the last words.

Another girl she didn't know passed her in the opposite direction. She looked at Lana, curled her upper lip, and snapped her head away.

If you only knew how I feel . . .

Lana's classes passed without incident. Most of the students and teachers didn't act any differently, but from time to time, she peeked around and noticed students look away and whisper to each other. But she made it through the day.

After school, Lana left the building and headed to the school bus, relieved the day was mercifully over. Someone stepped alongside her. Harrison Van Buren. A week before the fire, he'd asked her to be his science fair partner, and she'd politely declined. He was too impressed with himself.

As soon as Harrison passed her, he changed his posture. He stiffened his legs, stretched his arms ahead, and wobbled his shoulders.

Lana cringed. *Frankenstein's monster!*

After four or five steps, Harrison resumed his normal posture. He turned, smirked at her, and got on the bus.

As Lana stepped up behind him, she dug her fingernails into the palms of her hands to keep from crying. She wouldn't give him the satisfaction of seeing that. Harrison got off the bus first. Lana ran to her house and straight into her dad's study. She jumped into his arms and burst into tears. Something she'd never done during her three-month ordeal.

Dad listened to her tormented outpouring while he kissed her and stroked her hair. His own eyes welled with tears. He got her a glass of water and retrieved a folder from his filing cabinet. He showed her several photographs. The before-and-after pictures of some of his most challenging facial reconstructions. He then told her she was ready for facial remodeling.

Lana had hugged her dad. After she saw those photos, she knew she would never cry again over what Harrison or anyone else said or did to her.

~

James Madison stood in the hall outside his daughter's apartment. He pushed her doorbell. *She'll be surprised.*

Lana opened the door. "Hi, Daddy!" She gave him a big smile. "What brings you here so early? What do you have there?"

"Two coffees." He handed one to her. "I was over at Sawman's Hardware and thought I'd drop in and see if you'd like to take a drive to Lake Little."

"Love to. I don't have any classes this morning, and I can work a little overtime in the lab. But I promised my classmate down the hall I'd go over and help her with a math problem. Give me fifteen or twenty minutes? Then I'll be free."

Lana picked up a textbook and her laptop and hurried away.

Slurping air in with his coffee to cool it, James pulled a chair to the window of Lana's third-floor apartment and gazed out. Being with his daughter was always special, but the memories wouldn't go away.

He remembered sitting with her in the ICU at Quincy General eleven years ago. His brave, comatose little girl . . .

He'd stared at the wet bandages from her lower face to her neck and on the backs of her hands. The clinical scene was so familiar yet so different when it was his own child. Then he saw her start and heard her first words in three days.

"Fire, Daddy!"

He'd leaned over her and stroked the sleeve of her hospital gown. "I'm here, baby. Shhh. Shhh . . . Everything's going to be fine."

"Where's Jimmy? Is he . . . gonna be fine too?"

James had swallowed hard and, with a breaking heart, whispered, "Yes, darling, he's going to be fine too."

"Can I see him, Daddy?"

"Not now, sweetheart. He's getting special treatment in another hospital. At UVA."

"Jimmy was so brave when I ran down the hall with him in my arms. He never cried."

She was right. Jimmy had never cried. The medical examiner had said the shock and sparks probably jolted him backward. He'd hit his head on the hearth and was knocked unconscious. That explained why he didn't simply run out of the upstairs bedroom when the fire started. He'd died in the room and never suffered, thank God.

James parked the car at Lake Little, and he and Lana began a slow one-mile trek around the lake.

"Lana," he said, "I don't mean to be nosey, but there's something I want to ask you about."

"Sure, Dad. Anything."

"How did your date with Harrison go?"

"It didn't go." Lana chuckled. "I sent him an email because I was studying for an exam the night he wanted to go, and I told him he should feel free to take someone else."

"And?"

"He sounded a little huffy, but he told me Missy Farrell had been coming on to him. He thought she'd like to have dinner at the Panorama Restaurant, so I said he should make plans with her." She shrugged. "To be honest, Dad, I was relieved."

James smiled at her. "I'm glad to hear it. I hate to disparage the Van Burens' son, but I wouldn't be happy if you ended up with Harrison. I'm afraid there's not much of a solid foundation there."

"I totally agree. You don't have to worry on that front." They walked on for a few minutes in silence. Then Lana stopped and looked up into his face. "There's something I'd like to talk to you about."

"All right."

"Dad, I'm getting tired of the way Mom treats me. She really needs to stop hovering over me like I'm a three-year-old. I'm perfectly capable of running my own life."

"I agree, honey, and I told your mother as much after you left the other night." He put his hand on her shoulder. "I just want to ask you to be patient with her. She's still suffering from Jimmy's death, and she's afraid you'll make a bad decision and pay for it for the rest of your life."

"I'm trying, Dad, but Mom needs to let me live my own life. I'm afraid she's pushing me away by her constant meddling in my social life."

Chapter 7

Thursday, August 22

Dan arrived at the lab early in the morning. His new lab mate, Joe Stanley, was not in yet. *Unusual. He limped a little when he left yesterday.*

He reviewed his work list for the day, and a few minutes later, Joe appeared with a young girl by his side.

"How are you feeling today?" Dan asked. "I thought you were hobbling when you left yesterday."

"Just a leg cramp. I'm fine now."

Dan smiled and made a fist. "Glad to hear it. Who's your friend?"

"My niece, Victoria," Joe said. "We call her Vickie. She's in sixth grade and loves science. I told her about your laser, and she asked me if she could see it."

"Hi, Vickie. I'm Dan. Glad to meet you." Dan put out his hand, and she shook it. "Come over here, and I'll show you how my laser works."

Vickie beamed. "Thank you, Mr. Dan. I'm so excited. I have a science project due in December. Can I take photos and notes while you talk?"

"Absolutely. Let me show you the setup—we call it an apparatus—where I do my research. See that long, black, horizontal cylinder on the right side there? That's the laser."

"Looks like a fat hot dog," Vickie said and snapped a photo.

"Yeah. Now look over on the opposite side of my experiment. See that square thing? That's the light sensor, or detector, the laser beam will hit when I turn it on. The sensor tells us how bright, or powerful, the light from the laser is."

Vickie snapped a photo of the sensor and wrote in her notebook.

"Now I'm gonna turn on the laser," Dan said as he flipped a switch.

"I don't see anything," Vickie said.

"You can never see a light beam passing by you. You can only see it when it bounces off something like dust or water droplets in the air. Let me get my spray bottle. Now, I'll turn off the lights. Hang on, Joe. Looks like we still can't see it very well. Let's hit the beam with this spray." Dan pumped his spray bottle into the air between the laser and the sensor.

"Wow, that's beautiful," Vickie said as she snapped several photos of the experimental apparatus. "The red beam of light going from the laser to the sensor is so thin. Looks like a red strand of spaghetti. Before you cook it." All three of them laughed.

"Next, I'll show you how the sensor works. It sends an electrical signal to my computer that tells us how bright the laser beam is when it hits the sensor. Understand?"

"I think so. This is fun, Mr. Dan."

"I turned the laser off. What's the reading on the computer?"

"Zero. Let me write this down."

"Laser is on."

"Wow. The number jumped to one hundred."

"Yep. The computer adjusts the reading so we always start at one hundred when the laser beam first hits the sensor. Make sense to you, Vickie?"

"Yes, but I have a question. Why did the signal go to zero? Doesn't the sensor pick up the overhead lights?"

"Wow. You are definitely gonna be a scientist. All the lights in this room emit bluish light, while the sensor only picks up reddish light, like the laser beam. This way, we don't have to work in the dark or put the apparatus in an opaque box where we can't see what's going on inside. Also, notice the computer screens face away from the apparatus so their light doesn't get picked up either."

"That's cool, Mr. Dan."

"Take a look at this. It's a rod of yttrium oxide. We call it YO. How are you going to describe it in your notes?"

"Well, it looks like a glass cigarette. Clear as water. Its surface is smooth and polished."

"Good girl. More gold stars. Suppose I put the rod in the laser beam, between the laser and the sensor so the beam goes in one end of the rod and out the other. What do you think will happen to the signal on my computer?"

"Well, since the rod is perfectly clear, it shouldn't absorb any of the light. So the signal should stay at one hundred."

"Very logical. A scientist always tests her hypothesis—what she thinks will happen. Let's give it a try." Dan put the rod on its holder in the apparatus. "What's the signal?"

"Yikes, it dropped to ninety-five. The rod must be absorbing some of the laser light."

"Good answer! Most of the missing light got reflected backward when the laser beam hit the front and rear ends of the rod as it passed through. But you're still right. A little bit gets absorbed or scattered. Could be tiny specks or cracks or other kinds of absorption inside the rod. That's what I'm researching. To make things easier, I usually recalibrate once more after the crystal is in. Let's do that." Dan clicked his computer.

"Wow. Back to a hundred again! This has been amazing, Mr. Dan. I just got an idea for my science project. Suppose we put a clear drinking glass inside your apparatus, instead of the rod. And we record the signal. Then I fill it with water and record the signal again. Then I put some food coloring in the water. Different colors and amounts. Each time, we record the signal. We could tell how much laser light gets absorbed each time, couldn't we? Could you help me do it when you're not busy? Please?"

"Vickie, you are such a sweetheart. My answer is . . . ta-ta-ta-taah . . . yes!"

Vickie gave Dan a big hug. She then ran over to her uncle and whispered something in his ear and looked back at Dan. Joe laughed.

"Hey, I called Vickie's mom, and she'll be here in about ten minutes to pick her up. While we wait, maybe you could tell me more about what you're studying and what you hope to achieve."

"Sure," Dan said. "This frame that holds the rod can exert various forces and vibrations, which can make tiny optical changes or imperfections in the rod. If there are any imperfections created in the rod—distortions, cracks, whatever—they will absorb or reflect some of the light, and the laser signal will go down below the one hundred mark. For my research runs, I record all three decimal values as well. For example, the reading now has drifted a tad to 100.001. So, basically, I'm measuring the signal strength as I put different stresses on the crystal samples."

"Got it."

"By the way, I have a whole set of rods with different additives, called dopants, in them. Most of the published studies have involved a single dopant, like thallium or terbium, so we're looking at adding two dopants to the crystals. We took some of the best candidates from the earlier studies and started adding a second dopant."

Joe nodded. "That's good. I think I got the basic idea, but I'm still not sure why you're studying these imperfections."

"Yeah, I should have mentioned that too. By studying a series of optically clear crystals and their responses to stresses, we hope to find what effects high dopant levels may have on their mechanical properties. Yttrium-based crystals are used in many laboratory, military, space, and other optical instruments, including lasers. We don't want them failing or cracking under different kinds of stress.

"My stomach's growling," Dan said, rising from his chair. "We can talk more at the cafeteria if you two wanna come."

"Maybe I'll meet you there after Vickie's mom picks her up."

After lunch, Dan did some equipment maintenance and tests. Joe had already begun his experiments. When Dan was satisfied everything was working right, he powered up his apparatus. Next, he checked the position of the YO crystal rod, Sample 153, and turned to his computer screen. *All data monitors and laser detector signals look right.*

Joe glanced over from time to time. One of the students' duties was to look for problems or dangers their lab mates might face.

After about fifteen minutes, the *beep-beep-beep* of an alarm startled Joe, and he spun around in his chair.

"What's that?" Joe asked, his voice anxious.

"Nothing. No explosions or fires. One of the signals is changing in a way it's not supposed to. Never heard that alarm. Hang on a sec." Dan tapped his laptop keyboard to sequence through the plots that showed how the laser signals were changing as time progressed. "This is crazy. The laser signal *increased* from one hundred to over one hundred and one as the beam passed through the YO rod. The signal can drop more if there are imperfections in the rod, but it can't go up. Something's wrong."

"What? Are you saying the laser beam got stronger as it passed through the YO crystal rod?" Joe got up and came over to Dan's computer. "That's impossible. At least from what I know about optics."

Dan coughed nervously. "Me too. Must be a system problem of some kind. Let me run a few checks and then try again. I'll turn the alarm volume down so it doesn't drive us crazy."

After checking his equipment and finding no problems, he took more data.

Joe walked back to Dan's desk. "I know there has to be a mistake but think what it would mean if you could increase the power of lasers this way. Maybe in a big way, huh?"

"Interesting question," Dan replied. "I haven't thought about it a lot. Hmm. A bunch of possible uses come to mind. Like cutting through steel barriers and other dense materials faster. Blasting through rocks and digging deeper oil wells, maybe."

"Yeah," Joe responded. "Hey! What about sending laser signals farther out into space? And get this. We could destroy enemy missiles, airplanes, tanks, and soldiers at the speed of light!"

Dan laughed. "Talk about making mountains out of molehills. We just solved a lot of the world's problems and probably created a few new ones, all with a bad piece of lab equipment."

"What if it got into the wrong hands?" Joe asked.

"Get serious, Joe. It's just bad data. But let me ask you something. Have you noticed anything peculiar with your experiments?"

Joe shook his head. Dan got up and clicked the Print icon on his computer. Then he called his advisor and asked whether he could stop by.

"What's up?" Joe asked.

Dan grabbed his laptop and the printed plots. "My signal just went up to one hundred and two. See you later. I'm heading for Kromer's office."

Dan jogged up the stairs and down the hall, his heart pounding like a kid running from a bully. "Dr. Kromer, I gotta show you this."

Dan's advisor scrutinized his plots and asked several pointed questions. Shaking his head and wincing, the professor sat back in his chair and stared at the ceiling. "Dan, you're a careful researcher, but this is too crazy. Those oxide crystals can't make a laser beam get brighter, only dimmer. Here's what I want you to do. Check the system and your computer program too. Also, increase your run times. If the signal starts going up rapidly, shut everything down immediately. This effect you're seeing probably isn't real, but we don't want to risk damaging the equipment."

"I'll start first thing tomorrow."

"If you haven't found the problem in a few days, I'll come over to the lab and check out the system with you. If necessary, I'll arrange a meeting for us with Dr. Samstein, our solid-state optics physicist. How does that sound?"

"Fine. I'll contact you tomorrow evening. Thanks for the help."

As he closed the door, he heard his advisor muttering, "Light amplifier. What's coming next?"

Chapter 8

Saturday, August 24

Hey, Dan," Chumbo shouted down the hall. "I found some stuff in the refrigerator that still looks edible. You want lunch?"

Dan bounded into the kitchen in a T-shirt and blue jeans and dropped into one of the kitchen chairs. "Thanks, Chum."

"No problem." Chumbo dropped a package of presliced roast beef and a container of cole slaw on the table. "We'll have our own feast right here." He rummaged in a cabinet and brought out a loaf of bread and an unopened bag of chips.

Dan devoured his sandwich in a few bites and dumped the dishes in the sink. He leaned against the counter and turned to his roommate.

"Chum, I've been thinking. I appreciate the discussions we've been havin' about women. You've had plenty of experience, but I think you're better at finding women for yourself. I need some time to think this through."

"Take all the time you want. I'll be here when you need me." Chumbo gave him a thumbs-up.

Back in his room, Dan reached down to pet Angel. "Hey, little girl, tell me, what should I do?" He scratched her ears while she looked up at him with soulful eyes and woofed at him.

"Of course," he said and picked the dog up. "Of course, I need a girl to tell me what to do. I need a *female* love coach!" Dan picked up Angel and swung her around in a circle.

Woof! Woof!

"Come on, baby. Let's get rollin'." He made a few tap-dance moves while he carried his consultant back to Chumbo's room.

"Hey, man, I got it. The answer hit me like a sumo wrestler on steroids. We need a gender change."

Chumbo covered his lap with his hands and squeaked in falsetto, "No, anything but that!"

Dan flopped into a chair. Chumbo stared at him. "Dude, you look like you just had your first mouthful of Cap'n Crunch."

Dan shook his head. "More like Archimedes after he discovered how to find the volume of an irregular-shaped body and yelled 'Eureka!' Seriously, I need a female love coach to help me. That'll solve all my problems."

"It will?"

"Yes. She'll understand the female mind, spot my weaknesses, and show me how to behave with women. Also, we can practice whatever advice she gives with each other. I can go places with her. And, if the coach I find turns out to be good looking, imagine how complimented another woman will feel when she realizes I prefer her to the woman I'm with. It'll be perfect."

"Hang on a minute, Romeo. You think you can find a professional love coach in Quincy? Even if you can, I'll bet she charges fifty, seventy-five dollars an hour. Where are you gonna get that kind of money?"

"Not a pro. Maybe a college student. Somebody who could use a little spare cash by giving me a woman's perspective. Help build my confidence. What do you think?"

"A female love coach, eh?" Chumbo mused. "This might work out for you."

Chapter 9

Saturday night. Time to begin. *I'm gonna find a love coach.* Dan showered and put on a pair of charcoal-gray slacks, a lighter gray shirt, and a navy blazer.

Later that evening, Dan parked his Ingot Silver Mustang on a side street and walked over to The High Note café, which catered to the university crowd and some locals. The large room was divided into several areas with tables and booths near the front of the restaurant. Several students were talking and dancing to a soft-rock band in the central area. In the back, a small counter served snacks and drinks. Dan picked up a ginger ale at the counter and sat at a table for two.

As each half hour passed, Dan got another ginger ale or lime and tonic water and gave himself another half hour before he chalked up the first night of his adventure a flop. By 10:30, he'd had enough.

Dan slapped his palms on the tabletop and pushed himself up when someone new came in. He dropped back onto his chair.

She was tall and elegant with dark-blonde hair. She stood and glanced around the room.

A guy came up to her and took her arm. They both turned away to join the crowd listening to the band. Dan decided to have another drink, even though the woman was taken.

After he got a refill, he returned to his table. The young woman whispered something in her date's ear. The pair turned and strolled toward Dan's side of the room. The woman motioned to her date, and they sat at a nearby unoccupied table.

Even though Dan knew nothing would materialize that night, he was captivated by the woman. She was classy. Someone with an air of intelligence, grace, and beauty—like Michelangelo just put his chisel down.

The couple engaged in light conversation while they sipped their drinks. But as time passed, their moods changed. They looked bored, even irritated with each other. Suddenly, her escort got up and walked out the front door.

After her date left, the woman looked over at Dan for a few seconds, but he remained frozen. Neither person made eye contact again.

Ten minutes later, an older guy paraded over to the young woman.

"What happened to your friend? Looks like you could use some company," he said.

She frowned and raised her upper lip in displeasure, then said something and looked away from him. In the background noise, Dan could only hear the man's loud voice.

"Come on, beautiful, you can be friendly if you want. How about I order you a drink?" He sat in the vacant seat left by her date. She glared at him in silence, her elbows pulled against her torso.

"Oh, come on now. You can do better than that."

She turned and looked at Dan, her eyes wide open.

Dan sprang to his feet and rushed to her table. "Look, mister, can't you see the lady isn't interested?" he said, his voice soft but firm. "Would you please leave her alone?"

The man jumped up and shouted, "What? Where do you fit in, fella?"

Dan maintained his measured voice tone. "It'd be better for everybody if you backed off. Nice and quiet."

By this time, most of the people nearby were watching the scene unfold before them. The band still played. A few couples had stopped dancing.

The man picked up his chair and, raising it above his head, moved toward Dan. "Why don't you put the chair down?" Dan said, easing toward the front door. "We can talk about this outside."

"That suits me," he growled and dropped the chair behind him.

Once outside, Dan stopped a couple dozen feet from the door in the chilly night air. His antagonist kept moving forward. Several people followed them out, including the woman who was the focal point of the drama.

Dan tore off his blazer and handed it to her. He put his palm out toward his adversary. "Please, mister, don't do something you might regret."

Like an enraged bull, the man charged, swearing. He cocked his arm and with a grunt, let fly his fist at Dan's face. But Dan was quicker. He dropped down under the approaching missile. Lowering his elbow to his knees, he returned an uppercut to his off-balance assailant's jaw with an even louder grunt. The attacker's head snapped back. His body slammed backward to the concrete. He lay motionless, blood dripping from a large cut on the bottom of his jaw.

"I'm calling an ambulance!" someone shouted from the gathering crowd. Another said, "I'll call the police."

Dan stooped over his fallen enemy. A man from the crowd said he was a doctor and knelt beside the unconscious assailant. After examining the man and compressing his wound with his handkerchief, the doctor looked at Dan. "He's alive and breathing. We'll need to get him to a hospital, but I'll stay until the ambulance comes."

Then the doctor turned to the crowd. "Will someone please go into the café and ask for a tablecloth and a first-aid kit? And something we can use for a pillow."

"While we wait, may I see your right hand, Rocky?" he said to Dan, holding out one hand while continuing the victim's wound compression with his other.

After the doctor examined Dan, someone returned with the requested items, and the doctor turned back to his patient.

The woman from the café walked over and handed Dan his coat. "Don't forget this. My goodness, how can I thank you?"

Dan rose to her. "I'm happy I could help you—and so sorry about this fellow." Dan glanced at his fallen foe.

"That was some performance. Where'd you learn to fight like that?"

"My dad was an amateur boxer. Taught me everything he knew. Look, if you don't mind waiting for the ambulance to come, I wonder if I could talk to you about something. Somewhere quiet and warm."

The young woman smiled. "That's the least I can do. I'm Lana Madison."

"Dan Butler. Pleased to meet you."

After an ambulance came and drove away with the still-unconscious patient, a police car arrived. Two officers took statements from Lana and Dan and said they could go.

The pair strolled toward the Westwood Hotel, an old establishment with a quiet lounge that Dan had eaten in several times. Lana's presence, grace, and strangely familiar personality enthralled him and pushed the brief boxing match into the recesses of his mind, despite his aching knuckles. As he walked with her in enchanted silence, he felt he was breathing pure oxygen.

Lana walked past him as Dan held the door open. Her mind was alive with thoughts and questions as they entered the hotel lounge.

"Is this table OK?" She put her hand on a chair back.

Dan nodded. "Would you like anything to drink?" he asked and pointed at the food and drinks on the far side of the lounge.

"A Coke with ice, please."

In a few minutes, he returned with a Coke and another lime and tonic water.

"Well, Dan, what did you want to talk about?" Lana sipped the Coke.

"First, I want to be sure you're all right. Then I have a confession to make."

"I feel much better now, but I'm not a priest." Lana grinned.

Dan leaned forward in his chair. "I came to The High Note tonight with no intention of picking up a date. I came to offer a woman a part-time job."

"A part-time job? I never heard that one before. What kind of job are we talking about?" she responded, wrinkling her brow.

A blush crept into Dan's cheeks. "By way of introduction, let me tell you I'm a grad student in mechanical engineering here. I've got a few more years to finish my PhD. At the moment, I'm trying to find a kind woman, perhaps yourself, who'll help me overcome a—let's say, a personality defect."

"What do you mean?" She cocked her head.

"I get nervous and tongue-tied in the presence of any pretty or classy young woman with whom I'm trying to develop a romantic relationship. So I wonder if you might be interested in a part-time job as my . . . uh . . . love coach."

While Dan was speaking, Lana shifted in her seat. "I wonder, Mr. Butler, if you realize what you just said. Since you seem rather comfortable with me and are far from being tongue-tied, I assume you don't consider me pretty or classy—someone you could ever find interesting. Did I get that right?"

"No, no." Dan slapped his cheek. "That's not what I meant at all. In fact, it's just the reverse. You're one of the most attractive, elegant women I've ever met. But because of that, I know I don't stand a chance with you. That's why I've been so talkative." He touched her forearm briefly. "Lana, please say you understand and you're not mad. It's so like me to mean one thing and have it come across as the opposite."

Lana was torn between leaving—an unacceptable way to treat her hero—and being completely intrigued. "It helps to know I'm not detestable, but you want to hire me to be your love coach—to help you pick up women?"

Dan grimaced. "I thought that approach might be a good way out of my romantic dilemma, but it seems you don't agree. I can understand you refusing the job, but I hope I haven't done something stupid and hurt your feelings."

Lana put her fingertips on Dan's arm. "You didn't. Don't worry." *This has to be one of the strangest days of my life.*

After Lana took a deep breath and exhaled, she continued. "We didn't talk much about who I am, so let's start there. I'm a first-year PhD student in the new biomedical engineering program here at QU. Seems like we're comrades in arms. Have we ever met?"

"You'd think we would've, but there are a lot of engineering students at QU. Yet there is something familiar about you." Dan paused. "Nah."

"I'm still paying off my car loan, so I might be interested in your offer. Wow, a love coach. Let me think about it. I'll give you my answer soon. After what happened tonight, I feel like we're friends. Since my buddy Tom walked out on me tonight, is there any chance you'd give me a ride back to my apartment?" Lana wrote her phone number on her napkin and handed it to him. He did the same.

He drove to her apartment and accompanied her to the door of her suite. Moments later, she opened a gap in the blinds as he got into his car. He took something from his shirt pocket and kissed it.

Lana snapped her head back. *The napkin with my phone number? Good grief. A love coach?*

When Dan returned to his apartment, his roommate was spread out on the sofa watching a dinosaur movie. "I have some news for you, roomie. That is, if you can tear yourself away from the big lizards for a few minutes."

"Sure, pal, lay it on me." Chumbo sat up and clicked the TV remote.

"Tonight, I started looking for a love coach." Dan took his blazer off. "Went down to The High Note and met a possibility. Her name's Lana Madison. Smart. Classy. She's thinking about it."

"What's she look like?"

"This princess could've pulled Narcissus away from the pool and saved his life."

"You look like somebody who just got off the Heaven's Island shuttle. Who's Nabisco?"

"I said Narcissus. Google him, buddy."

Chapter 10

Monday, August 26

Dan didn't make much progress in the lab as the week began. *It's after three, and I still can't get her out of my mind. I'm heading to the library. Read some research articles on my list.*

As he crossed one end of the QU quadrangle and sucked in the late summer air, he said a prayer of thanksgiving. "Dear Lord, thank You for bringing Lana to me. Please let her accept my coaching job."

The bright sun warmed his face, and the campus was teeming with students and others. Several young couples lay on the grass, hugging or chatting.

Turning his head toward a small grove of blazing red maple trees at the edge of his path, he spotted a girl on her knees near one of the wooden benches surrounding a pulsating fountain. She crawled along, frantically pushing the grass from side to side with her hands. *A damsel in distress? Looks like an undergrad. Maybe I can help her.*

"Excuse me, but have you lost something?"

She turned and examined him, her startled look fading to a polite smile. "Thank you, but I'll be OK."

Dan stroked his chin. "Sure? There's a lot of grass on this campus."

She grinned. "That's very good. But I'm, well . . . maybe I could use a little help. Thank you for asking." She stood and extended her hand. "I'm Carter Edwards. And you?"

"Don Quixote, knight-errant, at your service." Seeing her quizzical look and quick glance at her watch, he tried again. "Sorry. Don Quixote is a fictional character who goes around trying to rescue young maids in trouble. I'm Dan Butler. What'd you lose?"

"The brooch my grandmother gave me on my twelfth birthday. It's silver with a ring of tiny diamonds and has both our names engraved on it. I can't believe I was so careless and stupid."

Dan's jaw dropped as he noticed the glistening tears in her eyes. "May I make a suggestion? Let's sit for a minute, so I can ask you a few questions. Call it a Sherlock Holmes game. It may save us a ton of time."

"But it's almost three forty-five, and I have a four o'clock class." Carter sat down on the nearest bench, and Dan followed her lead.

"Please tell me everything that happened from the time you first touched the brooch until you discovered it was missing."

Carter laced her fingers together and put her thumbs to her pursed lips. "OK. The bar pin on the back of the brooch was loose, and when it sprang open a couple of days ago, the brooch fell off. So this morning I put it in my leather bag—this one," she said, holding up her handbag. "I planned to drop it off at the jeweler's after classes. When I checked my bag after lunch, the brooch was missing. I've been retracing my steps for the past couple of hours. This is where I ate lunch today."

Dan nodded. "When you left your room this morning, what did you put in your bag and in what order? Tell me every time you opened the bag—as well as you can remember."

Carter's face brightened as she got up and paced, reviewing with Dan everything she'd done with her purse.

"Good. Good." Dan tapped his forehead. "When you put the lunch bag on top of the brooch, did it fit easily, or did you have to push and jostle the bag a bit?"

"Dan, where have you been all your life? Nothing fits easily into a woman's purse!"

"Fair enough. Where did you put the lunch bag when you were through eating? Did you crumple the bag?"

Carter's brows knotted as she pointed. "I put it in that trash can. I don't remember crumpling it. What's the point? There's no way the brooch could've gotten into the bag."

"We have a bit of work to do. I'm gonna empty the trash can, item by item, and you check each thing I take out. Ready?"

"But it's now three fifty."

It didn't take long for the pair to create a pile of cups, bottles, paper, and other trash. Suddenly, Dan grinned and made a slow, exaggerated dive of his hand into the can and pulled out a white paper bag with handles. His hand was inside the upright bag. "Does this look familiar?"

"Yes, but how are you keeping the bag from falling off your hand without holding onto it?"

"Because I'm holding the pin of your brooch!" With that he rotated his arm and showed Carter her lost treasure, its pin penetrating through the bottom of the paper bag. "Ta-da!"

She clasped her arms around his neck and kissed him hard on both cheeks. "Oh, Dan, I love you." Blubbering like a baby, she wouldn't let him go.

Finally, they moved apart.

He looked down at his watch. "Uh-oh, looks like your class begins in about zero minutes."

Dan handed her the brooch, and she put it in her handbag. "Dan, you have to let me take you to dinner. No refusals accepted. Can I have your phone number? I can't wait to tell my friends about Sherlock Holmes—I mean Don Quixote!"

"I'll accept your kind offer." He recited his phone number. "We'll decide later who pays."

Chapter 11

Lana Madison had just returned to her apartment from the drugstore that evening when her phone chimed. She put down her shopping bag and purse, then dropped on the sofa. *He's not letting any grass grow under his feet.* "Hi, Dan."

"Hello, Lana. How's your day going?"

"It's been good. I got a little cleaning and shopping done."

"Have you thought any more about my job proposal?" he asked.

"Yes, I have. Before I make up my mind, I have some questions. Some things we should discuss that we forgot in all the excitement at The High Note."

"Ask away."

"What exactly do you want me to do?" Lana asked.

"Since you already know a little about my difficulty with women, I was hoping you could observe me on dates. See the difference in my behavior with women depending on my interest level. Tell me what you think I'm doing right and wrong. Give me dating tips . . . let's see . . . Tell me how women react to different approaches. How they think. What they're looking for in men. Things like that."

"I'm not a professional counselor."

"I can't afford that. Besides, I feel comfortable with you. I'm confident that whatever you tell me will be valuable. Will you help me?"

Lana chuckled softly. "OK, but I'd like to have a trial period. A chance for us to know each other better and see how we both like this coaching concept before I go on the payroll."

"I don't want to take advantage of you and get a lot of free work. How long do you think the trial period will last?"

"I'm not sure. A couple of sessions. Then I can go on the payroll. The other question is, how much are you paying me?"

"Salary. Forgot about that. How about four hours a week guaranteed at ten dollars an hour? Wish I could afford more."

"That sounds fine."

"Awesome," Dan said. "Do you think we can start soon? I anticipate one or two dates coming and would love your help in planning and oversight."

Lana laughed. "In some ways, Dan, you are a fast mover. I'll check my schedule and let you know."

Chapter 12

Tuesday, August 27

The next morning, Dan was back in his advisor's mechanical engineering lab. He opened a box of transparent yttrium oxide rods and took out YO Sample 151 doped with lanthanum and titanium. *Looks like I need to shorten its mounting bracket. Where's my cutting tool?*

As he put the bracket in the lab vise and began cutting it, his mind wandered. *Easy does it. Not too fast. Oh, Lana . . . Lana. I love thinking about you. That Carter Edwards was something else after we found her broo—*

A sharp pain bit into his daydream.

"Ouch!" He sucked in air through his clenched teeth. "Dang it. I hate cuts."

He hustled over to the first-aid kit mounted on the wall and put some alcohol—initiating more sound effects—and a tight bandage on his bleeding fingertip. "Hey, Joe, I'm gonna see if Dr. Kromer is free for a minute, then go home and rest my hand."

Joe Stanley nodded. "I'm finished with my experiments for today, so there's no need for you to stay, partner. I'll hang around and do some reading."

"By the way," Dan said, "I forgot to mention it, but I decided to try to hire a female grad student to help me improve my dating techniques. I found Lana Madison, and she accepted my offer to be my love coach. Give me dating tips. Things like that. Might be a turning point for me."

"Congrats and good luck. You seem pretty upbeat about her. Sure you just see her as a coach?"

"Her personality and looks have me in a bit of a tailspin already. But she's out of my league."

"You never know. If you can't come in tomorrow, let me know. I'd like to continue my experiments, and I need a safety partner."

Small cotton-ball clouds dotted an azure sky as Dan headed for the engineering faculty office building where his advisor's office was located. He zipped up three flights of stairs with little increase in his breathing. *My workouts are sure helping.*

"Dr. Kromer, got a minute?" Dan called through the partly open doorway.

"Come on in, Dan. Got any graphs to show me?"

"Nope. Cut my finger and don't think I can do anything more in the lab today. But I've got a couple questions. And, you know how I keep complaining I can't meet any interesting girls around here?"

"Don't tell me!" Kromer slapped his desk.

"Yep. Two absolute winners. I could see myself with either of them. Unfortunately, I met the first one at the M-and-M and then lost her contact information. Have no idea what she looks like or even sounds like—she had laryngitis that day. The second girl is a bit more sublime. Too sublime. In simple English, she's out of my league. On the other hand, I talked her into being my love coach."

"Love coach? That's a new idea. If she agreed to be your love coach, maybe she likes you."

"Nah, she's doing it because I saved her from a guy who was bothering her at The High Note."

"Dan, you know how to complicate life, don't you? Hey, I have a suggestion. Pretend they're the same girl! Then you can stop worrying about the first one and concentrate on your coach." Kromer's face lit up with a Cheshire-cat smile.

"Very funny, boss. Now I know why you're my favorite thesis advisor."

"What are your questions?" Kromer asked.

"You said you wanted to review my lab work tomorrow morning. Just in case this cut gets infected and I need to get it looked at tomorrow, maybe we could do a quick review now. Then I'll go home."

"That's fine." Kromer pulled a folder out of his desk and riffled through it. "In your case, there's nothing much to review anyway. You've finished most of your coursework, and your research is coming along well. I've enjoyed having you in my group."

"Thanks," Dan said. "The other question was about the research seminar I gave yesterday. Did you notice the partially bald guy in the business suit sitting in the back row?"

"I'm afraid not. I came in a few minutes late and crept over to a seat in the front row. What about him? Our seminars are advertised on the university website several weeks in advance and open to the public."

"I don't know." Dan shook his head. "He looked so intense and wrote down almost everything I said. Then, as soon as I finished speaking and the questions started, something even weirder happened."

"What was that?"

"Someone asked a question about the system's stability. And, in the spirit of full disclosure, I discussed our increasing signal anomaly. Remember?"

"Of course."

Dan shook his head and leaned forward in his chair. "The visitor's mouth opened, and he started rubbing his chin and neck. Then he pulled out his phone and stood it on its side. I think he was making a video recording. When another person asked a question, he got up and hurried out through the rear door. I've been at our weekly seminars for years now. Never saw anything like that."

"Well, I bet he was from a large company." Kromer smiled. "Maybe we'll get a big research contract." Kromer's eyebrows shot up as he laughed.

"Fat chance," Dan echoed, and he got up to leave.

On his walk home, Dan mulled over his advisor's joking response to his concern about the bizarre visitor. Maybe his research could bring in funding for the university.

He'd been on autopilot as his brain directed him home. He couldn't get the mysterious stranger out of his mind.

Chapter 13

I don't care how many projects you're juggling. I want a plan as soon as possible explaining how you are going to follow up on the Quincy development." Sirius glared at Eos across his desk. "The board keeps pressuring me about the Vibricity Project. Got it, J. J.? So I . . . need . . . a plan to show the board and get 'em off my neck." Sirius slammed down a folder he had in his hands and huffed.

"Easy, Si, easy. I just heard the seminar yesterday and caught a flight back last night. As far as Quincy University goes, a grad student named Dan Butler is doing all the experimental work. He did something in a few weeks that we haven't been able to do in two years. Either he's doing something different or his crystal is different." Eos shook his head and took a couple of deep breaths. "How about we have a drink? Help me relax and think."

Sirius pulled a bottle and two glasses out of his desk. He filled them and put one on the far edge for Eos. "Tell me more."

Eos took a long swallow and placed the glass back on the desk. "Butler, who presented the seminar I attended, said the laser beam recently got a couple percentage points stronger *after* it passed through the rod. But the effect only lasts a few hours, then goes away for a few hours. It could be an instrumentation problem or something, but I'm pretty sure it isn't."

"How could you possibly know that?" Sirius frowned and shook his head.

"Because Butler takes the rod away from the laser beam and the signal reading is *normal*. He puts it back in and the signal goes *up* a few percentage points instead of going down. In and out, the story keeps repeating. Si, we've had a crew working full time on this for two years. We can get signal power increases, too, but never more than a tenth of a percent. Butler's only been getting a power increase for two days, and it's already twenty times higher than what we've seen in two years!"

Eos continued. "I suggest we develop a plan to surveille the Quincy lab and a second plan in case we need to bring Butler out here. If we get him and his crystal, or an identical one, here, we should be able to reproduce vibricity."

Eos took another swallow. "Suppose he's stubborn or super ethical or nervous. Then what? No vibricity. We need to treat him the right way."

"I know how to get information from our guests!" Sirius put his hands on the desk and stood. "Listen, J. J., I've got Kowalski, the Polish chemist, in our metal prayer cell right now, getting some electrical encouragement. The electrician has been keeping me informed. He's from an Eastern Slovakian border town and speaks Polish. Said he'd start with some psychological encouragement and then try a few volts if necessary. Yeah. That's how you get information out of people. Not playing toesies with them."

"What do they want from him?" Eos put his thumb under his chin with a curled forefinger against his lips.

"His company developed the world's most powerful explosive, and they want the chemical formula."

"There's another thing," Eos said. "Even if Butler cooperates, we might want to work together with his university. We made the theoretical discovery of vibricity. They stumbled onto it in the lab. We both deserve some of the fruits of the discovery if we work together."

"I don't want some fruit. I want the whole pie. I'd not make that my first offer." Sirius's phone rang. "Hang on a minute, J. J. . . . . OK, Ladi. How's he doing? Nothing yet? Try a little juice."

Sirius refilled his glass and glanced at Eos's half-filled glass. "Ladislav doesn't mind playing rough when he has to."

"Let's think about a master plan, and I'll write it up for you and the board."

"Hmm. OK. Remember—" His phone rang again. "Speak of the devil, and the devil will appear . . . Ladi, any luck? Too bad. Raise the voltage to level two."

Sirius rubbed his mouth in thought and took another swig. "Level three has a fifty percent kill rate. These Poles are tough."

"Seems like it. But back to Butler, my nephew's an engineer. I've spoken with him and some of his friends. I know how they think. Logic and fairness appeal more to them than threats and brutality. Let's start with the carrot and the stick approach."

"Carrots, eh?" Sirius pulled his head back. "Is that why rodeo riders wear spurs? Let's get real. Get tough."

"OK, OK. We can talk—"

The phone interrupted them again, and Sirius raised a hand. "That's too bad. Start playing with his head some more. Turn it to full power, and push the buzzer button. Keep repeating the kill rate. Psyche him up more. Call me back.

"Look, J. J., I'll let you play nursemaid to start with. You know something? What you said about the crystal rod going in and out of the laser beam is *pret-ty* convincing. I hope we can figure out what he's doing without having to bring him here. But I'm saving the best guest room for him just in case."

"Well, Si, are we finished?"

"Pretty much. Have you been watching any football lately?"

"Sure, Whenever I get any—ahem—spare time. Which is pretty much—"

Another chime sounded. "What's the latest? . . . How about that! . . . Fantastic job, Ladi.

"We did it! Kowalski said if it was just about him, he's ready to die. But he has a wife and four young children. He drew the structural formula of the chemical on a piece of paper. Yaa-hoo. Ten million enchiladas!"

Chapter 14

Wednesday, August 28

Lana patted her hair and pressed the doorbell. *Now I get to see the gentleman's quarters.* The lock clicked and the door opened. "Hello, coach of my dreams. Welcome to my humble apartment, and thanks for meeting me on such short notice." Dan bowed and swept his arm toward the foyer. "I think we'll have more privacy here. My roommate, Chumbo, is out tonight."

"Chumbo? I'll bet he's friendly."

"Yeah, sometimes too much so."

"Who is this little darling?" Lana asked as Angel ran up to her and sniffed her legs. She stooped down and held her hand out to the puppy. Then she petted the pup's head and shoulders.

"Angel. She found me in the park after I prayed for an angel."

"Why'd you want an angel?"

"Hang on a minute for that one." Dan took Lana's coat and led her to the den. No sooner had she sat on the sofa than Angel hopped up beside her and onto her lap. Lana held her head tenderly. "You are a little princess. Yes, you are."

"Would you like something to drink? We have Coke, ginger ale, and orange juice."

"Coke is fine."

"Be right back."

Dan returned with two Cokes and a plate of cookies, then sat beside Lana in front of the open laptop. "I'm looking forward to working with you. This is going to be amazing."

"I'm glad you're so enthusiastic. I feel the same way. Thanks for the snacks."

"My pleasure. Oh, I forgot to answer your question." Dan put an ankle on his knee. "I was praying for an angel to help me after I had a horrible date with someone, and this little pup snuggled up between my ankles."

"How interesting. Sounds like a quick answer to a prayer."

"Sometimes the Lord responds that way . . . Well, here's the output from the dating site I told you about." He pointed to the laptop screen. "You can see the summary showing I got three hits so far. I picked the best one. Judy Klein, twenty to twenty-four years old. That's good, 'cause I asked for twenty to twenty-nine. Lemme get her pic up."

"Hold on a sec. As your coach, I'd like to read about your winners and losers. It'll help me understand you better."

Clicking and touch typing at high speed, Lana perused all three bios and photos while muttering several "hmms" and a few "unnhs." Upon finishing, Lana turned to Dan and closed her eyes while tapping her chin. "So the person you chose seems to be the most intellectual and artistic, as well as the prettiest. Well, well."

Dan nodded and rubbed his palms together. "Yeah, I agree. Judy's got the edge. I thought she might be a better intellectual match. Math degree. Likes books, puzzles, classical music, museums. That kind of stuff. The other two are more activity oriented. They mentioned horticultural gardens, long walks in the woods, camping, and riding horses. They're all appealing in different ways, but I think I'll contact Judy first."

"Good choice. But if your coach may make a suggestion, here's what I think you should do. Message her to get her phone number. Just a few words. Then call. Keep it relatively short and relaxed, so you don't seem desperate or hesitant to ask her out. See how she responds. If she sounds interested, you can ask her out."

"Low key, eh?"

"Yes, phone calls are important. You're both doing a quick check out. You can hear each other's voice tone and get an idea of the other person's thought pattern. Also, she can tell you're not a weirdo or a bowl of oatmeal. Remember, she has your photo and bio. She probably already knows whether she's interested in meeting you."

"You understand women pretty well."

"I've been one for twenty-four years."

"Yeah . . . Uh-oh, I just remembered Chumbo wanted me to ask you a couple things."

"Go right ahead."

"This is going to sound funny since Chumbo is such a ladies' man—but would you be willing to give him a few tips? If you could just give him an hour, we would add it to your salary."

"Wow!" Lana pulled her head back and laughed. "What the heck. All right. Maybe I need to drop out of grad school and start a romance counseling practice."

Chapter 15

Friday, August 30

At 8:00 a.m., Eos placed his palm on the reading plate outside Sirius' office. The door clicked and slid open.

"Come on in, J. J." Sirius motioned toward the empty chair in front of his desk.

"Morning, Si," Eos said and took the seat.

Sirius picked up a sheet of paper and ran his finger down it. "I appreciate all your hard work. The board has approved the plan, and we're ready to go. According to your plan, let's start by you taking our audiovisual tech, Parton, and Young, the handyman, to Quincy. Young can get you access to the building and the lab—but only work in the wee hours. Parton can imbed some transmitting micro-video cameras in the ceiling. We'll need copies of all the files on Butler's computer and notebooks. The three of you need to leave tomorrow and start the lab surveillance—we'll call it Operation Q—so we can see what Butler's doing. We'll convert our vibricity lab here to mimic the lab at Quincy U so we can repeat Butler's every move."

"No problem. I'll get the admin to make the airline reservations for the three of us."

Sirius sat forward in his chair. "Speaking of vibricity, Halsey Powers's monthly update will be held here in an hour. Let's see if she has anything new. Why don't you hang around, and then you can pack right after the update?"

"Sure. Maybe I need to change my name from J. J. to yo-yo."

"Be serious, J. J. You know we have an offer of one hundred million for superpowered lasers. If we pull this off, there'll be some superpowered bonuses!"

After a cup of coffee and a sweet roll in the cafeteria, Eos was back in the CEO's office. A large portable screen and projector had been set up for the talk. The usual suspects were there: the CEO, who was in a private chat with the director of finance, and the directors of operations, information technology, and research.

Let's see what's new with our chief physicist. I missed her last update.

Dr. Halsey Powers walked up to the screen, and the lights dimmed.

"Good morning, everyone, and welcome to another monthly update on the Vibricity Project. As usual, I'll begin with a brief, nonmathematical review of what vibricity is, and then say a few words about recent developments. If we have time, I'll take questions at the end, as usual. OK?

"According to the theory I've been refining and reporting on for the past two years, energy can be stored inside certain—I'll say in a moment what certain means—transparent crystals like yttrium oxide, which is highly transparent." She reached into her handbag and pulled out a clear, cigarette-sized, solid rod. "This is a yttrium oxide rod. I'll pass it around."

While the rod was going around, she continued. "When a beam of light, like a laser beam, passes through the crystal, it absorbs some of the stored energy in the crystal and becomes more powerful. In other words, more powerful and more deadly. Can you imagine shining a flashlight through a pane of glass and have it come out brighter than when it went in? Of course not. Yet that's what my theoretical research says is possible with yttrium oxide and similar materials.

"So how do we do it? By a process I call vibricity. It rhymes with electricity. It takes three things to make vibricity work in a useful way, as shown in the slide on the screen.

"One." She pointed at the first line on the screen using her red pocket laser. "You need a polished piece of optically clear material like yttrium oxide.

"Two. The crystal must contain small amounts of three different atomic elements, called dopants. Which ones and how much of each? I'm still working on that." A sound of friendly laughter went through the small audience.

"I know, I know. But I've just made a theoretical breakthrough in that area, as well as being able to quantitate how much of a brightness or power increase is possible. I'm busy checking all the math before making an announcement to the directors. Let's just say, the power increase possible seems to be huge.

"People understand brightness pretty well. But how can light have power? Don't you need horses or engines for real power? Did you know that the total *power* of the sunlight hitting the earth is around 200 quadrillion watts, more than 10,000 times the world's total energy use? The sun is 93 million miles away from the earth. Mind-boggling.

"And three. You need an electromagnetic power source to provide the energy. Nothing is free. An AC coil or a moving magnet will nicely take care of that.

"Perhaps our director of research will say a word about how things are going in the lab?"

The research director stood and said, "In one word—terrible. As you know, we've been at this for two years and can't get any significant power boost. We can get enough power boost, less than a tenth of a percent increase, to know the vibricity effect, or something like it, is really there. But it's like trying to sell an expensive device for your car that increases your gas mileage by a hundredth of a mile per gallon. Good luck with that. However, we are waiting for Halsey to check out her work, so we can start buying the right materials."

Chapter 16

Sunday, September 1

When Dan returned from church the next morning, Chumbo was barefoot in cut-off jeans and a gray athletic T-shirt, lying on the sofa. Spotting a DVD case on the end table, Dan said, "Great movie you're watching. *Jurassic Park*. Very intellectual. Good way to spend Sunday morning, eh?"

"Lotsa people spend them nursing a hangover or pretending to be awake during a sermon, don't they, roomie? At least this movie teaches people about biology, even if the plot isn't realistic. Did you learn anything plausible at church today? Like how two—or was it three—guys built a boat big enough to carry mating pairs of every animal on earth?"

"Four guys. And are you going to start again, Chumbo? Don't you know the ark was huge, and it took Noah a long time—a hundred years to be exact—to build it?" Dan sat down and lifted his hands in the air.

"Where'd they get all the nails from?" Chumbo slapped his thighs in a fit of laughter.

"Keep on laughing, *roomeo*. That's what Noah's neighbors did until their knees went underwater—then they all put their thumbs out." That response wiped the grin off Chumbo's face, but he pumped his legs up and down, snickering.

"Dan, don't you see how some, in fact, many, of the bizarre things in the Bible, like three or four people building a ship big enough to hold animals of every species on earth, aren't realistic? And then rounding them all up. Like walking on water. Don't you see things like that are impossible?" Chumbo shook his head.

"Actually, they were impossible for humans to do alone," Dan answered. "But they weren't alone. Those who did or observed those things believed God, the creator of the universe, was at work. Speaking of creating the universe, how did that happen? The latest theory says universes are created spontaneously out of nothing, because of the laws of physics. But where do the laws come from? Where are these laws located before universes are created? And how did the laws get there? Does science just keep pushing the latest theory of the beginning further and further back, never explaining the ultimate beginning?" Dan smacked his lips. "To me, that's not a satisfactory answer to anything."

"Well, roomie, science is the best we got. Take it or leave it."

"Look, man," Dan said. "The reason you and I are so far apart in our views isn't because you believe in science and I don't. We both believe in science. It's because I believe there is something, someone, *higher* than science and you don't. The Bible says you will find God when you seek Him with all your heart. Why don't you try that?"

"I did when I was eight years old."

Chapter 17

As Dan drove to meet Judy Klein for their dinner date, he thought about the results of his internet research on her. He'd learned she played on the varsity tennis team in high school. She belonged to the campus Libertarian Party Organization and the B'nai B'rith. She also volunteered at the Jewish Home for Seniors.

He rethought the instructions Lana had given him. *Take slow, deep breaths. Tell her a joke. Talk about something you're familiar with.* She also reminded him she was going to bring Tom along, like at The High Note.

Dan stood near the reception desk in the restaurant, The Fowl Bowl, scanning the main floor for his date. He heard someone say, "The Butler-Klein reservation." Turning back to the desk, he saw her. *Wow. She's even better looking than her photos. Midtwenties for sure.* He prepared his opening line, then walked over to the desk. "I believe you're Judy Klein?"

"Hi, Dan. Nice to meet you."

While Dan searched his brain for another line, the receptionist came to the rescue. "The Butler-Klein table is ready. Please follow me." As the two walked silently to their table, Dan saw where Lana and Tom were seated. Lana smiled at him. She was facing Dan's table with her friend between them so Dan couldn't see Tom's face. He pulled out a chair for Judy so she couldn't see Lana, but he could.

"Would you mind if I sat in the other chair?" Judy's voice was friendly but firm.

Dan thought for a moment. "I have a little . . . let's just say I'd prefer it if you'd sit here. Do you mind?" Looking puzzled, she walked back to the chair Dan was still holding.

Well, that's strike one. "Um, would you like a drink?"

"I'll have a Twenty-First Century. How about you?"

"Time and Ionic. Uh, lime and tonic." *I don't see any servers around here.*

"Dan, please excuse me for a minute," Judy said and walked away.

Their server approached the table and leaned toward Dan. "What'll you have?"

"I'd like a tonic water, rocks and ice. I mean rocks and lime."

"Anything for the pretty lady?"

"Yeah, she wanted—I forgot, but it had a number, like a date or something."

"I bet it was a Twentieth Century, right?"

"Yeah, that's it. Thanks. You saved me."

After Judy returned, the server brought their drinks and left. She sipped her drink and frowned. "This isn't the drink I ordered. What did you order?"

He straightened up. "Uh, it was a something—a century cocktail. Twentieth, I think. Isn't that right?"

"Well, I wanted a Twenty-First Century. But what's a hundred years between friends?" Judy chuckled. "Don't worry, this is fine."

"Please forgive me. I should've waited and checked with you. I'll get you the right drink." He raised his arm to attract the server's attention.

She gently pulled it down and shook her head at the server. "No, I like it. The taste just caught me by surprise."

Dan nodded, then took a few slow, deep breaths. "I'm trying to remember what your background is. Computers?"

"Math, but you're getting closer now."

"I'm sorry, Judy. Let me be honest. I'm nervous. It always happens when I meet a pretty, smart woman."

"Is there a comma in there?" Judy asked while Dan tried to remember how to punctuate the sentence.

Throughout the evening, Judy tried to loosen Dan up. They had a quiet dinner, but like Karen, Judy did most of the talking. Dan remembered something from Lana's list. "I heard a funny joke recently. Let's see if I can remember it. A string goes into a bar and orders a beer. The bartender says they don't serve strings. He leaves and tells his string buddy, who's waiting outside, what happened. The buddy ties himself in a loop and messes up his hair. Then, he goes in and orders a beer. The bartender asks, 'Aren't you a string?' He answers, 'No. I'm a . . . I'm a . . .' Unbelievable. I forgot the punch line!"

Judy burst into laughter. "He says, 'No, I'm a frayed knot.' Dan, I love your half jokes."

While the embarrassment was cooling from Dan's face, Lana walked over to their table.

"Hi, Dan, fancy meeting you here." She kept her gaze fixed on him while she reached around his neck and adjusted the back of his shirt collar. "How's my hero doing? I'll never forget what you did at The High Note last Saturday. Let's get together again soon."

Dan smiled sheepishly.

Then Lana turned to Judy. "Please excuse the interruption. Hope you two enjoy your dinner."

But while Lana's appearance and flattery made Dan feel more relaxed and macho, it had a different effect on Judy. She picked up her knife and made tiny circles with it on the tablecloth. "Who was *she?*"

"Lana?" Dan rubbed his nose. "She's a girl I met recently. Just a friend."

Judy turned and looked over at Lana's table. "An interesting . . . friend. She's pretty, direct. You can take that with *or without* the comma. What did you do for her at The High Note?"

"Nothing much. She was sitting alone at a nearby table when an obnoxious fellow tried to pick her up. She looked distressed, so I went over and asked the guy to back off. He got mad, but when it was all over, he was out . . . of the picture."

"That was courageous. I'm impressed." Judy's broad smile matched her kind words.

The rest of the evening was cordial, but Dan remained tongue-tied. Finally, he thought of a relevant discussion topic. "Judy, I'm guessing from your name and online biography that you're probably Jewish. Is that right?"

"Yes."

"Do you mind if I ask you a question or two?"

"Not at all."

"Do you go to church—I mean synagogue—regularly? I hope that's not too personal. I'm just curious."

"Not really. I go to *shul* for the high holidays and maybe a few other times a year when the fancy strikes me. I was raised in an Orthodox Jewish home, but college squeezed religion out of my brain. Now, I'm not very observant, I guess. How about you?"

"College had a similar effect on me. But lately I've returned to attending weekly worship."

"What brought about the change?"

He pointed upward. "I developed an interest in astronomy. What I've learned showed me the universe is far too amazing to have evolved randomly from nothing. I took two electives in college, one called Introduction to Atomic and Molecular Physics, and the other was Introduction to Astronomy. The universe all comes down to the properties of three basic particles—electrons, protons, and neutrons. They make atoms. Atoms make molecules and everything else. Oh, I forgot another particle, photons. That's what light is made of."

Judy cocked her head. "So what? Matter and energy have to be made out of something, don't they?"

"Yeah, but those four particles are made from even weirder things called quarks and a bunch of other stuff. I accepted all that as random facts in college. But my thinking changed the last few years."

"How?"

"I just decided those particles and their constituent components couldn't have the unique properties needed to make up the universe by chance alone. Then, if you add the creation of life and genetic coding on top of that, the odds against a blind watchmaker go right out the window, in my opinion. So now I'm back in church again."

Judy smiled and nodded. "Are you aware that polls indicate only around half of American Jews believe in God? Largely due to the horrors of the past century." Judy's eyes narrowed. "I understand the fraction among Christians is higher. But you know what, Dan? I think I'm going to pick up a book on nuclear physics for dummies."

When the bill arrived, Dan paid it. He escorted her to her car. "Judy, I'm sorry I was so nervous and quiet at the beginning. It's not your fault. I'm working on loosening up with women. I'd like to see you again."

"I'd like that," Judy said as they approached her car.

When Dan got back in his car, he drummed the steering wheel. *The conversation picked up when we started talking about something I was familiar with. Hmm. My coach is already having a positive effect.*

Chapter 18

Monday, September 2

Lana knocked on the door of Dan's apartment. *This review session should be revealing.*

The door opened, and Dan grinned and swept his arms inward, beckoning her to enter. "Welcome again, my wonderful coach. Come in."

"Oh, what a terrific greeting. I'm happy to be of service."

"What can I get you to drink?"

"I'll try a ginger ale on the rocks, please." She reached down and petted Angel, who had rushed to her.

Dan went to the kitchen and returned with two glasses of ginger ale on a tray and a plate of cookies. "Hope you like these chocolate walnut cookies. I made them from scratch."

"A man who bakes. Now we're getting somewhere. Thank you very much." She picked up one of the cookies and took a bite. "Umm. Delicious." She sipped her ginger ale and put the glass on the table. "Didn't you tell me you had a roommate?"

"Yes. Chumbo. He's a biology grad student. He's out with his new semi-girlfriend, Kathy. But I think things may already be cooling off there. As you know, I've had my problems too. But with your help, I'm making progress."

Lana smiled. "You are indeed. Let's discuss your date with Judy last night. But first, what did you mean by Chumbo being out with his semi-girlfriend?"

"Well, he's working two women at the same time. Stevie and Kathy. Stevie's in the background right now, but I think he likes her more. Kathy seems to be more accommodating, if you know what I mean."

"I see." Lana chewed on her bottom lip. Let's get back to how things went with Judy."

"Gimme your hand." Dan gave it a slow, steady squeeze.

She grimaced. "Oh! I get it. You were pretty tight with her too? Brain lock? The noise level at the restaurant was low enough I could hear most of what you both said. Judy did most of the talking. I thought you loosened up at the end, and what I could hear of your spiritual discussion was interesting."

"You heard all my stupid remarks?" Dan said, then grunted. "Judy intimidated me at first. I don't think I would've gotten my birthday right if she'd asked. But, as you said, I finally loosened up. Should I give her a call and see if she wants to go out again?"

"I'm not sure Judy is your personality type. She's attractive, but *I* think she may be a bit too *intellectual* for you. You need a girl who's pretty and intelligent—definitely—but more *well-rounded* as well." She waited a moment for him to respond. "However, there's some good news also. Your date last night made me think of something that might help you overcome your difficulties."

"What?"

"Up till now you've been trying to memorize *lines*—sentences to use. That's too hard. Instead, choose two or three topics to talk about. Things you know. Movies. Cars. Boxing. Whatever. Even if your date's not interested in those subjects, they'll get you talking. Loosen you up. Then ask about her interests."

"I was thinking the same thing after the date. You're really helping my confidence." Dan winked at her. "Can I try one or two topics on you right now?"

"Sure."

"Let's try this—I love to read magazines about cars. Cars are majestic. Beautiful. Especially sleek sports cars. Jaguars. Corvettes.

Ferraris." Dan's hands moved through the air like exclamation points.

"Perfect. Now you ask me what *I* like. Call me, uh, let's see . . . call me Penny."

"So that's one of *my* interests, Penny. What do *you* like?"

Lana smiled broadly and spoke with excitement. "I love a good novel. I'm a sucker for an old-fashioned romance. How about you? Do you like them?"

"Romances or novels?" After he chuckled, Dan paused. "I like mystery novels. But not where you have to keep track of a lot of clues to figure out who did it. I like it where something mysterious happens, and as the story unfolds, you find out, layer by layer, how it happened."

"Bravo! You can keep a conversation going."

"Yeah. But it's easier when you already know the person and there's no anxiety."

"So when's your next date, heartthrob?"

Dan stood and made a soft-shoe step. "Tomorrow."

"Two dates in three days? Maybe *you* should be coaching *me*," Lana said as she picked up her drink from the coffee table and walked over to the van Gogh *Starry Night* print on the wall.

"Well, the one tomorrow isn't exactly a date. Did I mention Carter? She's the undergrad who lost the brooch her grandmother gave her, and I helped her find it. She invited me to dinner tomorrow. I think she's nine years younger than me, though, so there's no 'there' there."

"But she's taking you to dinner?" Lana asked as she turned to him and raised her eyebrows. "Sounds like maybe *she* thinks some there *is* there. I can't help you prep for tomorrow—I have a lot of work backed up. Anyway, since you don't think of her as a romantic interest, you'll be cool."

Lana looked down at Angel, who'd been watching the two of them from under the glass coffee table. She patted the cushion and said, "Come here, sweetheart, and say bye-bye to your new best friend."

Chapter 19

Wednesday, September 4

Eos, Young, and Parton sat in Eos's hotel room in Quincy, Virginia, eating their room-service breakfast and discussing the plan for the upcoming events.

"I hope everybody slept well because it's going to be the longest workday of your lives. Or, I should say, next several days." Eos put his fist over his mouth and faked a yawn.

"Nine hours," responded Young.

"Not that much for me," Parton answered. "I kept figuring all the angles—planning and camera. Huh."

"OK. Let's go up to thirty-thousand feet and review the big picture overview. If things go well this afternoon and tonight, we'll get the micro-video cameras in place and copy all the lab data and files we need. We may have to take some of Butler's experimental components out for analysis. After the StarWay Lab Q sees the results of Butler's protocols, we may have to make some adjustments, relocate the cameras, whatever. We could be here a few more days to get everything tuned up. But I want to be back in Shangri-La by this weekend.

"Now we drop to two thousand feet and review what happens today," Eos continued. "I see three phases to this, unless someone has a better idea. By the way, I was here recently to hear a seminar

Butler gave, but I wasn't paying attention to the campus—took a taxi right to the mechanical engineering building.

"Phase one. We scope out the campus this morning. We want as little exposure as possible in the area. But maybe two of us can take a walk around the whole school this morning on the sidewalks that border it. Parton can walk on the street side, so while we seem to be busy talking, you're turned to me but actually surveying the campus. Looking for how many students and older people are walking around, any video cameras, security people, maybe trying to figure which gate and path we should take to get to the mechanical engineering building where Butler's lab is. I'll turn and look as much as I can. We'll just move our lips and hands for any video cameras on the street, yet not distract each other. Here are your copies of the university map with our target circled. Try to memorize it. At least get a good idea of what's what. Any comments?"

They both shook their heads.

"Phase two is this afternoon. I want Parton to go in and try to plant a transmitting video micro-camera viewing the entire hall outside the lab, to check what time the night janitor goes in before we start at midnight. It'll also be our lookout in case he or anybody else comes down the hall while we're in the lab. The feed will come right to your laptop, Parton. Right? Oh, and check for door alarms and for a video camera in the back parking lot and which way it's pointing. Some time later, Young will go in and check that he's got the right tools to open the back door and lab door locks."

"I can open any lock," Young said and curled up a side of his mouth.

"I'm sure . . . Phase three. We go in at midnight. While we keep watching the video feed, you guys do what we talked about in Shangri-La. We'll review it again after we see the layout tonight."

At 11:55 p.m., they had parked their rental car, with a piece of cloth taped over its license plate, outside the gated faculty parking

lot behind the mechanical engineering building. They'd stopped and covered the license a block before entering campus.

Parton had said the video camera covering the hall had been installed, and the doors were not alarmed. Probably a feature of a moderate-sized Southern town in a country area. Young had reported the locks would not be a problem to open.

They carried their equipment, tool cases, and an empty carrying case to a spot outside the back door. Eos brought along his small laptop. They'd even brought a small, double fold-down ladder Eos had bought that morning. It was about the size of a large suitcase. Young did his work, and they entered the building and Dan's lab, which the handyman had identified by asking a passing graduate student.

"OK, this set-up will be perfect for us. We can keep our equipment and cases behind that table near the back wall. All those boxes stored underneath will make our stuff invisible from the front of the lab. Parton, you install the cameras. Young, photograph everything in the room and in the cabinets while I collect all the technical research information and copy any flash drives in Dan's or his lab mate's desks. Young, you have to keep an eye on the hallway feed on Parton's laptop while we all work."

"Hang on," Parton said. "I can turn on the automatic motion detector for the video. It'll buzz if something moves in the video. That way Young can get some work done."

"Thanks."

Both men nodded their readiness, and the work began. Things proceeded smoothly inside and outside the lab.

In less than an hour, Parton came down from the small ladder and folded it up. "All cameras installed and fully tested, boss," he said and beamed.

"Good work, Parton. It looks like Young and I need some more time."

Almost an hour later, Eos stood and shook two raised fists. "Got copies of Butler's data on the flash drives in his desk and photos of his recent lab notes. Young, did you get pics of all the lab equipment and of the contents of all the cabinets?"

"I just need another five minutes," Young answered.

Just then, the video motion alarm buzzer went off. Parton sprang toward it and silenced the alarm.

"It's the gol-dang janitor!"

"Grab your stuff, make a lightning check of the room, and shoot behind the back table."

Seconds later, everyone could hear the sound of keys and a door opening and closing. "Where did I lose them?" the janitor whispered to himself.

His footsteps grew louder. Everyone, now on their hands and knees, looked at each other with wide eyes. Eos slowly pulled a gun from his pocket.

"Yup. That's them." A rustling sound and retreating footsteps were heard, followed by a door opening and closing again.

Sighs of relief came from all three men.

"What was he was looking for?" Eos asked.

"I watched the whole time on my laptop. Those cameras work beautifully." Parton smiled and nodded.

"Eyeglasses."

Chapter 20

Thursday, September 5

The sun hovered low in the western sky as Chumbo drove to pick up Stevie. *Bet Stevie's gonna be a bit edgy tonight. She was cold when I called.*

He parked his car in front of her apartment building and texted her. A few minutes later, Stevie stepped out. She took her seat as Chumbo started the engine.

"Hey, Stevie. You're looking gorgeous, as usual. Been a few days since I saw you. I guess I forgot how good—"

"Skip it, Chumbo." Stevie's eyes pierced him. "Where've you been for the past—what is it—five weeks? Maybe my contact information dropped out of your phone, huh? Why'd you call last night? And why, oh why, did I say yes?"

Chumbo turned in the seat to face her and put his hand on her shoulder. "I know you're upset, honey, and you have every right to be. That's why I persisted last night. After full-time dating for six months—"

"*Ten* months."

"Excuse me, ten months. Anyway, I'm sorry that after we dated for almost a year, I dropped off the radar for—let's say a month or two. You know. Work. Exams. I've been busy, that's all. Look, I planned a surprise for you this evening. Will you give me a chance to make it up to you?"

"Better be good."

This is gonna be harder than I thought. Chumbo streamed mellow jazz music through the car's audio system. *She loves jazz.*

They drove mostly in silence for almost an hour—over rolling terrain and through colorful landscapes studded with hardwood trees. The road took them higher and higher into the hills northwest of town. The sun, low in the sky, gave a subdued, rustic tone to the early fall foliage. Farmhouses with extensive pastures displayed their stock of horses. They also passed wild ducks resting in the ponds as well as cattle, dogs, and poultry.

Chumbo glanced at the dashboard clock. *It's 7:50. Still some lingering sunlight. Perfect timing. Let's turn a lemon start into a lemonade finish.*

A front wheel dropped into a pothole, and the car shook hard. Stevie's hand clutched the dashboard. "Would you please slow down?"

"You don't wanna miss the show, do you?" Chumbo turned his voice playful again.

"What show?"

"You'll see."

The road forked. As Chumbo bore right onto a narrow dirt road, and the ride got even bumpier.

"I'm glad I didn't drink any milk before we left. Milkshakes, anyone?" Stevie's sarcasm was like a punch in the gut to Chumbo, and he squeezed the steering wheel.

They approached a ridge and stopped. Chumbo walked around to Stevie's side, opened her door, and took her hand. "Madam, we have arrived in Paradise."

She stepped out and took a deep breath of honeysuckle aroma. Before them lay a broad, green valley through which a rushing stream flowed. "This *is* a surprise and a beautiful one. How did you find it?"

"Research, milady, research. *One* of the things that I do best." Chumbo planted a sly smile on his face, but Stevie shook her head and frowned. He bounded to the trunk of the car and took out a blanket, a bag, and a cooler. "See what I brought? Let's have ourselves a sunset picnic." After spreading out the blanket on the grass, he placed the snacks and beer on it. "Time for the show to start. Look at the sun touching the top of the hills."

By the time the salmon sun sank and the glow from its passing began to subside, they were finished eating and drinking. Four beer bottles were in the small ice cooler—three of them empty. Stevie still held her half-full sparkling water bottle.

Chumbo leaned back on one elbow. "Stevie is an unusual name for a girl. Why did your parents name you that?"

Stevie sat up, her eyes brightening. "My father had a brother named Steven, who died from a hazing accident in college. I was the first child, and Dad wanted to honor his brother's memory by naming me after him. He and Mom decided on the name Stevia. It lent itself to the nickname Stevie. I don't think the sweetener had been developed yet."

Chumbo moved closer and looked into her eyes. "I have one more question, Stevie. Are you still mad at me?"

"Not mad, just feeling unsure. It was hard when you disappeared without a word." Her quiet voice showed no emotion.

Chumbo moved still closer and put his arm around her shoulders. "No reason to be unsure about anything, sweetheart." He pressed his lips against hers, lightly, teasingly.

Stevie pulled her head away. "That's not what I meant. I meant unsure about where you—where we—are going."

Chumbo's voice became more aggressive. "I was hoping you'd be glad to see me, and we would enjoy our meal together. Which we did. At least *I* did. I was hoping you wanted some affection. Like you did on all our other dates."

"I'm different now." Stevie brushed some crumbs off her skirt.

"Different? What do you mean, different?" Chumbo released her and backed away.

"Less sensual. More spiritual."

"Spiritual? Like Zen Buddhism, or Jesus and Mary?"

Stevie stood up. "The second one."

Chumbo got up, too and spun around with his hands in the air. "I can't believe this, Stevie. I knew you weren't a rocket scientist, but I didn't think you were a Neanderthal. My God—I mean, *your* God—what are you thinking, girl?"

Stevie gave him a wry smile. "I have a better question. What are *you* thinking, *boy*? Will you please take me home?"

"Get in the car." Chumbo grabbed the four corners of the blanket and dragged it with its contents to the trunk, carrying the cooler in his other hand.

Stevie was already seated when he took the wheel and floored the accelerator. The car skidded around in a circle and onto the dirt road. In total silence they drove down the hill, the car bouncing with every bump and pothole they hit. Back on the asphalt road, the ride was smoother, but Chumbo drove faster and the shaking continued.

Stevie didn't ask him to slow down. She sat back with both hands under her arms. After a half hour, a red light flashed on the dashboard, and she pointed at it. "What's that?"

Chumbo glanced down. "Can't you read? It says Coolant Overheat. Oh, darn! This is too much for one night. We're over halfway home. I'm not stopping now."

Fifteen minutes later, Stevie sniffed. "Do you smell that?"

Chumbo answered with a screech of the brakes.

Stevie knew she'd made Chumbo mad partly because of her comment about Jesus, but she wasn't backing down on that message. *Never again.*

"Shoot! Hang on a minute. Gotta call Dan." Chumbo took out his phone, made a few keystrokes, and tossed it on the dashboard. A moment later, Dan's voice came on from the phone's speaker.

"Hey, Chum. What's happenin'?"

"Where are you?"

"I'm still at work trying to track down this crazy laser aberration. You got problems?"

"I took Stevie on a sunset picnic. We're over halfway home, around fifteen miles out of town, and my car overheated. Think I can make it back?"

"Just let it cool off a while. Keep the speed down. Are you on level road now? How much traffic you got?"

"Slight downgrade. Pretty lonely out here."

"When the engine cools off, get back on the road and stay to the far right. As soon as you hit the speed limit plus five, put the gearshift in neutral, turn off the engine, and coast as far as you can. Then repeat. Speed up, shut off, coast. You'll probably go two or three miles each leg, and you probably won't overheat again. Got it?"

"You're a genius. We'll give it a try. Thanks!

Stevie smiled sympathetically. "I'm sorry I made you so mad you banged the car around."

Chumbo pressed his lips together, and the dimple in his left cheek deepened. "Were you the one who ignored the Overheat warning? Did you drive like a maniac? Look, Dan says we gotta wait half an hour, then we can creep home. But I don't wanna just sit here for thirty minutes. Why don't you explain to me what put you on the road to the convent? Sorry, to salvation, or whatever. I'll warn you in advance, Stevie, I don't buy that stuff anymore."

"All right." *Lord, don't let me blow this.* "It started with a couple of books I read. I fell in love with you soon after we started dating. I couldn't have done all those things we did without being in love. But I knew you didn't love me. Not as much as I loved you anyway. I knew you were seeing other girls. But I hoped your feelings would change."

"They did change. We're together again, aren't we?" Chumbo asked.

"As the months wore on," she continued, "I felt worse and worse. I told my friend Linda about the pain our relationship was causing me, and she recommended I read a C. S. Lewis book, *The Problem of Pain.* Lewis said that pain is God's megaphone to rouse a deaf world. I was so impressed I read another one of his books, *Mere Christianity.* I started reading the Bible and then going to church just before you disappeared. So, you see, Chum, God used *you* to bring me to *Him.* He does work in mysterious ways."

"Interesting story, Stevie." Chumbo took a deep breath. "I'm very happy for you. But it's just a story because there is no God out there. He's only an expression of human hope in a materialistic universe. People believe in God because it makes them feel good, makes them think they have a chance for eternal life. Look, I don't want to get into any deep theology now, but I'd like to talk to you sometime about what a human being can really know."

"What I know, Chumbo, is that the path to God is based on something higher than human logic and materialism."

"You think so?" He continued as though she hadn't made a worthwhile point. "I'm talking about how you can decide what's real. What's true. About the creation of the universe and life. The history of religion. The list goes on and on. Every intellectual— and I don't claim to be one—knows these things. Nietzsche said it all—'God is dead'." He shrugged. "Maybe we can talk more about this later."

Stevie grinned. "OK, but I'll have company with me." *Lord, help him to see the light like I did.* Chumbo's puzzled expression showed he didn't understand Who she was bringing, nor did he ask her.

Chumbo shrugged and pointed at the dashboard. "Right. Well, at least the engine temperature's back to normal. Religion class is over. Let's go home in Dan-omatic drive."

Chapter 21

Saturday, September 7

Lana approached the ticket counter of the Hartland Cinema with Dan. He'd followed up on her suggestion they go to a movie together. "How do you feel?" she asked. "Relaxed, I hope."

"I'm feeling terrific." Dan put a twenty-dollar bill on the counter and held up two fingers. "S and S, please."

"Don't forget, we agreed to pay for ourselves."

"You *are* dreaming, princess. Every man I know would give an arm and a leg to be able to take someone like you into a place like this. You think I'm letting you pay? Not in this universe."

"I love classic romance films, and *Sense and Sensibility* is one of my favorites." She waited for him to open the theater door.

"How about a Coke and some buttered popcorn?" Dan walked up to the refreshment stand. She nodded and thanked him.

After entering the Movie Six theater, they stopped to look around. The actors' names appeared on the screen.

"Guess the film just started," Dan said. "Sorry I got the time wrong. The place is almost empty. That's how I know it's gonna be a good movie."

"You're a beastly cynic. But rather perceptive, I must admit. Where'd you like to sit?"

"We'll need privacy." He grinned and pointed to the far-left back corner. "That spot looks good. If you're OK with it."

"That's fine. Remember, the purpose of this date is to pretend you're here with someone you want to fall in love with. Do you want me to go in first?"

"I know the guy's supposed to go in first to make the apologies for the woman, but no one else is seated in this aisle. So, please." Dan gestured into the empty row.

Lana sat in the corner with Dan next to her. "There's another reason too," he said. "If anybody tried to get to you, he'd have to kill me first."

"*One* of the reasons I like being with you is you make me feel so safe. And to think it all started with your magnificent performance at The High Note. Thank you, Sir Galahad." Lana chuckled.

After they munched and sipped for a while, Lana leaned toward Dan. "Thanks for choosing this movie for me. Let me know if anything confuses you. I practically have the dialog memorized."

"I don't know anything about it. How about a quick rundown?"

"Sure. It's Jane Austen's story of the love affairs of Henry Dashwood's two elder daughters, Elinor and Marianne. His youngest daughter is Margaret. That's Henry dying in bed right now. He inherited the use of his wealthy uncle's property during his life. After Henry dies, the property passes to his son, John."

"Got it. Thanks."

After they finished their snacking, the movie flowed into Elinor's uncertain romance with the handsome Edward Ferrars, who was constrained by a secret engagement elsewhere and Marianne's somewhat wild courtship with the dashing degenerate, John Willoughby.

Dan put his hand on Lana's arm and whispered, "Like you said before, this is an opportunity for me to practice. I don't want to rush anything, but what if I practice some romantic gestures? You can pretend you're interested in me."

She put her hand on top of his and whispered, "I was the female lead in a couple of romantic high school plays—shouldn't be *too* hard."

Later in the film, when Willoughby's duplicity had been revealed and Marianne began to value the love of her protector,

Colonel Brandon, Dan made his first move. He reached over and took Lana's hand.

But when the film was moving toward a resolution, Dan wasn't. They were still at the hand-holding stage.

"Dan, I need a short break. Be right back."

He smiled at her. "I could use a break too."

They walked together to the restrooms, sharing thoughts about the film. When Dan returned to his seat, Lana was already there. On the screen, Edward was just winding up the closing love scene where he proposed to Elinor, who looked like she was in ecstasy. "Uh-oh, looks like I missed all the fireworks, didn't I?" Dan asked.

"Fireworks? Oh, the movie."

Within minutes, they were walking through the main lobby again.

"How'd it go?" Dan asked with more than a little hesitation in his voice.

"The film was great, but the jury's still out on your performance."

"Let's fix that," Dan said.

He put one hand behind Lana's back and the other behind her head. He dipped her to the side until her head was inches from the floor. Straightening her up again, he put both hands on her waist and lifted her straight up over his head until she was horizontal. She gasped, looking down at him.

"You're staying up there until I get a passing grade, teacher!"

"Put me down!" Lana pleaded. "We'll stop at a drugstore, and I'll buy some gold stars for you."

Chapter 22

Monday, September 9

G ood morning, Dr. Wilson." Lana arrived at her advisor's office at 8:00 a.m.

"Come in and have a seat." He turned around from the back table where he was working and pointed toward an empty chair. "Any exams this morning?"

She shook her head and sat. "Not until my bioinstrumentation exam at two."

"I hated taking exams in college and grad school. But, you do what you have to. Right?" He made a slight scowl. "Let's see . . . you've been in my research group for about three months now, counting the summer. How are things going?"

Lana reached down and lifted her briefcase onto her lap. "If you'd like, I'll review my objectives for this semester and outline my progress."

With his approval, she summarized her research reading list, the status of her courses, and the practice measurements she'd made on artificial materials. "Also, I'm thinking of trying an unorthodox line of research I've been reading about. I'd like to study the effects of immersing my artificial skin transplants in gaseous atmospheres like hydrogen, helium, nitrogen, and others. Some research has shown this may affect a material's bioproperties and hasten healing.

It's highly speculative but not expensive. Anyway, I won't devote more than twenty percent of my lab time on these experiments, if you're OK with this."

"Hydrogen and helium, eh? You know the sun is almost completely made out of those two elements. Maybe that will throw some light on your research. What do you think?" Wilson wrinkled his nose, then broke into a broad grin.

"I think the somber halls of science can always use a little humor."

"Lana, you're just starting out, and spreading your wings isn't a bad idea. Yes, you can devote up to twenty percent of your lab time on this for a few months. Then we'll look at your findings and go from there. But don't get too hopeful. And don't let it distract you from your main line of research."

"I won't. Now comes the most important part. Here's a list of some supplies, materials, and test equipment. I'll also need some materials for my gas containment system. I hope your research budget can accommodate this."

He studied the list while rapping his fingers on the desk. "You want almost seven hundred dollars' worth of supplies. A bit higher than most students get. But . . . I think we can manage that. Give this list to our lab manager, and he'll order everything." He initialed her proposal and handed it to her. "Keep up the good work, Lana."

She stood and thanked him. On her way out, she thought of a phrase her uncle Ted, a Notre Dame football fan, used to say. *I want to win one for the Gipper! Develop natural-looking artificial skin.*

Chapter 23

Monday, September 16

Eos stood in front of Sirius's desk. "I haven't finished my written report yet because I didn't want to lose any time bringing you up to date."

"Thorough job, J. J. And fast." Sirius gave Eos a thumbs up. "We started receiving the video feed from the four transmitting cameras the morning after you installed them. The folks in lab Q have been analyzing every second of Butler's lab work. But before I get into that, what else have you found?"

"Plenty. Butler runs a clean lab and keeps meticulous records. We took high-resolution photos of his apparatus and his lab mate's equipment too. Also got photos of all the other equipment, tools, and supplies in the lab. Now comes the paydirt. Based on the dates and times of the data on two of the backup flash drives we found in his desk—he takes his laptop itself home at night—we know he keeps them both plugged into his laptop all day to make continual copies of all his experimental runs. His lab mate must also take his computer plus any backup flash drives home at night because we didn't find them in the lab either."

"Good. Good." The boss made another thumbs up. "I'm sure you have copies of those drives for us."

"Two copies of both drives. Butler usually takes his lab book home at night, too, but he forgot one night. We found an office with a copier, and Young made copies of all Butler's notes. Then we made two sets of copies for you."

"What about the yttrium oxide crystals they're using?"

"You'll love this, boss. But you might not love the price tag. We took the best crystal rods Butler has been using recently— IDed them from his lab notes—and had one of our associates in Charlottesville arrange for some overnight mass spectrometer runs to get a composition analysis of all the elements in the crystals. We then sent the results to our Q lab here so they can have identical rods made."

"Good decision." Sirius clamped his teeth together. "I wish things were going as well here. We've been mimicking in lab Q everything Butler does. Exactly! But so far—nothing. I know it's early, but I'm going to plan more aggressive operations for Mr. Butler. As they say, 'In for a penny, in for a pound!'"

"So you think 'It's love that makes the world go 'round'?" Eos grinned, even though he suspected his boss wasn't a fan of Gilbert and Sullivan musicals.

"What are you talking about? Butler is seeing a big effect but we are *not*! I'm getting nervous, J. J. We have a hundred million dollars riding on this. And our customers are getting nervous. I think our Quincy friend is going to do some long-distance traveling. We—that means *you*—will start Operation . . . uhh . . . Dogsled immediately. We'll bring Butler here so we can watch him work, duplicate his every move, and make suggestions. I'm not so sure those videos are allowing us to copy exactly what he's doing."

"Don't we want to give it more time?"

"Time? That's what we *don't* have! Right now, I'm sure people who are familiar with the situation are laughing at Quincy's results. But if a big, well-funded university or national lab jumps on this, they'll probably beat us! I want you to lay out two phases as part of the plan. Phase one is you try to lure him to StarWay on a two-week internship. We'll keep him here as long as necessary. Set up a meeting with him in Quincy *immediately* and make him an offer he can't refuse. Tell him our slots are filling up fast, and we need an answer right away. If that doesn't work, we go to phase two, an unexpected vacation for him in . . . Shangri-La."

Chapter 24

Tuesday, September 17

Stevie had accepted Chumbo's invitation to meet him at the Chatham Horticultural Gardens. She had an eye for plants and flowers, while he appreciated the diversity and beauty of the gardens from the biological perspective.

Where is he? She stood and sat, over and over.

Fifteen minutes late, Chumbo walked up to Stevie sitting on the front wall, waiting for him. "Hi, pie, you sure look nice. Thanks for meetin' me here. You saved me a lotta time since I came straight from work."

She rose and touched his arm. "I don't mind, Chum. Not at all."

With her arm through his, they walked inside and got their tickets and a map.

"I don't see any brilliant flower displays outside," Stevie remarked, looking out into the back gardens. "But plenty of things are going on inside, according to our map."

"Would you mind if we sit over there and look at the map together?" She pointed to a bench.

"Of course."

Stevie sat, but Chumbo stood with his raised foot next to her knee and placed the open map on his thigh so she could read it. As Stevie scanned the map, she rubbed her hands together.

"They've expanded since I was here three or four years ago. tropical flowers, mother's garden, aquatic plants, cacti and succulents, Amazon rainforest, and lots more," she said, reading him the botanical groups. "What would you like to see?"

"Why choose, when you can have them all?" He hesitated after looking at her pursed lips. "Let's get rollin'."

They strolled through the botanical exhibits arm in arm, just as they used to do. After they worked their way back to the front lobby, Chumbo stopped and took her hands. "Stevie, let's go back to the cafeteria we passed and get some pie and coffee, or whatever you want. OK?"

She smiled and turned back toward the dining area. *He's usually focused on himself, but today he seems to be sincerely thinking about me. Something must be going on.*

They returned to the cafeteria and picked out their desserts and drinks.

"This coconut cream pie is heavenly," Stevie murmured. "How's your bear claw?"

He took a big swig of coffee. "Very good, but their coffee is even better. I can feel the hair busting out all over my chest. Ahh."

Caught up in the joy of being with him, she couldn't keep the smile from her face. "Chumbo, I'm glad we're doing this."

"Two reasons I asked you to come here." Chumbo's voice was low and husky. "I wanted to see you again. Kinda help make up for my animal behavior the other night. I also wanted to talk to you about your new perspective on life. I'd like to hear more about what happened to you. What changed your carefree, give 'em . . . heck attitude?"

Looking down at the floor, she folded her hands in her lap. "My parents argued a lot when I was a kid. As I grew up, I learned about my father's chronic womanizing. I vowed I would never live that way. I would be the hammer, not the nail."

For the first time, she looked up at him. "I had other boyfriends before I met you, Chumbo. But you were different. I wanted to be with you all the time, but after a while, I became a carpet for you, just like my mother had been for my father. I felt myself rotting from the inside out. So I began looking elsewhere. I already told you how Linda and the C. S. Lewis books led me to the Bible and church."

Chumbo knitted his eyebrows together. "Why are you here now?"

She unfolded her hands. "Because I love you, and you mean more to me than I do to you." Tears welled up in her eyes.

He took her hand and led her to her car. She reached for the door, but he grasped her by the shoulders and hugged her.

He looked down into her eyes and spoke softly. "You mean a lot to me too, Stevie. I'm just no good for you."

Chapter 25

Lana peeked out her apartment window. Down below, Dan got out of his silver Mustang and walked into the building.

She moved a tray from the kitchen countertop to her glass coffee table.

The bell rang, and Lana opened the door.

"Come right in, Mr. Atlas," Lana said and made a sweeping gesture with her arm. "Please have a seat." She handed him a sparkling tonic with lime and ice. Lana lifted a plate of chocolate walnut brownies from the tray. "Sorry, I've had things pile up at work for a few days and had to put my second job on hold. What's on today's agenda?"

"Thanks. You remembered how much I like chocolate." Dan sat in the easy chair and reached for one of the brownies. "I had two ideas. I want to hear more about you and also what you think about the way I handled the dates from dinner with Judy to the movies with you."

"I'll answer your questions in reverse order." Lana sat on the sofa and took a sip of sparkling water. "To tell you the truth, I don't think you need a love coach. Yes, you were intimidated by Karen and stiff with Judy at first. But you're certainly relaxed with me. Just now, you asked me to talk about myself, and then you asked for my opinion. Two touchdowns."

"Yeah, but let's look deeper," Dan said. "Judy was a real test, and I didn't do very well. Carter doesn't count because I didn't see her as a prospect. Yes, I've been at ease with you. But as I said the night we met, it's only because we have a business relationship. So no fear of rejection or humiliation. Yet the job proposal opened the door to get to know you better."

Lana uttered an "ugh."

Dan's face reddened. "You don't agree?"

"No, no, it was sweet. Not at all maudlin. As to any possible weirdness in our situation, you'll eventually understand." She put her fingertips on his forearm. "OK, I'll tell you more about myself, but first I'd like a summary of your relationships with girls and women from your childhood to the present."

In fifteen minutes, Dan reviewed his love life. The dozens of boy-girl interactions ranged from "She kissed me in the alley, and I disappeared" to more mature affairs of the heart, after the girl herself or her friend confessed her feelings to Dan.

"Wow, let me think about this." She took another sip of water and stared at him. "I know what's causing your difficulty. You're a sweet, sensitive person, but you're seeking a nearly perfect woman in body, mind, and spirit. Good luck finding her. Like many men, you're too focused on a woman's appearance. You think a beautiful woman must not be approachable." She tilted her head to one side. "You should think more about what's going on under her skin."

"That's interesting," Dan said.

"Lots of girls were attracted to you, even fell in love with you, and lots haven't. But you won't approach one unless she hangs out a big sign saying, 'I really like you!' However, the minute she does that, her value drops in your eyes. You want the ones that run away from you. Is this the 'forbidden fruit' syndrome?" *Therein lies my problem with him.*

"I never thought of it that way before," Dan whispered.

"Yes. And because you think you're not attractive to women, you clam up, get tense, whatever. These traits turn off a lot of women. Still, when romance isn't on your mind—such as when you came over to save me at The High Note—you do fine. I'm not a psychiatrist, but I imagine with some practice, you could overcome these limitations. Maybe I can help you do that."

"Impressive. You understand me better than I do."

"It's often easier for someone to see things from the outside."

"You sound like my roommate," Dan said. "He's had a lot of experience too. His girlfriend, Stevie, recently had a spiritual awakening, and Chumbo's somewhere between an atheist and an agnostic. Probably more of the former."

"I'd like to meet them." Lana tapped her chin several times. "Now, I'll say a few words about myself, as you requested, sir." Lana hesitated. "I was a skinny tomboy in Cedarwood Falls. Average looks. Above ave—well, let's be honest, excellent—grades. I kept to myself, except when I was outrunning or outclimbing the neighborhood boys. I have loving parents. My mom was a hospital administrator and a town socialite. She still is. Dad was a top-ranked plastic surgeon. And I had a younger bro—" Her voice broke.

"Pardon me." She spoke with difficulty and hurried out of the room.

Lana returned two or three minutes later with a balled-up tissue in her hand. "Would you mind if we save the rest of the story until we know each other better?"

Without a word, he moved to the sofa next to her.

They sat hand in hand for a long while. The sun went down, and the room darkened. Only Lana's sniffles broke the silence.

Chapter 26

Wednesday, September 18

Dan was back in the lab earlier than usual in the morning. Joe wasn't in yet, so he asked Ron Steinberg from Dr. Kromer's second lab next door to be his lab safety backup for a while.

Let's see if we have a signal increase today, and if so, is there a connection with anything else? After two hours of data acquisition, Dan saw no signal boost. *This is crazy. I need a break. Plenty of research articles to read.* "Ron, I'm quitting for a while. Thanks for the help. I'll return the favor as soon as you need it."

When Joe arrived in the late morning, Dan was on his hands and knees feeling under a large wooden equipment locker.

"Lost something, eh?" his lab mate asked.

"Yeah, the handle and retaining pin on my nail clipper popped off, and I can't find them. They have to be under here, but I can't get my arm in very far, and the locker is too heavy to move."

Joe went to another locker and came back with a wooden meterstick. "Try this."

Dan soon pushed the lost parts out from under the side of the locker. "Thanks. I'd be lost without this baby. Clip my nails every few days. Better addiction than biting them or smoking." He reassembled his clipper and put it in his pocket.

Joe started up his acoustics experiments in pressurized gases. "Sorry for being late. I had an appointment this morning and forgot to text you."

"No problem." Soon, Dan was back on his testing apparatus with the same null results regarding the laser signal. "Hope your results are more consistent than mine."

"So far, so good."

"How come you're still wearing your jacket?" Dan said. "Are you cold? Coming down with something?"

"This lab is so drafty."

"Funny, I never paid much attention to that."

By midafternoon, the unexplained laser signal increase was back, but the effect was smaller this time, only up one point to 101. After asking for indulgence from his lab mate, Dan followed through with his plan to look for associations of the signal increase with other phenomena. He measured the laser beam strength with the overhead lights turned on and off. No changes. But with a small alternating-current electric coil placed at various distances from his apparatus, and when he waved a strong magnet near the apparatus, the signal increased substantially. *Unbelievable! Getting signals up to 106. That's up six percent from where it's supposed to be. The closer the coil or magnet is to the YO rod and laser beam, the stronger the laser signal gets. It looks like the coil is transferring some of its energy to the laser. Absolutely nuts! Gotta call Kromer right away.*

Ten minutes later, Dan's advisor was in the lab, and they went through all of Dan's tests together. "This is wild, Dan. I wonder if I can get Dr. Samstein from the physics department over here. Keep that AC coil turned on and near the YO rod from now on. When the rod is active, that coil is the energy source for most of the additional laser power."

"I agree." Dan made a sign that read "LASER ON, COIL ON" in two-inch high letters and hung it on the wall near the experiment.

By 5:30, Joe had left, but Dan, his advisor, and Dr. Samstein, who had just come in, continued working in the lab. After the demonstration was complete, Samstein smiled and nodded. "Your light show is impressive. Unorthodox according to current knowledge, but it doesn't violate the fundamental laws of physics. At least we understand the additional laser energy is coming from the electrical coil or the moving magnet—assuming this effect is real. But how is that happening?"

"Any suggestions about what to try next?" Kromer asked.

"Yes," replied Samstein. "Let's put the coil and wave the magnet near the crystal at the same time. That will tell us if both effects together produce a bigger signal than either one alone."

Dan did as requested, and it worked. The signal increase was significantly larger than either one separately. But thirty minutes later, the increase was less than half of what they had previously observed. Now Samstein had a puzzled look. "Hmm, let's turn everything off and wait a while. Maybe something got overheated."

But when the experiment was repeated, there was hardly any signal increase at all. Samstein shook his head. "Gentlemen, you know the basic rule of experimental science. If you can't repeat an observation, it's not real."

"But Dan has seen this phenomenon many times, even without the coil and magnet. They only made it larger." Kromer grunted. "Where can we go for help?"

"I don't understand what happened to the laser signal boost we all witnessed earlier," Samstein said, "but I think I'll call my old college friend, Wilbur Jenkins. He's on the physics faculty at Loman College and does research on the electro-optical properties of crystals, including yttrium oxide. Meanwhile, Dan can try to revive the 'Butler Effect'."

"I *can* repeat it," Dan said. "Just not every time. I'll keep trying to find out why."

Chapter 27

Thursday, September 19

Dan was alone in the lab at 7:30 in the morning. He paced and muttered. "Hurry up, Joe. I need to get my experiment started."

His lab mate came in a few minutes before eight, and Dan began another series of experimental checks. By midmorning, the vanishing laser-boost phenomenon was back, now showing a reading over 110, a 10 percent increase. When Dan tried a different crystal containing a new dopant set, lanthanum and cerium, both lanthanide elements, the laser signal worked its way to almost 125.

His computer clock read 11:05 when he picked up the lab phone. "Dr. Kromer? It's Dan. The signal boost is back. First, it went to 110."

"That's fantastic," said his advisor.

"But get this. I tried another rod containing a different dopant set. This one had lanthanum and cerium. Now it's up over 25 percent to 125."

"Good heavens! I'll cancel my afternoon appointment and be there at three o'clock. OK?"

"Absolutely. I'm not going anywhere. I'll be taking data until you get here."

By 1:20 the laser signal boost had crept up to 133.

Joe finished his sandwich and started shutting down his experiment.

"You going someplace, Joe? I need you here."

"Sorry, gotta run over to the computer store on the other side of town and pick up another internal hard drive for my laptop. Mine is starting to generate errors. If I get done in time, I'll come back to work. Maybe Ron can sub for me."

"Hope you find what you need." *Ron walked by a few minutes ago. Probably on his way to the cafeteria.*

Dan shut down his equipment. He typed his main findings into his laptop and did some calculations on the data he had.

At 2:45, Dr. Kromer came into the lab. "How's the signal looking?"

Dan grinned. "That new YO rod with the lanthanum and cerium looked great."

"May I see your run record for today?"

Dan vacated his chair for Kromer, who took a seat and studied the information logged in Dan's laptop. "You quit at one thirty? What happened?"

"Joe left. No safety partner. He had to get a part for his laptop. I couldn't find Ron Steinberg to sub for him. You know the rules. They're your rules."

"Safety first, last, and always. *That's* my rule, Dan. I'm here, so let's fire her up again."

The effect showed up as before, but it wasn't quite as strong. And by 5:00, after two maddening hours of watching the effect slowly dwindle from 118 to 102, only a couple percentage points above normal, they quit. Dan banged the countertop.

"Take it easy, Dan, we'll figure it out. Unstable experimental results are usually caused by instrumentation or environmental problems. But sometimes a new phenomenon is on the verge of discovery. In that rare but exciting case, the variation may be caused by one or more uncontrolled systems or environmental parameters. For example, room temperature or humidity."

"Yeah. But we keep getting big effects, and then they disappear. It's infuriating!"

"But even if it's bad equipment, you have to track it down." Kromer put his hand on Dan's shoulder and looked straight into his eyes. "Otherwise, none of your future research data will be trustworthy. Keep at it, and make sure *all* your data gets recorded, even when you think everything is junk. You never know."

That's my problem. I never know when or if the effect is going to be there!

Chapter 28

When Dan returned to the apartment, Chumbo was waiting for him.

"I need to talk to you about something, pal." Chumbo cocked his head. "It's only six o'clock. Let's grab our furry roommate and head for the park. We can eat the chili I made when we get back."

"Sure. I'm not that hungry anyway. Bad day in the lab."

A short time later, the three roommates arrived at Community Park. As they strolled along, a frisky Angel followed them, more or less, with numerous brief excursions. Dan took a deep breath and exhaled slowly, sighing. "What a day for a walk in the park. Blue sky and beautiful."

Chumbo pointed at a bench. "Let's grab a seat over there. We can watch those kids kick their soccer ball around." They headed to the unoccupied bench and sat.

"Hang on a minute." Chumbo got up and raced Angel to retrieve the soccer ball rolling toward their bench. He kicked the ball back to the group of girls. They all waved to him. He bowed at them from the waist and got a bunch of smiles and giggles.

Chumbo returned and sat again. "Stevie's gone silent lately. She's been tryin' to educate me about the Bible, God, all that stuff. But when my eyes glaze over, she gets frustrated. Said she needed some private time. But I miss her, so I wanna try again."

Dan nodded. "I think you two will work it out."

"Look, roomie," Chumbo said. "Let's you and me try it by the numbers. I know it makes sense to *you* because you already believe this stuff. But I believe in sensory perception and thought. I gotta see, hear, smell, taste, or touch something to believe in it. It has to make sense to believe in it. I gave up on God when I was eight and my father died."

Chumbo raised his hands and crossed his two forefingers. "To explain the universe and the world you need two things—matter and life. Matter, or let's say matter plus energy. Or let's say anything physical wasn't created out of nothing. It always existed in one form or another and was transformed into the universe by . . . the Big Bang or something."

"I see." Dan puffed his cheeks.

"Yeah, and the second thing is life. You start with a big soup of the right ingredients, add a few billion years for the stuff to percolate, and you get microorganisms. Wait a few billion more years and you get . . . Einstein! It's called evolution. Dan, my god is Charles Darwin." Chumbo flailed his arms around.

"So your gods are Einstein and Darwin," Dan said. "Have you ever heard of Occam's razor?"

"Nope."

"The philosophical principle called Occam's razor is named after a fourteenth-century logician and friar William of Ockham. It says if you have to choose between competing ideas, then choose the simplest one. That's one of the reasons I choose the Lord God Almighty, Jehovah, Hashem, Jesus, and any other name He is known by in any language. Everything, physical or nonphysical, that ever was, is, or ever will be, exists through Him, although I don't completely understand what He's doing. Think about this, Chumbo . . . think about it. One Magnificent Being explains everything you've ever seen or ever will see. Everything you've ever thought or ever will think. Ockham would be proud of that."

Chumbo stood up. "Hmm. Occam's Razor. Interesting way of looking at things. If you apply that to your relationship with Lana, doesn't that mean she's into you?"

"I don't think Occam's razor applies to relationships."

Chapter 29

As Lana backed out of the driveway to her apartment, she stopped before entering the street as usual, but this time the pause was longer and her breaths shorter. She was on her way home to tell her parents about her business relationship with Dan.

Lana pulled onto her street, headed west two miles, then turned north for a straight shot to the Falls. A forty-minute drive in good conditions. She turned on the radio and got a station playing Adele's "Crazy for You," one of her favorites. Eased into relaxing, her thoughts drifted to Dan. Would he ever understand her feelings for him on his own? Would she eventually have to just come out and tell him? She needed more patience. After all, their meeting at The High Note was less than four weeks ago. She turned up the radio volume. The music and her musings made the drive go faster.

Fifteen minutes later, she let herself into her parents' home. "I'm here," she called, and her parents met her with hugs and words of welcome. Dad took her hand and walked down the long hall with her to the den, her mother following.

Lana sat in her favorite of the three recliners. "I always love being home again. By the way, I drove through some dark storm clouds on my way here. We may get some cymbal crashes during dinner." She pulled the handle on her recliner and her feet went up. "So much is happening at school, it's hard to get home anymore."

"I'm sure it is, darlin'," her mom said, "but you need to try harder. Dad and I miss you terribly. Don't we, James?"

"Absolutely. I can hardly fix a toaster or leaky faucet without my trusty electromechanical assistant to help me."

Lana felt a wave of melancholy wash over her remembering how much fun it was to be her father's helper.

"Well, Lana dear, tell me how your graduate school is coming." Mom never engaged in small talk for long.

"I'm still enjoying it. My new advisor, Dr. Wilson, is tough, but I'm learning how to work with him."

Dad chuckled. "Still my little therapist, eh? Always trying to understand what makes other people tick. It's a wonder you didn't go into psychology."

Mom stood up and walked toward the hall. "Excuse me a minute, I'll check with Clara about dinner."

"It's ready!" Mom called from the dining room doorway.

The dinner was delicious. Clara served a bottom round pot roast with potatoes and asparagus. Then she brought out a large tray containing a homemade apple pie, tea, and coffee.

"Wow, Clara," Lana said. "That looks great. Beats anything I'm getting in Quincy."

Mom started the after-dinner conversation. "Well, dear, anything new happening in Quincy? We lead such a quiet life in the Falls. Pleasant but quiet."

"Well, I met another grad student, Dan Butler, who's mentioned several of his friends I'm hoping to get together with soon." Lana felt her cheeks get warm.

Mom smiled and raised her head. "That sounds wonderful. You need a social life. Can't study all the time. Who are they?"

"Well, let's see." Lana considered the safest way to explain the situation. "Dan is in mechanical engineering. His roommate is Chumbo Porter. Chumbo's girlfriend is Stevie Morgan. Oh, and there's another girl, Carter Edwards."

"Oh, that's nice. Is she Dan's . . . *friend?*"

"I'd say they're friends. But Dan and I have formed a relationship—a business venture."

Lana's mother put down her fork. "You haven't said a word about that. What kind of business?"

"Well, I'm coaching him."

Her mom took a last swallow of coffee and put her napkin on the table. "Lana, I'm afraid I wouldn't make a very good dentist. So rather than having to pull out any teeth, why don't you just explain to us what's going on?"

Dad, who'd been eating his pie and listening, also put his fork down. "Coaching him to do what?"

"I met Dan at a café. He's a very nice guy who's insecure about approaching women he's interested in and thought I might be willing to coach him about relationships. I can use the money for my car payments."

Her mom frowned. "I've never heard of such a thing. A single man hires a single woman—a beautiful one at that—to teach him how to pick up women. That doesn't ring true. Apparently he didn't have any trouble approaching you. I'd like to meet some of these women he wants to . . . to . . . approach."

Lana saw an opening. "That's a good point, Mother, and I asked him that myself after he offered me the job. He said he knew he had no chance with me, so he wasn't intimidated."

"That sounds like a pickup line to me. What do you think, James?"

"*I* think Lana has excellent judgment. If she's comfortable with Dan, I'm sure he's fine."

Her mother adjusted her sleeves. "Tell me the truth, darling. What are your real feelings for Dan? You said it was a business relationship—and a screwy one at that—but is that all it is? Do you have any, shall we say, *nonbusiness* interest in Dan?"

"Dan is good-looking and honorable. Why does that matter if he's not going to try to form a romantic relationship with me?"

Mom frowned, and her voice turned shrill. "So you're not dating him, just giving him advice. Is that right?"

"Take it easy," Dad said. "This isn't a prosecution in court."

Her mother threw her napkin down on the table. She went into the kitchen and came back with a glass of red wine. "Talk to her, James."

"Lana, why don't you invite Dan to come here for dinner this weekend? It might ease your mother's concern. I'd like to meet this young, and rather enterprising, man myself."

Mom's shaking hand caused wavelets in the wine. She put her glass on the table.

Lana rose from her chair. "Well, it sounds like the storm *outside* has passed anyway. I'd better get back to Quincy." She kissed her mother.

Her father walked her to the front door and gave her a kiss. "Hang in there, girl," he whispered.

"Thanks, Dad. Love you both." *If Mom could just meet Dan, I know she'd come around.*

Chapter 30

Friday, September 20

After scanning the area around Reading Room 2 a second time and seeing no one in this part of the Quincy library, Dan entered and took a seat at one of the tables, tapping his knees. *That was one unexpected email.*

Dan smoothed his navy sports jacket and adjusted the dark gray tie on his light blue shirt. He pulled the folded sheet he'd printed last night from his jacket.

To: djbutler@quincyu.edu
From: jjeos@starwaylabs.com
Subject: Internship Interview

Dear Mr. Butler:
My name is J. J. Eos. I represent StarWay Labs, a young but highly successful industrial research organization headquartered in the Research Triangle Park, NC. We offer short-term internships to graduate students conducting research in a number of areas of interest to our organization. These are designed to expose them to modern industrial research while minimizing disruption of their present educational or professional careers. Upon

completion of their education, StarWay interns are offered positions in one of our laboratories or assisted in obtaining job interviews with our industrial associates. You can learn more about our organization at starwaylabs.com.

I will be conducting interviews in Quincy the next two days and am interested in interviewing you about a possible internship with StarWay Labs. I have an opening at ten tomorrow morning in reserved Reading Room 2 of the Quincy University library. I apologize for the late invitation, but I had to move up my trip to Virginia on short notice.

Please let me know by return email whether you are interested and available tomorrow. If you are not available at that time, then perhaps we can meet when I return to Virginia next week. A short evaluation questionnaire is attached. Please fill it out and return it with your email.

Sincerely,
J. J. Eos, MS
Director, Academic Recruitment

Dan refolded the paper and replaced it in his jacket. *Their website was interesting but kinda brief. Kromer was OK with me following up but said not to jump into anything.* He looked up through the window and caught sight of a middle-aged, bald man in a dark gray pinstripe suit heading toward the room. Dan swallowed and looked down again. *He looks familiar.*

Seconds later, the man opened the door and smiled. "Daniel Butler?"

"Yes, sir. You must be Mr. Eos." Dan stood, and they shook hands.

"I am indeed." He handed Dan his card, laid his laptop case on the table, and took a seat. "Sorry I'm late. I like to take a short walk between meetings. Relaxes me. Shall we get started, Daniel? Or is it Dan?"

Dan sat down again. "People call me Dan."

"Dan it is, then."

"Mr. Eos, you look familiar. Did you attend my research seminar a few weeks ago?"

"No, I haven't been in Virginia for several months. But I'm always being mistaken for other people."

"A visitor in the back row looked a bit like you, but I couldn't see him very well."

Eos shrugged. "Let me give you a quick rundown on StarWay Labs and our internship program. We recently celebrated our twentieth anniversary as a corporation, although several of the top managers and scientists had previously worked together. In a nutshell, StarWay conducts company-confidential research for us and our commercial partners on high-risk, high-payoff science and engineering projects. Of course, we don't get into those details on our webpage."

"Does that mean you don't publish your research?" Dan asked. "I'm interested in a scholarly career."

"Practically no industrial research ever gets published." Eos raised his eyebrows and leaned back. "Except in cases where the work has scientific but no commercial value. Inventions considered workable and profitable are patented, sometimes by StarWay and sometimes jointly with our partners."

Eos smiled. "Now, here's something most companies don't do. All StarWay employees who work on a project share in the income earned by any patents from the project. In fact, we've had several cases where this included our interns as well."

"How do the internships work?" Dan interlaced his fingers and sat back.

"We try to custom fit them to each person's situation. You choose anything between a two- to four-week commitment. Renewals are usually available."

"Why did you select me?" Dan asked.

"Excellent question. And by the way, a candidate's questions are part of the interview score." Eos made a few keystrokes on his keyboard. "Your area of research, opto-mechanics of lasers in yttrium oxide, fits well into one of our current research interests. So I decided—"

"How could you possibly know that," Dan interrupted, "when we haven't published anything about—"

"Not formally, that's true, but the mechanical engineering department's website lists the research projects of every graduate student and gives a short summary. Yours was one of them. Part of my job is to search the websites of technical universities in the Southeast."

"Wow, that's amazing." Dan tapped the table.

"How is your research going? In broad terms, of course." Eos leaned forward and put his chin on his palm.

"It's going, uh, fine." Dan spoke slowly, careful not to reveal too much information. "We're studying yttrium oxide rods doped with various metals and under different conditions. Right now I'm trying to get rid of a nutty problem in my experiment."

"Nutty problem?" Eos focused on Dan.

"Yeah, the instruments show the laser beam gets stronger after it passes through the crystal rod, when it should actually be reduced by a few percentage points. My advisor and I both know that's abnormal behavior, but I haven't pinpointed the reason yet."

"These things happen in research. I'm sure you'll figure it out." Eos removed a bottle of water from his case and took a prolonged swallow. "Getting back to your candidacy, here's what we'll do. Based on your research area, the excellent evaluation form you emailed me, and my rating of this interview, StarWay Labs will offer you one of the internships I described. You choose the time, with room and board and all travel expenses paid. And with a stipend of . . ." Eos took another drink and thought for a moment. "How does seven hundred and fifty dollars a week sound, Dan?"

"Wow. Thank you very much. But I want to think about this and talk to my advisor first. Can I let you know next week?"

"I wish I could hold the offer that long but funds are limited, and I have several other excellent candidates waiting to hear from me. I'm afraid I can only hold this offer until tomorrow. Because of laboratory availability, the rescheduling restricts my flexibility. We would like you to start right away, but I *could* give you a week to get your affairs in order before you report."

Eos stood and shook Dan's hand. "I enjoyed meeting you, Dan. This will be a unique opportunity for you. Of course, it's your choice, but you might regret it if you pass this up. I'll call you tomorrow for your decision."

What a day! A guy offers me a fantastic-sounding job with huge enticements and wants an answer by the next day. Crazy.

Glittering above the building across the street from his apartment, the planet Venus greeted the oncoming night. Dan put his head against the armrest of his sofa, pulled out his phone, and tapped Lana's icon.

"Hey, Lan, it's Dan. Bet you didn't know I was a poet."

"I *like* the way it sounds. What are you up to?" Lana's voice was as smooth as warm honey.

"I got an email yesterday from a guy at a research organization, StarWay Labs, and he wanted to interview me on campus for a short-term industrial research internship. I met with him this morning, and get this, he offered me a two- to four-week gig at seven hundred and fifty a week and all expenses paid, but he wants an answer by tomorrow."

"Did you talk to Dr. Kromer about it?"

"He said it was an unusual offer, but he could spare me for two weeks if I wanted the industrial research experience."

"Where is this StarWay Labs? And why are they so interested in you? Could it have anything to do with your research anomalies?"

"He said the headquarters were in North Carolina, but their brief webpage didn't list an address. Weird, right? But they are interested in laser opto-mechanics of yttrium oxide. After talking with Dr. Kromer and you, I realize the offer sounds pretty strange. I'm gonna think about it tonight and make my decision tomorrow."

Lana's voice tightened. "The offer is generous. Maybe too generous. In fact, it sounds too good to be true. And you know what they say about those." There was a pause. "Are you going to talk to the campus police or somebody?"

"It does sound suspicious, but Eos didn't say anything threatening or illegal."

"It's your call. But be careful."

"Hmm. Sounds like my love coach is starting to worry about her student. Why might that be?"

"Of course, I care about you."

"You have to, right? After all, I'm paying you a salary."

"Good night, Dan."

"I mean . . . come on . . ."

"Good night." And the call ended.

Dan dropped his phone on the couch and slapped himself on the side of his head with the palm of his hand. "Idiot."

Chapter 31

Saturday, September 21

At 8:00 a.m., Dan's phone alarm sounded. *Dang it. The only morning I get to sleep in.* It was a local call, so he picked it up. "Good *morning.*"

"And to you, too, Dan. This is your friend, J. J. Eos. I apologize for the early call, but I have a plane to catch. There's been an interesting development regarding your StarWay internship candidacy, and I wanted to tell you before I go *incommunicado* for several hours on the plane. Do you have a moment to talk?"

"Sure. Go ahead."

"Dan, I reviewed your qualifications and research area against the others on my list. I'm convinced you are the best one, so I called the lab director and told him all about you. I asked him to give you another week or two to decide. He reiterated that would conflict too much with the current lab utilization schedule, but here's the good news. He authorized me to increase your salary from seven hundred and fifty to one thousand dollars per week. He's also upgrading you to the premium visitor's room in StarWay Labs. I've seen it, and it's better than *my* room. Is that enough sugar to perhaps entice you? The lab director is *very* enthusiastic about your coming. I'll bet he'd even give you dinner and a tour of his magnificent country estate.

I've been here for twenty years, and he's never been this excited about another intern. What do you say, Dan?"

"How much time do I have to think this over?"

"I'm packed and ready to leave in fifteen minutes. I'd have called earlier but didn't want to disturb you even a minute before eight. Let's say in ten minutes?"

"Can you hang on for that long while I think this over?"

"How about if I call back at eight fifteen. OK?"

"Sure. You're making it difficult for me to say no."

"Talk to you then."

Dan jumped out of bed. He threw his jeans and slippers on and ran into the bathroom. Two minutes later he was back in the bedroom on his knees for a quick prayer and plea for guidance.

It was clear StarWay really wanted him though he wasn't sure why. He knew it wasn't because he was an academic superstar. There was no time to call Dr. Kromer or Lana. Practically no time even to think.

The offer is fantastic. They sound like a reputable lab, except for the high-pressure job I'm getting. Why me? It has to be the laser boost. But everyone says it's wrong. So how would they know it's right? And if they do know, why do they need me? This is too crazy.

His end table digital clock said 8:11. Nothing left but to wait it out. His heart pounded, and his hands trembled. Four minutes that seemed like eternity.

When his clock changed from 8:14 to 8:15, his phone sounded. He almost dropped it.

"Hello."

"What's your decision, Dan?"

"Mr. Eos, I am so thankful for your wonderful offer, but I can't accept it. My hesitancy is—"

"Daniel, there are three things I want you to know. I am very disappointed. The laboratory director will be very disappointed. And if you ever find out more about StarWay, you will also be extremely disappointed. Good luck at school." *Click.*

So now it's Chumbo Porter, eh? What a nickname. Lana chuckled and laid her phone beside her on the couch. *It's ten a.m., and he's coming at eleven.*

She toed her flats off and tucked her legs under her on the sofa.

When she pulled an afghan over her lap, it triggered a painful memory. Eleven years ago, Lana had sat next to her dad on a sofa. He'd held her hand. In those days, her anguish over her little brother was constant. *Daddy, I never saw Jimmy again after the fire. You said I had to stay in the hospital during the funeral. You said the coffin was closed. Maybe Jimmy wasn't in it.* She closed her eyes, willing the memory to go away, and drifted off to sleep.

The ring of her doorbell jolted Lana awake, and she sat up. She slipped on her shoes and ran to the bathroom, where she swished a swig of mouthwash. Then she hurried back to the door and opened it.

"Hi, Chumbo. Come on in. It's good to meet you. Would you care for something to drink? I have fruit juice, tonic water, and sodas. Got pretzels too."

"I'm fine on the eats. But, uh, sodas?" Chumbo's expression sagged like a flat tire. "Listen, I have a six-pack in my car. Mind if I run out and get it?" He put his palms together like he was praying.

"Chumbo, I hope I'm not being dull, but would you mind drinking something else? I keep a dry apartment."

"A tonic would be fine." Chumbo managed a weak thank-you and took the easy chair. "It looks like things are improving for Dan under your supervision. And I can see why. When you two first met, I asked him to talk to you about my dating problems. I assume he did, right?"

"Yes, he did. I'll help if I can, but I'm not a professional counselor. To start, maybe you could give me a rundown on your immediate family and a few words about your childhood."

Chumbo spoke for several minutes about his parents and younger sisters. He was more verbose about his childhood. But even with Lana's gentle prodding for him to be more succinct, he ended twenty minutes later with, "Of course, I'll pay you for your time. Although, I expect it won't take as long for you to help me as it'll take for Dan."

"I suspect it may take you longer than Dan. So how about if I throw in a free discussion or two?"

"I appreciate that." Chumbo crunched on a pretzel and slurped some tonic. "For whatever reason, I've always had an easy time hooking up with girls. I take what I can get and wait for Ms. Wonderful to appear. I'm dating two girls right now—Stevie and, to a lesser extent, Kathy. Kathy is mostly for fun, and Stevie stopped having fun since she found God. But I like her, even though she puts restrictions on our relationship."

Chumbo stopped and stared into the air. "On top of that, she and Dan are working hard to convince me God is real. So I'm kinda mixed up right now. Any advice?" He sat back, folded his hands on his stomach, and raised his brows.

"I'm confused too. It sounds like your life is pretty much driven by alcohol and sex." Lana spoke without emotion or drama.

Chumbo's face turned a dark shade of red, and he croaked out, "What's Dan been telling you about me?"

"He's told me nothing. You drove here with beer in your car in case I didn't have any. The last time I was in your apartment with Dan, I opened your refrigerator for some OJ. Found four six-packs of beer. That covers the first charge."

"Well, I think you're making—"

"Then we come to the sex. You mentioned you date multiple women and used 'fun' and 'take what you can get' regarding both. When I was with Dan that night, he brought the mail in with him. We were gabbing away, and he was looking at me and absent-mindedly opening envelopes. When he saw my embarrassed expression, he looked down at what was in his hands. He slipped it back in the envelope and with a red face said, 'Sorry, Lana, that wasn't for me.' Nice magazines you're reading, Chumbo."

"I don't think that makes them addictions. They're just ways—"

Lana crossed her hands over her chest. "Listen, I know what addictions are and what they can do. Two addictions killed my little brother in a fire when he was seven years old. I was alone with him because my father had gone out to buy liquor for his secret binge drinking while Mom was out of town. But I wasn't watching my brother. I was watching a TV series I was pretty much addicted to. Jimmy's been dead for over a decade, but I still grieve for him. So please don't tell me what an addiction is."

"I'm sorry, Lana. I didn't know. Look, maybe this coaching idea was a mistake. I'd better be getting—"

Lana unhooked her arms and took a deep breath. "Hang on, Chumbo. I apologize for going off like that. I just wanted you to know that my family also has some baggage."

"I understand. What do you suggest we do?" Chumbo took a small pad and pencil from his shirt pocket.

"Let's identify what your issues are based on what you said and go from there. Let me think." Lana sat back and closed her eyes. "Your problems with women fall into three general categories. Your alcohol problem. The personal versus sexual aspects of your interactions. And your relationship with God. Did I miss anything?"

"Sounds right to me." Chumbo checked the notes he'd jotted down while Lana was speaking.

"Good. Why don't you think about those three areas, and maybe we can get together another time? You might want to write down how you've been handling them . . . and also, what you think a truly good man would do. I'm not saying you're not a good man."

"Roger, coach. Thanks a lot."

"While you're thinking about the way you treat and use women, ask yourself how you'd like it if somebody did those things to your sisters."

After Chumbo left, Lana lay on her couch and tried to deep-breathe away the tension that built up during Chumbo's visit. Bringing up the problems her family had experienced, and especially the death of her seven-year-old brother, Jimmy, had drained her.

As she closed her eyes and slowed her breathing, she felt her arm slip from her stomach to the cushion . . .

She was thirteen again and standing outside the door of her parents' bedroom. Slowly, she opened the door, and there he was again, with his toys strewn about.

"Get away from that outlet before you kill yourself, Jimmy! Where'd you find that screwdriver?"

"Daddy fixed the circuit. Now I can too. Where is he? When's Mommy comin' home?"

"I'll bet you can. Dad's at the store. And I told you Mom's coming home tomorrow." She strode into the bedroom and held out her hand. "Give me the screwdriver."

He clamped his jaws together and frowned. After a few seconds, he sighed and handed it to her.

She put the tool on top of the mantel. "Now listen, Jimmy. Take your toys downstairs where I can see you. Right away. *The Dodson Family*—my *favorite* TV show—is coming on."

"Those Dodson girls. I hate 'em." Jimmy leaned back on his elbows.

"Do it *now*, SpongeBob. I mean it." She flew downstairs and jumped onto her chair in the den, turning on the TV. Lana reached for the mug she'd left next to the chair. Her favorite peach tea.

While Amber Dodson applied her makeup, Lana looked up at her own image in the mirror behind the TV. She only had three more years until, hopefully, she might be as glamorous as Amber. Mimicking her TV idol's signature full-moon eyes, Lana held her breath when Chad pushed Amber Dodson's doorbell. *Is he finally gonna ask her out? Ooh, what a hunk!*

The house lights flickered a few minutes later.

When the first scene ended, Lana savored the last swallow of her tea and checked her watch. *Why isn't Dad back yet? Better check on Jimmy again.*

Putting her mug on the table, she glanced toward the staircase. Smoke drifted out of the upstairs hallway. She gasped and sprang to her feet. Dropping the TV remote on the floor, she bolted up the stairs. Her eyes and nostrils stung. A glow flickered under the door of her parents' bedroom.

"Dear God, the screwdriver!"

Lana shot down the hall and grabbed the doorknob. She shrieked and jerked her hand back. Covering the other hand with her sweater, she opened the door. Scorching air slammed her to the floor. She took a deep breath. Her lungs stung like she was inhaling pins and needles.

"Jimmy!" Smoke billowed from the room and curled on the hall ceiling. Orange and yellow, the flames lashed at her. Crawling into the hellhole under the fire and dense smoke, Lana wriggled lizard-like toward the fireplace.

"Jimmy! Jimmy! Where are you?" She strained to hear his voice through the roaring fire.

Her vision blurred with tears and smoke. As the back of her neck and hands began to singe, she screamed.

"Dear . . . Lord, save . . . us!" After she choked out the prayer, she bumped against Jimmy's leg.

Remaining low, Lana dragged Jimmy to the door. Once in the hall, she picked him up and ran, still screaming, to the staircase. When they reached the landing at full speed, she jumped the top steps. They landed halfway down and tumbled the rest of the way. She held fast to Jimmy, who ended up on top of her, motionless.

Lana made a wet, throaty sound. While she lay on her back, impotent, tongues of fire licked the walls and spilled down the hallway. With one arm still wrapped around Jimmy, her other arm covered her eyes . . .

Lana gasped and jerked upright on the sofa. Her heart raced, and she was covered in sweat, as she had been those many dozens of times this had happened in the past.

Chapter 32

James donned casual attire to meet his daughter's new client that evening. His wife had been in a tizzy all day, thinking about how to handle Dan and about preparing dinner, since Clara was ill. Ann and Lana had spoken, somewhat more civilly, earlier in the week, and they'd decided it was time for James and Ann to meet Daniel Butler. Lana told her mother the evening was part of Dan's coaching—how to behave when meeting the parents of the woman he was dating. Of course, James knew Ann hoped this was not the case.

Lana warned me this morning, "Tonight, if Mom becomes the flint, you and I have to be the firefighters."

"James! I need you," Ann called up the staircase in a rhythmic cadence. "I'm ready for you to carve the turkey."

He came down and did his usual duty. "I love the way you decorated the dining room table. Your prize-winning red roses look stunning on our buffet."

"Isn't it surprising what a nonprofessional with gangrene of the thumb can do? The ladies in the Flower Society always flatter me." Ann's voice had an upbeat lilt that belied her modest words. "Lana sounded positively enchanted this morning, didn't she?"

James picked up on his wife's relative enthusiasm. "I'm looking forward to meeting Dan. Aren't you?"

"Let's just say I'm hoping for the best. For her sake."

Lana and Dan arrived at the correct time. After they entered, Dan greeted James and Ann and handed Ann a gift.

"My mother wanted you to have this, Mrs. Madison. The vase is handcrafted, and the flowers are from her garden."

She thanked him and took the flowers to the dining room. After a few more words of introduction, Lana walked Ann to the kitchen, while James escorted Dan upstairs to see his prized collection of first edition medical textbooks.

Everyone spoke in upbeat tones during dinner. Lana reached for seconds on the homemade panko asparagus, and Dan scarfed down two big servings of turkey and dressing. While Ann smiled pleasantly, she spoke less than the rest of the party. *She must be waiting for dessert.*

James eyed the gorgeous rose display on the buffet. Dan's wildflowers looked so lonely sitting beside them. It seemed rude to have put them there.

After dinner, Lana took Dan to the den. The Madisons went to the kitchen, and when they returned, Ann carried a tray with apple pie and vanilla ice cream. Dad brought after-dinner beverages.

"Well, Dan," Ann said, taking her seat, "I know Lana is enjoying her . . . coaching job. She explained it to us, but I'm a bit confused about what you two are doing. Would you mind explaining it to us?"

Dan looked at Lana, and a wide smile spread across his face. "Of course, but first, I want to express my gratitude to both you and Dr. Madison for having me to dinner," he said. "After all the frozen meals and cafeteria food I've eaten, this dinner was delicious."

Lana beamed. James smiled broadly. Ann grinned, but one eyebrow rose while the other fell.

Dan frowned. "As far as the job goes, I saw Lana at a café and asked her to be my dating coach."

"That's surprising," Ann said. "Lana told me you were shy around attractive women."

"My situation is a bit complicated, Mrs. Madison. You see, my reticence disappears if it isn't a romantic relationship. No fear of rejection."

James's eyes widened at the last few words. "Sounds like you just wanted advice on how a shy fellow could meet women."

While Dan was nodding, Ann jumped back in. "I'm still trying to understand the arrangement, Daniel, but if you and Lana are working together, her father and I would like to get to know you better. Is your family from this area?"

Dan moved back in his chair and picked up his coffee cup. "Yes, ma'am, we're from Hockson's Creek. About ten miles southwest of Quincy."

"I see." Ann cleared her throat. "What do your parents do for a living?"

Dan choked on his coffee and began a fit of coughing. Lana developed a definite frown.

"Ann," James said, "maybe it's time to give your . . . inquisitive nature a rest and see if Dan has any questions for us."

"It's OK, Dr. Madison." Dan put his coffee cup on the table. He paused, then replied, "Dad worked at the sawmill outside of town before it closed about ten years ago. Since then, he's been with the parts department at Masterson Toyota in South Quincy. Mom's a homemaker. She also crafts and sells pottery and cultivates her wildflower garden. She makes beautiful pottery, like the vase I brought you."

"It's very nice." Ann turned and looked at the buffet. "I'd like to see some more of them." She tapped her fingertips lightly on the arm of her chair.

"Sounds lovely." James smiled at the new direction of the conversation. "I don't think of pottery as a hobby or a craft. It can be an art form as elevated as sculpture. Of course, that depends on the artist."

"Dan has shown me several photos of his mother's pieces," Lana added. "Talk about talent. Dan, do you mind bringing them up on your phone?"

"Sure, be happy to." Dan smiled and took out his cell phone. After tapping it a few times, he passed it to Ann.

She scrolled through a few pictures. "Your mother's very talented." She handed the phone to James and said, "Dan, I'm interested in hearing about your research, but please, no jargon or math terms."

He gave her a two-minute summary, appropriately simplified.

Ann tried to look interested and then continued her cross-examination. "What's the job market like these days in mechanics? Sorry, mechanical engineering. What kind of salary do you expect?"

Dan stared dumbfounded at Mrs. Madison.

Lana sprang up. "Wow," she said, looking at her watch. "It's almost nine o'clock. I have an early appointment tomorrow. Mom and Dad, your dinner and hospitality were sublime, but I think Dan and I should say good night now."

On the ride back to town, neither said a word for the first several miles. Then Lana put her hand on Dan's. "If you're mad, you have every right to be. As a matter of fact, I'm pretty upset myself. My mother doesn't know how to be diplomatic."

"Lana, I'd rather not have this discussion while I'm driving. Chumbo texted me that he's going out tonight, and Mrs. Haynes isn't available, so he's going to leave Angel alone. I don't know if he fed or walked her. Do you mind if we drive straight to my apartment and talk there?"

Lana turned and looked at his compressed lips. "That's fine," she murmured.

Not a word was spoken for the rest of the drive, except when Lana asked him a question about his plans for the next day and received no answer.

When they arrived at the apartment, Angel was at the door yipping. She sniffed Lana and then wagged her tail vigorously. Dan walked to the kitchen table, and Lana sat on the den sofa.

"He left a note," Dan called from the kitchen. "He fed and walked Angel. We can have our discussion now."

He came back into the den. Lana looked straight ahead and remained quiet. She petted Angel, who'd jumped onto her lap.

"It's the silent treatment, is it?" Dan walked over and stood in front of Lana. "Then I'll start. Look, Lana, I know Hockson's Creek isn't as elegant as Cedarwood Falls. I know plastic surgeons make a lot more money than mechanical engineers. You told me your mom is the president of the Cedarwood Falls Flower Society. Mine is the treasurer for the Hockson's Creek Pottery Club. I get it. Your mother looked down her long nose at me all night. And she knows nothing about me."

"Dan, I want to—"

"Your mother made it clear that I'm not welcome as your friend, even though we're just business partners. But *you* need to be around your mother. Our relationship is causing a serious problem between you and your mother."

Lana put Angel down. "Wake up, Dan. You have it backward!" She stood and grasped his arm. "I want to continue being friends with you, to keep seeing . . . working with you, Dan. I will not let my mother's controlling attitude and snobbery come between us. My mother is a good-hearted woman who loves her family very much. She just—"

"—doesn't understand that her ideas and ways of doing things don't necessarily apply to others," Dan blurted out. "And another thing. She treats you like you're still in high school."

"I know all that. But she lost a child, my younger brother, when I was thirteen, so I try to excuse her attitude."

"Yes, I assumed there'd been some sort of tragedy from what you started to say that evening when we sat in silence on your sofa. I sympathize with you and your family, but I'm not sure that gives her the right to try to control the life of her other child—who is an adult."

"You're talking like . . . like you don't think we can keep working together."

"I'll tell you what I think. She's your mother. And I don't want to come between the two of you."

"You're worrying that you're coming between my mother and me," Lana said. "But did you ever stop to think that she . . . that she is coming between *us?*"

"Is teaching me about romance more important than the love between a mother and her only surviving child? Is it?"

"You're hopeless!" Lana shouted. "You don't get it, do you?"

"I get it perfectly. You're the one who doesn't understand. It would be a different story if you had strong feelings for me." Dan raised his eyebrows. "Then we wouldn't be having this argument, would we?"

Lana turned and grabbed her bag. Her world was shaking. "Take me home!"

Angel jumped off the couch and into the breach. She licked Lana's hand, then stood on her hind legs, taking Dan's hand in her mouth and pulling it toward Lana, while the two continued glaring at each other.

"Maybe Angel has more sense than either of us," Dan said, his voice returning to normal. He stooped and stroked his dog's head, then looked at Lana. "I'll take you home."

Neither said anything on the drive to Lana's apartment. Angel sat in Lana's lap and whimpered periodically. When Dan parked the car, Lana turned to him with tears streaming down her face and scooted Angel off her lap.

Angel, alone on the seat next to him, whimpered as Lana rushed toward the building. Alone.

Chapter 33

Monday, September 23

Early in the morning, Lana lay in bed staring at the ceiling after a second miserable night of tossing and turning. She didn't want to take her morning run. She didn't want to go to the lab. Reaching over to the nightstand, she grabbed her phone and typed a few letters, then tapped the Call icon.

"Hi. It's me. Hope I didn't wake you."

"No," her dad said. "I've been up for over an hour. Just finished breakfast."

"Dan and I had a fight at his apartment after our dinner with you and Mom. I kind of lost it. Do you think I should call and apologize, Daddy, or wait for him to call me?"

"A fight. How about that," her dad replied. "It seems Mom's intuition is better than mine. Maybe I'm old-fashioned, but I think a woman should play it cool in such circumstances. Give him another day or two. I'll bet he calls."

"I was leaning that way, but it never hurts to get your opinion. And please don't tell Mom. OK?"

"Mum's the word, sweetheart."

Dan arrived at the lab early, determined to focus on the laser boost phenomenon and set aside his preoccupation with the argument with Lana.

By late afternoon, research with the crystal rod containing the lanthanum and cerium dopants had repeatedly confirmed several aspects of Dan's mysterious laser power boost. The effect was sporadic, and the cause of its appearance and disappearance remained unknown. Laser power increases over 200 points were now commonplace. *But getting super results in the lab isn't making me feel any better about Lana.*

By increasing the output of the electric coil's power supply, the laser signal became several times larger than the earlier values.

But none of the faculty members except Dr. Kromer believed the effect could be real. He'd informed Dan earlier that day that Dr. Jenkins, who had been out of the country, finally called Dr. Samstein back. After receiving the latest results, Jenkins said such behavior had never been documented before.

When Joe left the lab at 6:15 p.m., Dan was forced to power down all his equipment. *Time to go home and cry in my beer.* Except, he didn't drink.

He picked up his laptop and walked toward the light switch, then remembered he wanted to call Lana before he left. He took out his phone. No answer. Her phone rolled over to voice mail.

"Hello, Lana. It's Dan. I've been thinking about our situation. We need to talk. I'm gonna stop at the supermarket on the way home. I'll give you a call tonight after I eat. Bye."

Dan switched off the overhead lights and headed for his car. Outside, no moon was visible. With only trees and an occasional building, this part of campus was isolated. An icy wind cut across his face.

As Dan approached the nearly empty lot, he noticed a white, unmarked van parked next to his car. The van had no windows behind the front seat. *Kinda creepy the way that van is so close to my car. It wasn't there this morning. Oh, come on, man. You can handle yourself.*

Then he stopped cold at the entrance gate. *I don't like this. Commercial vans don't usually park in the student lot.* He thought about his options. Campus police was only five minutes back.

Dan turned around and retraced his steps. Every minute or so, he looked back at the van until he rounded a bend in the path and lost sight of it. When he was a few hundred feet from his destination and could read the sign marked Campus Police, he paused again and looked at his watch. 6:38.

What am I going to tell them? "There's a van parked next to my car in the student lot. Would you please come with me and check it out?"

He turned around and headed back to his car.

BOOK TWO

Chapter 34

Dan's heart raced, and his head tingled as he approached the chain-link fence surrounding the student parking lot a second time. He picked up his pace to a jog and passed through the entrance gate. The sooner he got out of the lot the better.

Pulling out his car's remote, he pressed a button and heard the doors unlock as the headlights flashed twice. Dan peered into the front seat to check it was empty as he squeezed into the space between the two vehicles. Like those childhood nightmares where a bear or dinosaur was chasing him, his mind went into slow motion as he reached for the handle and opened his door.

Dan heard the side door behind him slam open. He spun around and looked into the van and at a gun barrel aimed at his head. Behind it sat a bearded man with dark glasses, wearing a black overcoat and hat.

Dan froze. *Oh, God.* "What do you want? I only have a few dollars. And a wristwatch."

The gunman waved his weapon at him. "Get in! Move!" he said in a strained voice that sounded artificially low.

With no escape possible, Dan climbed into the van. Chills danced along his spine, and his breathing became labored.

Only two single seats faced each other near the front, and a floor-to-ceiling metal chamber about three feet square in the right rear corner occupied the main compartment of the customized van. A young man, who bore an eerie resemblance to himself, knelt behind the open door.

"Give him your car keys and your jacket!" shouted the gunman, keeping his weapon trained on Dan. "And sit down."

Dan reached over, and with a trembling hand gave the man his keyring and remote, as well as his jacket.

The accomplice grabbed the keys and shrugged into the jacket. He quick-stepped out of the van and entered Dan's car. Then the kidnapper slammed the van's door closed. A flat metal wall with a small sliding door separated the driver's and the main compartments. The only access to the back of the van was through the side and rear doors.

What do I have that they could possibly want? This job was set up so carefully . . . The laser? . . . The laser! . . . Good Lord!

Dan heard his car pull away. *Clever people. This is no car theft. That's me driving away for the security camera.*

The gunman took Dan's laptop, cell phone, watch, and wallet and put them in a briefcase on the floor beside him.

"Well, Mr. Daniel Butler, I should introduce myself." The gunman no longer used an artificial voice. Removing his sunglasses and stripping off his beard and hat, the man said, "No need for these during our trip, is there?"

Eos! God help me! Dan stared at the face of his captor. *It's the lasers.*

"This'll be a long ride with one transfer," Eos said. "That's a restroom back there if you need one. Just like in a jetliner."

Dan nodded. "I have to use the bathroom."

Eos's cell phone chirped. "I have to answer this text," he said. "Go ahead but don't take too long. There's no lock on the door."

Dan got up and walked to the back of the van. When he returned, Eos was setting his phone down. He took a set of handcuffs out of his case and tossed them to Dan. "I'm tired of holding this gun. Put on these bracelets with the chain passing under your armrest. Make sure you snap them both closed. I want to hear the clicks."

Beads of sweat ran down his forehead as Dan secured the handcuffs.

"You look nervous, Dan. I gave you a chance to do this in a much more civilized way. But you didn't like my internship offer, did you? Now, we play hardball."

"I guess this is about you and your associates stealing the laser boost technology from QU, isn't it?" Dan started to bring his hand up to wipe his forehead, but the chain ran out. "It's amazing that nobody but you and I think this stuff is real."

"We aren't stealing anything, and we're not the only ones who believe in it. You'll have to wait until we arrive in Shangri-La before we can discuss that."

"Shangri-La? What are you gonna do with me?" Dan said, his voice trembled.

"Shangri-La. Our home lab. Now chat time is over. From now on, I do all the talking."

Dan felt his eyes grow large when Eos took a syringe out of a bag on the floor.

"I'm going to give you a sedative." Eos's voice was matter-of-fact. "We have a long trip ahead, and it will be much easier for both of us if you're asleep."

Before Dan could react, there was a sharp jab in his upper arm. His mouth dropped open, and he immediately felt the effect of the tranquilizer. He was barely conscious when he heard the front door of the van open. The left side of the vehicle dropped a little as someone took the driver's seat. Once the door shut, the engine started, and the van lurched forward. Then Dan's world went black.

Chapter 35

He sounded serious when he called and asked to come over at 7:00. Stevie put on the finishing touches of her makeup and closed her cosmetics organizer.

She went to the kitchen and made a pot of coffee. She had just filled her cup and taken it into the living room when there was a familiar seven-rap knock on the door of her apartment. *He's on time. Unbelievable.*

"Hi. Come on in, Chum," Stevie said. "Go on in and sit down, and I'll get you a cup of coffee." She poured a cup of coffee and placed it on the table in front of him.

"Thanks for letting me come over." Chumbo sat on the couch, crossed his ankles, and put his hands behind his head. "I hope I didn't interrupt anything."

"No, you didn't," Stevie said.

"Had a meeting with Lana."

"Lana? Who's Lana?" Stevie asked as she sat beside him.

"She's been giving Dan dating tips, so I thought I could use some help too."

Stevie laughed so hard she spilled her coffee. "You're getting dating tips? What a riot." She stood. "Hold on while I get some paper towels."

"Now hang on, Stevie," Chumbo pleaded as she left the room. "Dan's problem is he needs help to loosen up with women. Mine is I'm too loose."

"You think I don't know that?" she called back from the kitchen.

"Of course, you do. But after talking with you and Lana, I'm trying to do something about it. And you, Dan, and I've been talking about something else a lot lately. Faith."

"I'm sure you've noticed the connection between your two problems," Stevie pointed out as she returned, then wiped up the spill.

"I guess so. But I thought we could talk about the first one."

"It's your quarter, Chum. Why don't you *ply* and I'll *reply*?"

"Fair enough. I've been like a sailor drifting on a sailboat in the South Pacific. Getting blown from one beautiful, sun-drenched island to another by the prevailing winds."

"Sounds like a pleasant life."

"Yeah, but there's something missing. Something important. Even before the issue of morality or theology comes in."

"What might that be, Mr. Philosopher?" Stevie asked.

"I've been doing a ton of traveling, but I don't have a destination."

"I know what that's like. Any ideas about what to do?"

"I think I want to get closer to someone I really trust. Respect. Admire. Have feelings for."

"And?"

"Someone like you," Chumbo said, with a warmth and conviction Stevie had never heard from him.

"I didn't expect you to ever talk like that," Stevie said, choking up. "You already know my feelings toward you. And you know what my restrictions are, don't you?"

"I'm willing to accept your purity standards and quit drinking." He ran his hands through his hair. "But don't get any ideas about me going to church, though."

Stevie stared at him for a long time. "I want to believe you, Chum, and I want to give our relationship another chance. But I've learned things from your past behavior. If you break my heart again, you know what that would mean. Right?"

"Yes. I understand."

Chapter 36

Sitting in her easy chair, Lana stared at her watch. 8:30. He said he'd call after dinner. This wasn't like Dan. Why was he calling? To apologize? To break off their relationship completely? Something else? Did something happen to him? God forbid!

Lana snapped up her phone and called his cell. No answer. His lab. No answer. *Don't panic! Try his roommate.* "Hello, Chumbo, it's Lana. . . . I'm fine, but Dan said he'd call me tonight. He hasn't contacted me, and I haven't been able to reach him." She took a deep breath. "Are you in your apartment?"

"Yup. Just got in."

"Is he there?" she asked.

"Haven't seen him."

Oh, Good Lord.

"When he . . . comes in, will you ask him to call me? . . . Thanks." Maybe she shouldn't have waited for him to call first. And she shouldn't have lost her temper at his place. Yes, he was obtuse, but he had a right to be. She should have been first to break the silence. . . . *I'm going to his lab. Now!*

Fifteen minutes later, Lana was at the entrance to the student parking lot. *His car's not here. Maybe he walked to work this morning. No, he said he would stop at the supermarket on the way home. But which one?*

Lana wasn't in the mood to search the parking lots of all the local food stores. She slouched back in her seat and thought some more.

Maybe his phone battery is dead. Maybe he got a flat tire or his car broke down driving back. This is insane. I'm going back to my apartment.

By tomorrow morning, hopefully, it would all be explained.

Tuesday, September 24

At 7:00 a.m., Lana woke to the sound of her phone melody. She stubbed her finger reaching wildly to answer it. "Hi, Chumbo. Is he back?"

"I stayed up until midnight, and Dan never showed up. By then it was too late to call you and too early to call the police. I moved his pillow to the middle of his bed in case he came in late and left early. The pillow hasn't been touched, but I went out and checked the backyard. His car is here. But no sign of Dan. That's weird. I notified the campus police. What do you think is going on?"

Lana's heart thumped, and her words came out in short bursts. "Maybe he stayed with his parents. Maybe they picked him up. Do you have his parents' phone number?"

"Yes, I have it."

"Text it to me, please. I'm going to phone Mrs. Butler. I'll get back with you soon."

Breathing hard, Lana said a prayer for Dan. She tried his phone again and left a message. Then she called Mrs. Butler, using the number Chumbo had texted to her. Mrs. Butler picked up the call, but she knew nothing of Dan's whereabouts. She said she'd get Dan's father involved and call Lana back later in the day.

Lana had a couple of classes to attend, so she packed a lunch and went to campus. First, she checked Dan's lab. Joe didn't know anything about his whereabouts. Next, Lana walked to the office of her advisor, Dr. Wilson, and peeked in the half-open door. "May I come in?" she asked.

Dr. Wilson looked up from the paper he was reading. "Sure, Lana, have a seat."

"I'm sorry to bother you with a personal issue, Dr. Wilson, but I can't locate a friend of mine, a fellow grad student, and I'm beginning to worry." She clasped her hands in her lap. "His name is Dan Butler. Do you know him?"

"I don't know him personally, but his name sounds familiar. He might have taken my Physics for Engineers course a couple of years ago."

"I feel rather foolish, like I'm jumping to conclusions. I talked to him yesterday afternoon, but his roommate says he didn't return to their apartment, and he's not in his lab. I sense that something is wrong. Dan isn't the type of person to just disappear." She bit her lip in frustration. "Do you think I should get Dan's friends involved in helping to find him?"

Dr. Wilson tapped his fingernails on his desktop. "In my experience, it isn't unusual for a graduate student to take a little time off, even go into hiding for a day or two, if they're under a lot of stress. But let's remember this missing person case is barely a day old. I'm sure everything will be fine. However, if he doesn't show up in a day or two, the police should be notified." He leaned back in his chair. "I don't see anything wrong with you getting together with his friends to gather information that could be valuable to the police. But let me repeat what I just said—I'm sure everything will be fine."

Late that afternoon, after her Advanced Bioinstrumentation class, Lana got a call from Mrs. Butler. "Lana, I'm concerned about Dan. Arnold called the police, and two of them came to our house to take a statement from us. I told them you know as much as anyone about the situation, and they're going to contact you soon. They said it's too early to get worried. I hope it's OK I gave them your phone number."

"Of course, that's fine, Mrs. Butler. I spoke with my thesis advisor about Dan. He was upbeat that everything would be all right. He seemed to have no doubt about it. Maybe we both can take some encouragement from that."

Mrs. Butler's voice choked up. "I hope so, Lana. I hope so."

Lana forced her voice to sound upbeat. "I'll be praying for him day and night, Mrs. Butler."

Chapter 37

D an woke up in bed in nothing but his underwear feeling like he'd been asleep for days. His eyelids were crusted shut. Groaning as he rubbed them open, he sat up and recollected the tragic play he was an unwilling actor in. He shook his head to clear the fog in his brain.

He peered at his dim surroundings. The large room was set up like a hotel room but had no windows. A lamp on the nightstand beside the king-sized bed emitted a low-level bluish-white light that gave the room and its IKEA-like furnishings an eerie look. The air in the room had the faint odor of pine. His wristwatch lay on the nightstand. It was 8:55.

Dan jumped out of bed and ran to the door. Locked. He looked around for a door key or card. Nothing. There was a dresser on the wall opposite the bed, and he yanked the drawers open. Plenty of pairs of brand-new underwear and socks but still no key. He scanned his surroundings again. This time he noticed a small envelope with his name on it lying on the large, modern hardwood table. He removed the enclosed card and read:

Dan—when you wake up and are ready, please pull the chain.

Dan dropped the note back on the table and gritted his teeth. *I'll pull your chain after I finish checking out this place, buddy.*

Locating a rotary knob on the wall, he turned it, and a recessed ceiling light came on. Dan continued his inspection.

There was a walk-in closet that contained a leather jacket, three sets of clothing, and two pairs of shoes—all expensive looking but staid. There were sets of dumbbells and resistance bands on the shelf.

Dan put one hand on the wall to steady himself and the other on his head. *Am I still asleep? Am I dead?*

A sliding door led to a modern bath with a vanity, toiletries, and towels. Along the back wall were two compartments, a shower, and a commode.

Dan returned to the bedroom and inspected a large, hardwood bookcase filled with a three-row set of red leatherbound classics. There was even a King James Bible. Next to the bookcase were two easy chairs facing each other and a tall reading lamp.

"Looks like Hotel California," he mumbled. "You check in but never check out."

With his hands still quivering, Dan made the bed, took a quick shower, dressed, and pulled the chain. A few minutes later, he heard a knock, and the doorknob clicked. Eos stepped in, carrying a black briefcase.

"As you probably guessed, you're in Shangri-La. How do you feel? Hungry?"

"How should I feel when my world imploded on me? But, yes, I'm hungry, like I haven't eaten for days."

Eos nodded and sat at the table. He opened his briefcase.

"Here's the breakfast menu." Eos handed a card and a pencil to Dan, who sat down across from him. "Check off what you want, and I'll do mine. Then we can talk and eat at the same time."

Dan chose scrambled eggs, toast, orange juice, and coffee and handed his card to Eos.

Eos made a little flourish with his hand holding the cards. "Now we put the cards in this slot in the dumbwaiter here and push the blue button. The food will come up to this compartment when the green light comes on. The dirty dishes go in the same compartment, and you push the yellow button here. Questions?"

Dan eyed Eos. "Am I in some kind of a prison?"

"I meant questions about the food. But this is one of the best rooms in the place." Eos tried to make a sympathetic smile, but it didn't convince Dan. "The food will be up in a few minutes. Let's start."

Eos took Dan's laptop and two other items from his briefcase. "Here's your computer and phone back. Like I said, you get your wallet back when you leave."

"Thanks." Dan snorted. "You're a real great guy."

Eos exhaled deeply. "I appreciate your attitude, Dan, but let's not waste time. You can ask questions, but not about our location, the time frame of your visit, or the people or projects involved. I'll be telling you anything you're allowed to know. For example, you're not in Virginia anymore, courtesy of an overnight ride we took in a small business jet."

"You have me over a barrel," Dan interjected. "When you're ready, I'm extremely anxious to know what's going on."

"I will repeat what I told you before." Eos held up one hand and touched each finger as he talked. "I'm a technical consultant retained by an international group of wealthy entrepreneurs and research professionals who created StarWay Labs. The group does not engage in military research, rather in proprietary and modest-cost science and engineering projects with high risk and higher potential payoff." Eos shrugged. "Spiriting you away is the first time StarWay has engaged in anything unlawful. You had the bad luck to drift into our sphere of influence. Now the question is, can we work together?"

"I want to go home."

"Good. If we all cooperate, that can happen soon. Days or weeks, not months."

"Weeks?" Dan said. "Look, Mr. Eos, my parents will be frantic when they find out I'm missing. They need to know I'm safe. Now."

"Not my problem. If they're worried, it's because *you* turned down our rather generous internship offer. But if you work hard to replicate what you did in your lab, your visit here could be over in a few days.

"In the van, you accused us of stealing the property of Quincy University. I'm going to explain now why that isn't true. One of our scientists, Dr. Powers, a theoretical solid-state physicist, developed a remarkable hypothesis two years ago."

"What was it?" Dan asked.

"She solved some quantum mechanical equations that indicated that if certain crystals, like yttrium oxide, were doped with at least three atomic elements, they could create highly unstable energy storage zones by a process she calls 'vibricity'."

"My crystals only have two dopants, not three."

"But maybe there's a third element there. Maybe vibricity can sometimes work with two dopants. Or with trace amounts of the third dopant. Who knows?"

Dan couldn't help the fact he was intrigued by what Eos was telling him. "What's that have to do with increasing a laser's power?" he asked.

"The way Powers explained it, two factors are at work here. One is the well-known physical principle of energy transformation. That shows up all the time. Three examples she gave were falling bodies where gravitational energy becomes kinetic energy of motion. In absorbing light, like sunshine, where . . . uh . . . electromagnetic energy becomes heat energy. And in electric motors where electrical energy becomes kinetic energy."

"I understand that."

"The second factor is more mysterious." Eos shook his head. "At least to me. These vibricity zones can behave like lasers. Light passing through the zone can stimulate the creation of more light that moves parallel to the original light, and the new light creates more and more light until it all leaves the vibricity zone. But to be useful, the crystal has to be transparent, preferably optically clear, so the light can come out."

"Aha!" Dan cried. "That's what I'm seeing in my lab at QU. We're transforming energy from the electric coil and the moving magnet into increased laser energy. Right?"

"As far as I understand." Eos gave him a weak grin.

"But if this 'vibricity' exists, why hasn't anyone discovered it?"

"Vibricity has never been observed because it operates at extremely low levels in most materials. Too low to be detected, especially since no one is looking for it."

"Looking for it?" Dan accented each word. "They don't even believe it when it's staring them in the face."

"And neither would we. Until Dr. Powers's theory came along. Unfortunately, she has been unable to prove which elements, or atomic types, must be present in the crystal—although she had recently made great progress in that area—and how much you need of them to trigger the effect. We've been observing tiny levels of vibricity in our lab for almost two years, hundreds of times smaller than what you've seen. We picked up on your idea of the AC electric coil. That did increase the laser energy somewhat, but it's still too low to be useful."

"I have no idea why we're seeing what you call vibricity at QU, so how can I possibly help?" Dan asked. "If you apologize for kidnapping me . . . make some restitution . . . maybe they'll let you do joint research with us. That way you'll get to do research on the actual crystals I've been using."

Eos gestured toward the dumb waiter. "Ah, the food is here. Let's eat and then take a walk outside. But no tricks, please. I know you're trained in boxing, but I have twenty years' experience as an instructor in Krav Maga. It was perfected in Israel and kills people." His eyelids drooped. "I'd hate to have to use it on you."

After the meal, they left the room. Eos led Dan down a long hallway to a stainless steel elevator. He placed his palm on a glass plate and motioned for Dan to do likewise. The elevator door opened, and they went in. After they ascended one floor, the door opened to a dimly lit chamber. Eos used the palm key on one wall of the room to open a door exposing a short stairway leading up. Above it was a metal hatch, and Eos opened it. Sunlight filtered down.

"This isn't the main entrance, obviously," Eos said. "You're in a high-security area."

The two men climbed the stairway and stepped out into a luxurious green forest filled with a dank but invigorating aroma.

No building. Proves StarWay is underground. And these don't look like Southeastern trees.

"This is the only way to keep sane when we're here for long periods. If you cooperate, you'll be able to come here without an overseer and relax or eat." Two paths led away from the stairway.

Eos motioned toward the one on the left, and they walked into the woods.

"You were asking about getting the crystals from QU. No need for that, Dan. We've been watching you ever since your advisor advertised the work with yttrium oxide crystals. Soon after you first saw laser light boosts, we borrowed the crystals from your lab after closing time, had them analyzed overnight, and replaced them before morning. Then we made two copies of each crystal. We've been testing them here using a copy of your research apparatus. Nothing new. So it must be something you're doing in running the experiments. That's why you're here. Maybe you can lure some vibricity out of our crystals."

"I doubt it."

"We're almost finished refitting one of our labs for you, a replica of your Quincy lab. We're doing it at lightning speed—and lightning cost. We'll video you working in our lab on our invention with your equipment and crystals."

"I'm not doing anything special."

"You'll *have* to try if you *ever* want to leave this place." Eos's mouth turned up in a slight smile, and he blinked. "If you make a sincere effort and succeed, we'll pay you and QU big-time."

"Look, Eos, even if I cooperate, there's no way you're going to let me go home. What you're doing to me is a crime, plus I would have to divulge everything I know about StarWay. You're going to make me disappear no matter what I do. Under these circumstances, I'll be a nervous wreck and useless to you."

Eos acted as though he hadn't heard. "Let's meet again tomorrow morning," he said. "In the meantime, forget about all this. Start on the library we installed in your bookcase. You'll need a clear head to be of any help."

Eos pointed back toward the elevator, and they returned to Dan's floor. He went into his room and flopped on the bed.

Forget about all this, said the spider to the fly! Like what? My future? My life? How can I trust these people? I have to protect my parents. Lana. Myself. I have to let Lana and my parents know I'm OK. Lord, I need Your help now.

Chapter 38

Wednesday, September 25

Dan woke with a throbbing headache. After several hours of pacing and agonizing the previous evening, he'd decided to play along in the lab and stall for time until he was rescued. If he was rescued. Then he had read himself to sleep with Plato and Psalm 77, where Asaph sought the Lord in the time of his trouble.

Someone knocked on Dan's door. "Are you still in bed? Time to get up."

Sounds like my friendly cell boss. "Hang on a second. I'll be right there." He grabbed his wristwatch from the night table. 7:10 a.m.

Dan did a quick hygiene routine, dressed, and opened the door. Eos stood there with his briefcase. "How about if we eat breakfast together? To save time, I'll reorder our last meal."

"Come in. And breakfast would be welcome. The food and accommodations here are excellent—no doubt about that. By the way, calling you Mr. Eos seems a little formal, and J. J. sounds too friendly. Do you have another suggestion?"

Eos put his briefcase on the table, took out four meal cards, and handed three to Dan. "Call me J. J. if you like. Why don't we wait till the food comes up to start our discussion?"

"Fine." *Eating or starving is one of the few options I have.*

"I have some good news. I explained your position and concerns to the boss. He came up with a plan that will make your stay at StarWay Labs much easier for you."

"Oh, yeah?" Dan put his chin on his fist.

"I have a present for you from the boss. We call him Sirius, after the star." Eos opened his briefcase and took out an ebony wooden box.

Dan opened the box and withdrew a gold wristwatch. The twelve hours on its golden face were marked with twelve glittering stones that appeared to be diamonds. "Why's he giving it to me?"

"A thank-you for your cooperation. Wear it every day. If you help us, you'll be able to keep it when you leave. See if it fits."

Dan removed his wristwatch and slipped his left hand through the open clasp of the new one and, after a momentary hesitation, snapped it shut.

A whirring sound and a green light announced the food had arrived. "Would you mind getting the food while I respond to a text message?" Eos said.

Dan got up and brought two plates and hot coffee to the table.

"More good news." Eos's smile didn't give Dan any comfort. "More ways to make your stay here much easier. But first, I'll ask you a few simple questions. Ready?"

"Do I have a choice?"

"The questions are easy to answer. Where are you?"

"I believe I'm at StarWay Labs," Dan replied, and his left hand quivered. "But I'm not sore—I mean, not sure."

"Relax. Everything will be fine. Where is StarWay Labs?"

"Hmm." Dan thought for a moment. "I don't know."

"Good. Last question. If Lana invited you to stay overnight at her apartment, would you accept?"

"No."

Beep! The watch sounded, and the top diamond began flashing.

"Well, well. A little prevarication, eh?" Eos said, obviously pleased with his test. "Looks like you're human after all." He pointed to Dan's wrist. "That watch is one of our proudest developments at StarWay. Keeps people honest. Of course, if you decide to take it home, the mother chip will be replaced with something less intelligent."

"How does this watch make my job here easier?"

"Simple. You're an ethical person. You want to go home without providing us any help. On the other hand, we'll do whatever we must to get that help. You probably know that, considering all the trouble, expense, and risk we took to bring you here. So what would be a good plan for someone in your position? Stalling, maybe? Going through the motions but changing your behavior a bit here and there? Think of a helpful idea but don't reveal it. Right?"

"I wasn't thinking of doing that."

Beep!

"Dan, Dan, you're proving how this watch is going to help both of us. I have a contract here. We'll pay you a year's salary if you help us, and we are *unsuccessful* after three weeks. But we'll pay you five years of salary if we strike *pay dirt*. We're only asking you to try. We've been at this for two years. We should reap the benefit because we were first."

Eos took a big mouthful of breakfast and washed it down with coffee. "The cooperation contract also provides for Quincy U to receive ten million dollars if they work with us. One million to be paid to them upon fully executing a research contract. Of course, you'll be required to tell everyone back in Quincy that you understood *our precedence* regarding the discovery and our desire for cooperative work with substantial remuneration to you and the university. And that this made you view our little excursion here as *voluntary*, not a kidnapping, with the period of silence necessary until we had a mutually satisfactory agreement."

Eos continued with a sinister smile. "Dan, I need to make something perfectly clear to you. We developed the theory of vibricity. We spent millions over the past two years on research and are spending another million now on the operation to bring you here and support our joint research. After two years of experimental research, we know vibricity actually exists. But the magnitude of the effect we are seeing is too small to be useful.

"You stumbled onto something you don't understand, nor do we, that already increases the vibricity effect enough for practical uses, and the amount of increase may likely be further magnified.

Therefore: one, we have every right to the discovery. Two, we hope you and the StarWay people working together will be successful. If we are, you and Quincy University will be generously compensated. But three, if we become convinced you are not trying hard enough, we are prepared to do absolutely whatever it takes to make you try harder. There's nothing magical about Quincy, Virginia. We will do very unpleasant things, if necessary, to you, your family, friends, whatever, to reach our goal. And judging by how expertly this operation has been carried out, I'm sure you know we can do it.

"Just work for us wholeheartedly, and at quitting time each day, I'll ask you a few questions to keep you honest. It's that simple."

Family and friends? No way! "Well. I don't seem to have much choice in the matter." Dan rubbed his neck and stared at the ceiling. "My biggest concerns *are* my family and friends. We have to let them know I'm well and will be working in a private lab for a few weeks. Something like that."

"I'll look into it. But remember, you only have one option, Dan, and it's the easy one. Think about it tonight, and tomorrow we'll both sign the contract."

Chapter 39

By midmorning, the policemen had left Lana's apartment. She stared into her mirror at the dark circles under her eyes after another restless night. She'd called her departmental main office to inform her advisor she'd be absent from work for several days to assist in the search for Dan Butler. *Dan, Dan, where are you? Oh, Good Lord, please let him be safe. Oh, my heart races whenever I think of him in danger. . . . Maybe Mrs. Butler knows something.*

She pulled up a contact on her phone. Every ring seemed to take an hour. "Good morning, Mrs. Butler, it's Lana. Would it be all right if I come over? I'd like to find out what you've been told about Dan, and I have an idea I want to run by you. . . . Don't worry." *Listen to me talk about not worrying.* She added the address Mrs. Butler gave her into her map app.

Lana arrived at the Butlers' house just after 11:00. Dan's mother looked pale and disheveled, her hands kneading a damp handkerchief. "Come in and sit down, Lana. Please pardon my appearance. I haven't slept well."

"I share your concern and lack of sleep, Mrs. Butler," Lana said as the two women sat in the living room. "What information have the police given you about the investigation? Dan's roommate, lab partner, and I might be able to help find him."

"The university president called this morning. He assured me their people were working closely with the city police, and they would leave no stone unturned." She wiped her eyes and sniffled.

"He said the campus police were reviewing the video from the security camera in the student parking lot, and they would email us the report today. He felt sure Dan would be located soon. Then the police came. They wanted a lot of details about Dan's behavior and characteristics—why someone might kidnap him. They said they'd talk to his university contacts."

"That's wonderful," Lana said, putting her hand on the woman's forearm. "I've been thinking of getting some of Dan's friends together to see if we could come up with any information that might help the police. That is, if you approve, of course."

"Of course, we approve. Why don't you stay a while and have a piece of homemade pecan pie? I made it for . . . for Dan."

Mrs. Butler went to the kitchen and brought back a tray with one serving of dessert and two cups of tea.

"The pie looks delicious, Mrs. Butler." Lana had no appetite but couldn't turn down the kind gesture from Dan's mother.

The two women drank tea without much additional conversation, until Lana noticed a basket at the end of the couch with what appeared to be colorful sweaters. She gestured toward the basket. "What are those pretty woolens?"

"Just some dog sweaters I knitted for my sister's pet accessories store in town. Seems they are very popular with her customers. Every month she brings me a list of colors and sizes for the sweaters and the appropriate skeins of wool to knit them with. Then she picks up the sweaters as I finish them. I've been making them for over ten years now. If she ever goes out of business, I'll probably keep knitting the sweaters and give them away. I don't think I can stop now. It's how I quit smoking!" She handed a blue and white sweater to Lana.

Lana held the sweater up in front of her. "This is beautiful, and these are the colors of Quincy U." she said. "You're very talented. Could I buy this one?"

"That's very kind of you, Lana, but you don't have to . . ."

"This would be for Dan's little dog, Angel. How much?"

"After what you're doing for Danny? Please, just take it," Mrs. Butler said and went to the kitchen to get a bag to put the sweater in.

Lana smiled and put it in the bag. "This is wonderful, but I'd better be going. I want to talk to some others who know Dan. Maybe we can get a clue to where he is."

"Until they find Dan," Mrs. Butler said, "will you promise to call me every day? And I'll call you if we get any news on our end." She walked Lana to the front door. "Thanks very much to you and your team for all you're doing for my son." She hugged Lana and then wiped her eyes.

On the ride back to her apartment, Lana called Chumbo and gave him the update. She volunteered to set up an email distribution for Dan's friends and send daily updates. Then she took a long shot and asked him if he knew Carter Edwards's phone number.

"Hold on, I'll check Dan's desk." After a few minutes, Chumbo returned to the phone. "Sorry to take so long. Dan didn't have anything in his desk, but I have the password to his iPad, and I checked his texts there. I've got Carter's number."

"You have the password to Dan's iPad?" Lana was surprised.

"Yeah. We exchanged passwords a few months ago when he was in the lab and needed some information, but he had left his laptop at the apartment. We decided it would be a good idea to be able to get into each other's electronic devices, just in case there was ever an emergency." Lana heard him blow out a long breath. "We never expected anything like this, though." He read off Carter's phone number to Lana.

"Thanks, Chumbo. I'll be in touch."

That afternoon, she received an email with the campus police report forwarded by Mrs. Butler.

QUINCY UNIVERSITY CAMPUS POLICE DEPT
INV REPORT: 251027-2
REPORT SUMMARY (*EDITED FOR DISTRIB*)   VIDEO
SURV CAMERA 14SP
SUBM BY: L.D. COMPTON, SR OFF
——— BEGIN REPORT ———
SUBJECT(S): DANIEL BUTLER (DB), QU GRADUATE
STUDENT, MECH ENGING;

DRIVER OF VAN (DV) PARKED NEXT TO BUTLER
SEDAN
07:11 AM: DB SEDAN ENTERS SPACE 247 IN STUDENT
LOT #2
07:12 AM: DB EXITS VEHICLE AND LOT
07:21 AM: VAN ENTERS SPACE 246 OBSCURING VIEW
OF DB SEDAN
07:21 AM: DV EXITS VEHICLE AND LOT
6:42 PM: DB ENTERS LOT AND WALKS TO DB SEDAN
6:44 PM: DB SEDAN EXITS LOT
7:05 PM: DV ENTERS LOT AND VAN
7:05 PM: VAN EXITS LOT
—— END REPORT ——

Lana drummed her fingers on the desk as she considered the report. If Dan drove away in his car at 6:44, that was just a few minutes after he had called Lana. The van parked between the camera and Dan's car bothered her, but there was no mention of anyone else approaching his car between the time he arrived and left. She read the report through again and called Carter.

"Hi, Carter. This is Lana Madison. I'm a friend of Dan Butler's."

"Hi. What's up?"

Lana tried to keep her voice from shaking. "Have you seen Dan recently?"

"No. Why? Is something wrong?"

"I apologize for bothering you, but a problem has come up, and I'm checking with Dan's friends." She took a deep breath. "Dan seems to be missing."

"Missing?" Carter's voice went shrill. "Since when?"

"Since Monday night. I was one of the last people he tried to communicate with, so the police interviewed me this morning. I was thinking we—maybe you, Chumbo, and some other friends— should get together this afternoon or evening and review what we know."

Carter didn't wait long before answering. "I'll do whatever I can to help Dan. You obviously have my phone number. Just let me know how I can help. Dear God, I hope and pray he's all right."

Lana sat at her desk and began to create a plan. She texted Dan's friends with the reason, date, and time of a meeting to discuss how to help Dan.

She called Chumbo and asked him if he'd bring Angel and her supplies over when he came. She wanted to keep her until Dan returned. Chumbo agreed and told her Mrs. Haynes would be willing to watch Angel when Lana had to be away from her apartment for a long time. He asked if he could invite Stevie to the meeting, and Lana agreed.

By late afternoon, she had acceptances from Joe and Carter as well.

At 7:10 p.m., Chumbo and Stevie joined the others at Lana's apartment. "Sorry we're late." He carried Angel and a large bag of her supplies. The pup leaped out of his arms and ran to Lana.

"Come here, sweetheart. And please have a seat, Chumbo and . . . Stevie?" Lana said.

"Oops, sorry. This is my good friend, Stevie Morgan."

"Hi, Stevie, and welcome aboard." She motioned to the oatmeal cookies and soft drinks on the table. "Help yourself."

Chumbo and Stevie sat, and he glanced at the cookies but shook his head. "Not now."

Lana opened the meeting with a prayer for Dan. By the end of the prayer, Joe's nose had reddened, and Carter sobbed openly. Lana went to the kitchen and fetched a box of tissues.

Then she asked everyone to say a few words about themselves.

Chumbo spoke last. "I know we're all hurtin' over Dan, but he's *my* roommate. I talked to him every day. We're like brothers. I feel like I lost an arm. This is rotten." He rose and paced for a few seconds. "Why would anybody want to kidnap Dan Butler? That doesn't make sense."

Stevie clenched her fists. "I never thought I'd wish ill-health for anybody, but I sure hope this ends up with Dan being unconscious or suffering from amnesia in an emergency room somewhere, rather than bad people getting hold of him."

"That might be the case if someone knocked him out and lifted his wallet—otherwise the hospital would've contacted his family or the university by now." Carter shook her head.

Lana made eye contact with each person. "Maybe we can do something for Dan. I'd like to begin by updating you on what information I have. I've been in touch with Dan's mother, partly because I may have been the last person Dan tried to communicate with. So here's what I know . . ."

After a summary, Lana continued. "I made some copies of the police report on the parking lot video they sent to the Butlers. After you read it, I'd like your comments. Then we can discuss what we could do. Please be careful with this report. Even though I have Mrs. Butler's permission to gather all of us together to discuss the situation, the information is confidential."

After a few minutes of reading and reflection, Carter spoke. "It all boils down to two facts, as far as I can tell. Dan parks his car in the grad student lot at just after seven a.m., and he leaves almost twelve hours later at quarter to seven that evening, if my brain is working right. So, the question is, where did he go?"

Stevie nodded her assent, and Joe mumbled his.

Chumbo shook his head. "I have a problem with that," he said. "Did anyone else notice the van conveniently blocked Dan's car from the camera's view all day? I doubt the camera recorded him getting into his car."

"That bothered me, too," Lana said, "but I'm not sure why since the video shows him driving away."

"Yeah," Joe added, "especially since the report doesn't mention a single person approaching the area from the time the van driver parked it in the morning until he returned that night." Joe tapped the table for emphasis.

Chumbo shot back, "Sure 'nuff, Joe, but it doesn't prevent people and stuff from moving between the van and the car, especially if its side door faced the car. A second van occupant could've entered Dan's car at any time. I don't want to jump to conclusions—just sayin' lotsa things are possible with that van blocking the camera."

The group talked a while about the van, then they shifted to possible future actions. When they finished, Lana recapped the main points.

"Here's a summary of what we've decided. One. I'm going to ask Mrs. Butler if she can get us a copy of the surveillance video. If she does, Chumbo will follow up with that. Thanks, Chum.

"Two. Assuming the worst, that somebody snatched Dan— maybe related to his laser work—we need to think what he might have done to escape or at least to pass on information to us. That's a super long shot, but Stevie agreed to focus on that. Thank you, Stevie.

"Three. Since Carter likes to read, she's going to do some research on kidnapping. Also, she's going to provide Stevie with ideas on how Dan's mind works, based on the techniques he used to find her lost brooch. Go for it, Carter.

"Four. Joe will do some internet searching on laser research and development. Try to find out who the major players are. That may be difficult, given the huge number of organizations and people involved, but we have no easy options here. Good luck, Joe.

"Meanwhile, I'll keep in touch with the Butlers and monitor the media to see if the news of Dan's disappearance is made public. I'll contact Dan's advisor, too, and let you know if I learn anything new. I'll also type up our meeting notes and start a computer file of everything. Let me know if you learn anything that could help us find Dan."

Lana looked at her watch and stood. "Looks like it's time to say goodnight. I haven't been sleeping well. Can we meet here again tomorrow night at seven?"

After the team had gone, Lana sat on the sofa, and Angel jumped into her arms. "Dear God, please let him be safe. I beg of You, please!" She stroked the puppy, who curled her forepaws. "We both miss him, don't we, little girl?" Her throat tightened so much it hurt. "When my mother stomped all over him, I knew I had strong feelings for him, but now . . . oh, Angel, I'm sure I love him."

Her tears flowed freely, and Angel licked them off her cheeks.

Chapter 40

Thursday, September 26

Eos was back at Dan's room for breakfast. "Good morning, Dan. I have two copies of the contract. I can tell you our organization keeps its promises, but that doesn't matter because we hold all the cards anyway." He handed Dan the contracts. "Read over the details while we eat the pastries and coffee I brought." He placed a small shopping bag on the table.

Eos started eating while Dan painstakingly read through the fourteen sheets of paper. "Look, J. J., I'm willing to take a chance on the contract even if I don't get paid. What choice do I have? But I want my family and friends to know I'm OK, so they can stop worrying about me, and I can stop worrying about them."

"Now that we've agreed to work together," Eos said, "we can send an email to your parents."

"What will it say?" Dan scratched his jaw.

"You can help write it."

"Good."

"I need a one-word answer from you." Eos placed a pen on the table. "Will you sign now?"

Dan thought for a minute. "Yes—and God help me."

Eos handed Dan the pen, and they signed both copies of the StarWay contract.

"Now, let's take a look at your new lab." Eos gathered the papers. "And then we'll get some fresh air. Ready?"

Dan ate his last bite of apple strudel and nodded.

Eos opened his briefcase, placed the contracts inside, then took out a single sheet of paper. "Your request to send an email has been approved, but upper management wants to see it before it's sent. I'll get you the requirements for what needs to be in it tomorrow."

They left the room and walked a short distance down an empty hall to the next door on the right. On the stainless steel door were the letters *DB*. Eos held his palm on a glowing glass plate. A green light spread across the pad, and the door lock clicked. Eos opened the door, and they entered the lab, triggering the overhead lights to come on.

Dan looked around the room. "This is an exact replica of my lab! Same layout, equipment, furniture, and cabinets . . . everything. You even have Joe's stuff in here."

Eos looked pleased. "Yes, since we don't know what is causing what, we decided to make this lab as similar as possible to your Quincy lab. In the drawer where you keep your crystal samples, you'll find clones of them. Also some new samples you can try that the people in the main lab found interesting. After we take a walk outside, you can come back and get organized."

They stepped out of the lab, and Eos pointed at the keypad on the wall outside the door. "Hold your right hand on that palm plate, fingers splayed." Dan complied, and a flashing red light activated as a buzzer whined. "Hold still while I type in a code." The noise stopped. The red light turned green and then off.

"Now you can enter any room in the facility to which you have access, but there aren't many. If you try to gain entrance to a prohibited room, the pad will turn red, and security will appear.

"Ready for another elevator ride?" They walked farther down the corridor to an elevator door with a blue light overhead. Eos turned to Dan. "Do what I do." He put his palm on the plate and stepped into the elevator, and Dan followed suit. On the wall were a button panel and a screen displaying a large number one.

Dan felt the elevator lurch upward, and the number decreased to zero. *Zero? That's a funny floor in a building.* They stepped out into a closet with a short stairway leading up to a large hatch. Eos palmed the access plate, and the hatch opened to dull sunlight. They climbed up the rest of the stairs into a forest and the familiar organic smell of decaying leaves.

"You can't access the elevator or this hatch unless someone is with you," Eos said. "But the paperwork for your access to privileges is being processed."

"Thank you. I'll bet there's an electric fence or something around this area."

"Yes, we have a perimeter fence, and the lot is huge. Something else you should know. The fence is not only there to stop *human* traffic." Eos made a growling sound.

Is he trying to scare me? If so, it's working!

"This place has me wired," Dan said. "Wild animals are the least of it. I'm averaging five hours of sleep. I hate to take pills, but if I don't get some sleep soon, I'm going to crash."

"Hmm." Sounding concerned, Eos wiggled his lip. "That would be bad for you *and* the project. Let me think on it. I may be able to come up with a better option than pills."

Chapter 41

Lana started the meeting promptly at 7:00. "It's great to see the four of you again. By the way, there's no reason I have to be in charge of our meetings. Anyone else want the job?"

"You're our commander-in-chief now," Chumbo said. The others nodded.

Lana asked if someone would like to offer a prayer, and Stevie volunteered. Then Lana began the meeting. "Does anyone have any pressing information to share first?" No one spoke, so Lana continued. "I spoke with Mrs. Butler, and she said the campus police chief okayed Chumbo's viewing the video recording. He also agreed to make a copy of the video for us but said the material should only be shared on a need-to-know basis. Chumbo's going to update all of us on what happened today after I finish my part."

"Can't wait," Joe said, scratching Angel's head. The pup rolled on her back. "I see a lot of potential information coming from that video."

"I hope so," Lana said. "Well, my other job is to monitor the media, particularly television, for information on Dan. I didn't check every news report, but I haven't heard anything at all. Anyone else heard or seen anything? . . . No? OK, Chumbo, your turn."

"Everybody ready to hear the findings of the video voyeurs who spent two hours with Officer Krupke this afternoon?" Chumbo drained his coffee cup. "Thought you might. He loves playing detective. Found out he also loves science fiction movies, which gave me a chance to chum up with him—pun definitely intended.

Since I knew this would involve some investigative work"—
Chumbo turned and put his hand out toward Stevie—"I took the
liberty of inviting Detective Morgan here to come along, and she
kindly obliged. She and I decided to work as a team. Is that all right
with everybody?"

"Works for me," Joe said. "Carter and I did some research
together already. Want to make it official, Carter?" He looked at her
and extended his hand, palm upturned.

"Absolutely," Carter answered, and gave his hand a slap. "We
can bounce ideas and results back and forth before reporting them
to the rest of the team."

"Excellent," Lana said. "Stevie, can you tell us what you and
Chumbo discovered?"

Stevie nodded. "It was a commercial van with no windows
behind the front seats. You wouldn't be able to see a gorilla moving
around in the back. I snapped photos of a few images of the monitor."
She passed her phone around. "If anything funny was going on, the
van would've had to arrive soon after Dan parked to make sure
the adjacent space was open, but not immediately, because that
would've aroused suspicion when the video was viewed by the
police. That's exactly what happened."

Chumbo continued their story. "The three of us went over the
footage, looking for any evidence, including shadows, that somebody
was moving around between or inside the vehicles. Nothing. No
action taking place between the two vehicles, if there was any, was
visible to the camera. But we saw two suspicious things on the video.
As Dan walked into the parking lot, he seemed nervous. His pace
was faster than normal. More like a jog. He kept looking around.
Anybody know what might have scared him?"

Lana frowned in thought. "Maybe. Dan told me an industrial
recruiter had contacted him—I can't remember the name, darn
it—and offered him a high-paying, short-term internship with their
laser-research group. But the man wanted an immediate decision.
Dan said he was going to turn it down. The story sounded a little
strange to me."

"There's something else," Stevie said. "I saw a slight sag toward the far side of the van a few seconds after Dan went off camera, and it moved in several other places too." She moved her hands in opposition to each other to demonstrate the oscillation of the van. "When I pointed them out, Chumbo and the officer said they weren't sure, but *I'm confident about what I saw*. If nobody was in the van, why was it moving?"

"Yeah, Stevie and I are going to think about that some more."

"Thanks, Chum. Keep us informed. Joe, what do you and Carter want to tell us?"

"Carter and I spent a couple of hours in the campus library," Joe said, looking at his partner. "We were doing our assignments on researching laser R and D labs and the psychology of kidnapping. Not much so far, but my teammate here has an interesting idea."

Carter moved to the edge of her chair. "If they find the van we think Dan was taken away in, we might get more information. Dan's a smart guy, and if he could've left us a clue, he would've. One of us needs to go through that van with a fine-tooth comb."

"If we can get access to that van, maybe Stevie and I should look it over," Chumbo said. "I know Dan's habits and idiosyncrasies. I might be able to spot a clue someone else would miss."

"Go for it, you two." Lana looked around for any objections. No one said a word.

Chapter 42

Friday, September 27

Chumbo had invited Stevie to lunch at the pizza place near campus at noon. As usual, he was late. But not as late as usual.

"Hi, Stevie. Thanks for meeting me here. Would you like to order?" Chumbo asked, and they walked over to the food area.

"Hi. You didn't tell me if this was for the rescue team or pleasure."

"It's always for pleasure when we're together. But actually, it's a little of both."

After they had ordered and Chumbo paid, they took their meals back to their booth. Chumbo gave Stevie a peck on the cheek, and they sat across from each other. "How about if we do the business part now and then take a walk around campus? It's a gorgeous day." Stevie took a small bite of her veggie pizza.

"Suits me fine. I wanted to follow up on your observation that the van might be moving."

"Not might be, *was*."

"OK." Chumbo had a swig of his Dr. Pepper. "Was. We'd agree that the motion was pretty subtle since Krupke and I didn't really see it. I wonder if we could nail that down some way."

"How?"

"That's what I thought you might be able to suggest," Chumbo replied. Stevie cocked her head and tightened her lips.

They were both silent for moment, then he piped up. "Hey, I've got an idea. Let's call Joe. He's a mechanical engineer." Chumbo took out his phone and dialed. Chumbo frowned. No answer.

"Well, what about Lana? She's an engineer, too, and darned smart."

"Good idea, Stevie." He pointed a finger at her and made the call.

"Lana, it's Chumbo. Got a sec? Good. I'm sitting here with Stevie talking about the video. Can I put you on speaker? Thanks." He pressed an icon and laid the phone on the table.

"Hi, Stevie. Having fun?"

"Loads. Chum and I were just discussing the moving van. Hey, that's funny. Anyway, do you think there's any way we could use modern technology to magnify the movement? To analyze it or something?"

"That's a great idea, and I may know somebody you can talk to. There's a grad student named Amy Welch in the computer science department. I had a couple of classes with her. She's a super bright woman, and she told me she was doing research on some kind of image processor. She might be able to help."

"You're a champion, Lana. We—at least I—would never have thought of that," Chumbo responded in an excited voice. "Thanks a bunch."

"No problem. Have fun. If you find anything, we can talk about it at the meeting tonight. Gotta run. Bye."

Fifteen minutes later, they were standing outside the door that said *Image Processing Lab.* in the beautiful new computer science department building at Quincy University. Stevie knocked on the door, and a woman's voice called out, "Come in."

They entered and saw a dozen desks in three rows. Each one had a large desktop computer with a big computer monitor. Six of them had people who looked like grad students staring at them. A woman at the closest desk stood and said, "Can I help you?"

"We're looking for Amy Welch," Chumbo said.

The young woman approached them. "You've found her." She extended her hand. "I'm Amy."

"Amy, I'm Chumbo Porter, a zoology grad student here, and this is Stevie Morgan. We're working with the police about the disappearance of an engineering grad student, and Lana Madison said you might be able to help us."

"Yeah, I heard about that. Terrible." Amy tightened her eyes and shook her head.

"It's worse than terrible," Chumbo said. "Dan Butler is my roommate."

"Sorry," Amy replied. "How can I help?"

"We have a flash drive here." Stevie looked at Chumbo and put out her hand toward him, and he pulled the drive from his pocket and handed it to her. "This has a small section of the footage from the student parking lot the night of the disappearance. We—at least, I—think the possible kidnapping vehicle, a van, moved a couple of times. Chumbo and the campus police officer who looked at the video and gave us the drive couldn't see it. Is there any way to enhance that motion? Maybe quantify it?"

"Are you guys psychic or something? Maybe just lucky . . . or blessed. Some of the other students call me the Omega Queen." Amy took a mock bow. "My PhD topic is to develop a software program to do precisely the kind of thing you are talking about. It's called Omega Plus. My dissertation is almost finished, and the program works better than we expected. Can I have the flash drive for a minute?"

"I need to explain something first, Amy." Chumbo held both index fingers up. "Officer Krupke, who gave this to us, made us promise we would only let others see it on an absolute need-to-know basis. Do we have your word you'll keep the video information secure?"

"Definitely. And I think I can help, but it's your call."

Stevie handed her the drive. "This will be educational."

"Why don't you grab two of those rolling chairs by the wall. No sense standing up." Amy sat, plugged the drive into her computer, and started typing away.

By the time the pair had returned, Amy had rotated her chair around and was holding the drive out. Chumbo took it. "So here's what happened in the fifteen or twenty seconds you've been away. First Omega Plus read and stored the entire video sequence on the drive. Then it did a preliminary analysis of the image frames. Yours had sixty frames per second. That's very good. High resolution, meaning sharp images, not out of focus. Excellent. And the noise—like the snow that used to be in the TV image when the reception was bad, which rarely happens nowadays—is very low. Super. All three are very important for what we're going to do. We should get outstanding results." Now, I'm—or I should say, Opie, my nickname for OP, is going to get to work."

"How long have you been working on Opie, Amy?" Stevie asked with a broad smile.

"About four years. Let's see. OK, here's the first image out of the thirty-six thousand frames I ran from the parking lot camera. That's a ton of data, explaining how the results can be so super accurate." The lot, with a few dozen cars and a van, appeared on the computer screen.

"Looks like it was taken at night. Daytime is better, but the floodlights there were bright enough to give us the good results I told you about. There's the object of interest, the van you mentioned." Amy put the cursor on it. "I'll use my mouse to draw a circle around the van." Opie automatically magnified the van until it filled the large screen.

"This is impressive," Chumbo remarked.

"And Opie adds that smaller image of the entire frame in the bottom corner, so she can analyze and we can see anything else going on in the lot. Now I'm going to put four fiducial markers anywhere near the four corners of the roof of the van. Opie will search and find the exact positions of the actual corners and put small red dots there. If the corners move, the red dots will move with them. By watching how those dots move, Opie can tell us with great accuracy about things we can hardly see. If Opie detects any motion of the dots, she goes into slow motion and runs the video back and forth three times, so we get a better look."

"Amy, I can't believe what you've done." Stevie put her hand on her forehead.

Amy grinned and clicked on the four corners of the roof. "Oops, I forgot to tell you the most important things Opie will do besides telling us something moved. She'll analyze and compare the positions of the four dots, which is basically the position of the van. When they all move down or up, which tells us if weight has been added or taken off, she also looks at whether the vehicle is tilting and in which direction, which tells us if people are walking around inside the vehicle and where they're going."

Chumbo put his head in his hands. "I know I must be dreaming."

"Here we go." When Opie asked the question: GO? Amy typed Y, and Opie was off and running.

Stevie said, "I saw the motion of the van just after Dan disappeared behind it. Let's see what Opie says."

"It's been seven minutes, and Opie's done with your ten-minute video section." Amy raised a thumb. "Here's what she found."

"Are you telling me she recalculated the positions of four fiducial markers in thirty-six thousand video frames and that other stuff you mentioned in seven minutes? Impossible."

"Impossible but true. Now, as I was saying, let's look at the results. I'll pick out one instance to go through with you in detail. Then I'll summarize the others. I'll change the gobbledygook into English, and we'll do it by the numbers. I turned my voice recording and speech-to-text converters on. Leave me your email addresses, and I'll edit and send all this to you before dinner."

"Thanks so much. This is incredible."

Amy perused the list on the screen and clicked on one of them. "Someone, probably a man, definitely entered the parking lot, walked behind the van, and got in it. The person weighed about 180 pounds. I'll have Opie show us that segment of the video."

"Yes, it was Dan. We saw it in Officer Krupke's office. But let's see the video again and whether Opie sees the sag," Stevie said excitedly.

The video came on, and a few seconds later, a man with a large, flashing blue dot Opie put on his back appeared, jogged behind the van while the flashing dot stayed with him, and then both disappeared. The entire screen shifted to a close up of the front of the van's roof showing all the red fiducial dots, which turned blue and suddenly started dropping. Two blue vertical lines appeared next to their dots, showing how far the van dropped.

"Yay," shouted Stevie. "It *is* Dan, and the van *did* move. And the blue lines show how far each corner dropped."

"You got it, Stevie," Amy said. "Notice both far side lines are much longer than their near side companions. That tells us he got on *behind* the van, and his weight made the far side go down more. If you sit on a mattress, which side goes down more?"

"The side you're sitting on," they both answered, almost in unison.

"Alright" Amy continued, "let me quickly summarize the whole analysis now and email it to you both late this afternoon. By the way, I've set the time to zero when your guy got on the van.

"Hold onto your hats, lady and gentleman. Here we go.

"One: thirty-two seconds before Dan got on, someone moved from the front-center of the van to a position just to the rear of the side door.

"Two: twelve seconds before Dan got on, the van tilted backward and shook a little, which probably indicates the sliding door opened.

"Three: time zero is when Dan, weighing one hundred eighty pounds, got on and immediately went to the center of the van."

She paused a second to catch her breath and then continued, "Four: two seconds later, a downward shake indicates someone sat down. Probably Dan.

"Five: ten seconds after that, the one standing near the door, weighing a hundred sixty-five pounds, gets off.

"Six: three seconds later, bigger vibrations and a brief tilt indicate the side door closed.

"Seven: after thirty-five more seconds, the car next to the van drives away. That one was obvious."

Here she took another pause. "And finally, eight: two minutes later, someone walks from the center of the van to the right rear corner, and after another two minutes, returns to their seat."

"Oh. I asked Opie to compare the weight and facial features of the person who drove the car in with those of the outgoing driver. She says the probability that the weights are the same is less than one percent, and the probability their faces are the same is less than a tenth of a percent."

Stevie clapped her hands. "Hallelujah! We turned the van into a position-sensitive scale! Dan did not drive his car away like we assumed. He remained in the van. We need to get this information to the police after the meeting tonight."

"There were no further movements for the remainder of the ten-minute video clip." Amy requested they ask the campus cops for the whole day's video, and she'd let Opie analyze all of it—a mountain of data that would take hours to complete.

"Amy," Stevie's voice was husky with emotion. "You may have just saved a man's life."

Chapter 43

After their walk through the forest, Dan and Eos took the elevator back down to level one. Eos's phone chimed, and he read the text message. "Guess what, Dan? You are authorized to enter your room and your lab by yourself. You can also use the elevator alone to take a walk outside." Eos flipped on the Hold Door switch. "We can talk here, in your room, or your lab. Whichever you prefer."

"The lab is fine."

They stopped in front of the lab door. "You have access to your lab, but let me remind you what happens if you try an unauthorized entrance. Try that palm plate on the door across the hall from your lab."

Dan put his hand on the white glass plate. It flashed red, and a loud, continuous buzzer sounded. When Eos laid his hand on the plate, the plate turned white, and the buzzer stopped. "That cancels your mistake—otherwise, the security people make an unannounced appearance. We insist you be careful. Now try the plate on your lab."

Dan complied. This time the plate turned green.

"Understand? The system knows which rooms you have access to. Do you remember them?"

As Dan entered, he smirked and puffed through his nose. "Sure. My room, my lab, and the elevator, for walks outside. However, I need an insider, like you, to accompany me in other cases."

"Don't forget." Eos beckoned for Dan to enter his lab.

"Let me start with the big picture first." Eos sat in one chair and motioned toward another for Dan. "Our main objectives are to study your process and see if our camera in your campus lab missed anything. We have eight cameras here, so we can see everything no matter where you face and stand. Our research team in the main laser lab upstairs will scrutinize the video feed, and if the vibricity effect starts up again, they will try to mimic and enhance your results. The lab folks may send you suggestions, or if they are certain about something, directions on what to do next. Also, if you want to try a crystal with a new dopant, we can consider that, but remember, we already have a copy of your lanthanum-cerium crystal that gave fantastic results at QU. We just have to figure out what the missing activator or technique is."

"Just? Seems like *just* finding a needle in a haystack."

"Time will tell. Let's see. Next topic is your work schedule. We'll be in the lab for ten hours every day, excluding lunchtime and dinner, six days a week. We'll synchronize your schedule with the lab team's. Eight to noon, one to five, and six to eight in the evening. You choose your day off, and the team will match it. When do you want to start working?"

Dan sat forward in his chair. "I can start with the evening session tonight, but first I want to write the email to my folks. And I want Sundays off."

"OK. Here's a list of specific things to put in the email. You can add general and personal comments—information that will prove it's you and anything else you want to say—within reason. Bring the draft email with you when we start work tonight. I'll read it and take it right up to upper management for final approval."

Dan took the list. "How long will that take?"

"I'll personally ask that they expedite it. If they approve it, I'll send it over the weekend—Monday at the latest."

Dan looked at his watch and drummed his fingernails on the table. "Well, it's lunchtime now. I'd like to eat and work on the email draft."

Eos placed his fingertips together. "Any other questions?"

"I couldn't get my watch off to wash my hands. It's a bracelet, not an expansion band. How do I remove it?"

"You don't. You'll wear your Shadow for two years. It's waterproof, so you can shower with it on. I have more to say about the Shadow, but what are your other questions?"

"When you release me, how can you trust me not to finger this lab when the authorities start debriefing me? What if I tell them about StarWay's shady practices? Or maybe you won't release me. Maybe you'll kill me."

"We already discussed that. Holding people against their will is illegal. But we are taking good care of you and paying you rather than extorting money from your family and their connections. The punishment would be fairly mild. The same with the intellectual property issues. But murder is something else. Decades, to life, in prison."

"What if you hole me up in Utah or somewhere for years?"

"You're figuring all the angles. But so did we. We think Shadow is the mutually acceptable solution. It will give your location and transmit everything you say and everything others say to you. Every night you'll have to recite a series of statements. For example, 'I have not transmitted any information about Eos, StarWay Labs, or my stay at Shangri-La to anyone. I have not contacted and have no intention of contacting the authorities about StarWay.' Things like that. If Shadow detects lies or you do anything to remove or disable it, an agent will pay you a visit within minutes. A human shadow will always be nearby. If you discover the secret to vibricity, we'll get it the same day because that's covered in one of your nightly recitations.

"We would have started this already, except they installed an improved new upgrade to the Shadow software when you arrived. The IT folks tell me it has a bug, and the lab computer isn't receiving its transmissions."

"Why don't you plan to keep me here indefinitely? Then you won't have to share anything with QU or me."

"We've already indicated a willingness to share vibricity with QU, since both sides played a role in its discovery and reduction to practice. Besides, we think your virtuous character is not compatible with prolonged confinement. We'll let Shadow do all the work."

"Maybe it can find vibricity too."

At 6:00 p.m., Dan and Eos met in the lab, and Dan handed Eos the email.

Dan opened the drawer that held the test rods. "I'll start with the lanthanum and cerium-doped rod—the one that gave the biggest power boost."

"If you've been doing something subtle in the Quincy lab, we need to pick it up here," Eos said. "Behave *exactly* the same way as you did there. Try to relax." He sported a mischievous grin. "There are some good-looking single women here. Maybe you could take one of them for walks in the forest. Just remember, there are microphones and video cameras everywhere. Plus Big Brother on your wrist."

"No thanks, J. J. Let's get to work." Dan turned on some switches and looked back at his new lab assistant.

He had his cloned system set up and calibrated in less than an hour. They spent another hour measuring the laser power. The signal enhancement was insignificant, like the earlier null results at QU.

Eos removed his safety goggles. "Eight p.m. Quitting time."

"Why does StarWay think the power boost comes and goes?"

"We have no idea, but we hope your expensive visit here will provide the answer. I've sat in on a few meetings with the scientists working on this project. We get steady results here, but they're miniscule compared with your boosts. A hundredth to a tenth of a point on your scale. Our results are useless for practical device development." Eos let his pen drop on the table.

Dan nodded. "I suspect something was changing in my QU lab, which caused the unstable results. Maybe you can arrange a meeting between the scientists and me to discuss some of these things. If personnel secrecy is a problem, we can do it by phone."

Eos put his lab notebook in his briefcase. "Not a bad idea. I'll pass it on."

I sure hope we figure this out before they decide my life is expendable.

Chapter 44

Lana was preparing for the third meeting of the rescue team when Chumbo called her to say he and Stevie would be late but had some unbelievable news. Joe and Carter arrived on time and helped themselves to drinks and snacks Lana had set out on the table.

"It's ten after seven—why don't we get started. Would either of you like to say a prayer?" Lana touched a tissue to each eye.

Carter volunteered, and afterward Lana asked for an update.

Carter took a quick swig of her orange drink. "After a long discussion, Joe and I decided the most important thing we could do is assist Chumbo and Stevie, assuming the van is recovered. Especially since I had that lost brooch experience with Dan and know how he thinks. Of course, we have to wait and hear what they found out about whether or not Dan *was* in the van."

Joe cleared his throat. "That's right. We went on the assumption Dan would have been sitting in his seat in the van the whole time, unless the ride was so long he had to leave it for a restroom stop somewhere. Of the various ways we could think of for him to leave a message or clue, we liked two. If he had access to paper and a pen—unlikely—he could have written something on a snippet of paper and hidden it. Probably near his seat. Or maybe he used the point of his nail file to scratch something somewhere near his hands. I've often seen him cut his nails with the clipper he kept in his pocket. Once the clipper came apart in the lab and we had to fish out some of the pieces from under a cabinet."

"But the problem with the clever clue concept," Carter pointed out, "is he has to leave significant information even if he had little time or knowledge about where he was going. It's not easy to think of what to do and then do it without being seen, especially if there's something pointed at you." Carter extended a thumb and forefinger.

"Please, Carter, I don't want to think about such a horrible possibility." Lana put her head in her hands.

The doorbell chimed, and Lana jumped up and headed for the door.

Chumbo and Stevie barged in. "Hi, gang. It's me, Sherlock, of Holmes and Watson," Chumbo wisecracked while he put his jacket on the back of the empty chair. Stevie pulled her coat off and gave everyone a big smile and wave.

Chumbo rubbed his palms together. "Anybody want to hear the most amazing scientific hypothesis since Galileo, who said the lightweight ball would fall as fast as the heavy one?"

The others sang out, "Yes."

"Listen to this." Chumbo sat on the couch, grabbed a cookie, and stuffed it in his mouth. "That was delicious. I've been running on fumes since lunch."

Stevie took one of the chocolate chip cookies and nibbled it while Chumbo continued.

"Lana gave us a great suggestion today when she told us to check with Amy Welch to see if we could figure out if Dan actually entered the van." He nodded to Lana. "It was a super idea." He grabbed another cookie and stuffed it in his mouth.

Stevie took up the narrative. "We took the flash drive with us over to Comp Sci and talked to Lana's friend Amy, who has this unbelievable system she's developed. In just a few minutes we saw how much the van sagged."

"Kudos to Chumbo and Stevie!" Lana exclaimed, and everybody clapped.

"I don't understand how it works and what you're trying to find out," Carter said.

"Before I slam you with the group's findings, let me explain. The idea is to measure small vertical movements of the van and slight tilts. When someone or something is put into the van, it drops down. When they get out, it rises back to where it was. The heavier the item, the more it drops. If you move around inside the van, the tilt changes. It drops in the part of the van you move to while it rises in the part you're moving away from. The farther you go to the side or corner, the more it tilts. Now it may only drop or tilt an inch or less, but that's plenty for Omega Plus. From this, the team can deduce when a person gets on or off the van, how much they weigh, and track their movement inside the van. Unbelievable."

"That's cool," Lana said. "How accurate is it? Like, how accurate is the weight measurement and the positional determination?"

"Amy just sent us a long email with a summary of the results and the system's capabilities. I brought copies for everyone. The program has data on various types of vehicles—sedans, SUVs, vans, and so on. From the video, the team determined the make and model. So the answer to your question is it's accurate to about five pounds' weight measurement and can locate a person's position within one or two feet. The high accuracy is possible because the campus police installed new hi-res digital video cameras everywhere a year ago after a student was attacked at night in one of the parking lots."

"Wow." Joe made a fist and popped it into a palm. "You can weigh somebody by putting them on a van while you video the vehicle and get it right within five pounds."

"Yep. Hang on, everybody, while I pull up my notes." Chumbo took his phone from his pocket and tapped it a few times. "I asked the Omega Plus folks two questions. One, can you say for sure if somebody got into the van? Answer—yes. Someone—let's call him Dan—absolutely got into the van ten minutes into this video clip—a few seconds after Dan moved into the hidden space between the two vehicles, and he never got off. Even if Dan only weighed five or ten pounds instead of one eighty, Omega Plus still would have been sensitive enough to detect him getting on and staying in. The person who entered the van weighed about one hundred eighty pounds. Dan always kept his weight right at a hundred eighty pounds."

"Fantastic," Carter interjected.

Chumbo and Stevie summarized the details from the Opie report.

Stevie clapped her hands. "See, we turned the van into a position-sensitive scale! Dan did not drive his car away. He was in the van. We need to get this information to the police right after the meeting."

"It's also clear the driver of Dan's car was in the van when it first arrived," Carter suggested.

"Definitely," Chumbo replied. "One other person had to be there to restrain Dan. Otherwise, he would have run away after the car driver left. Remember, the car driver was inside the van to the rear of the door when Dan got in. The Omega Plus team said they would ask the campus cops for the entire twelve-hour video and let the program analyze the whole dang thing—a mountain of data that will take hours of work."

"Hang on, everybody." Joe put a finger on his temple. "Anyone care to summarize what we know and think we know?"

"I will." Carter rubbed her hands together, then picked up her notes.

"Dan drives in first, parks, and walks out of the lot. Then the white van parks next to Dan's car and blocks the security camera view of it. In the van are three people. The van driver is up front. Hidden in the back compartment are the car driver and another person—maybe a gunman, to get Dan aboard and guard him during the trip. At some point, the van driver leaves the vehicle and walks out of the parking lot.

"That evening Dan returns to the lot and disappears between the van and his car. The hidden side door of the van opens, and Dan gets in and sits. The car driver, who looks like Dan in the video, gets out with Dan's car keys, enters Dan's car, and drives away. Someone goes from the center of the van to the right rear corner and returns a little later. Wonder what that was all about? Finally, the original van driver returns and drives the van away. Did I miss anything?"

"Great job, Carter," Chumbo said. "The campus police told me Inspector Bakewell was handling the Butler case. I'll get in touch with him as soon as possible tomorrow morning."

"Three cheers for all of you," Lana said, "and the unbelievable progress we're making. I was hoping and praying Dan hadn't been kidnapped, but now that we know what happened, we can put together a plan to find him." Lana high-fived each of her four friends. "When should we meet again? How about seven o'clock again tomorrow evening?"

After everyone had left, Lana collapsed on the sofa and said more prayers for Dan.

Should she phone and tell her parents about Dan's disappearance? Would Mom use the crisis as more ammunition against him? She mulled over the matter and then made the call.

"Hi, Daddy. Sorry to call this late."

"No problem, sweetheart. Everything OK? Mom's here, so I'll put you on speaker."

"Hi, Mom. I just wanted you both to know that Dan Butler is missing. His friends and I formed a rescue team to help the police. On the condition you'll both keep this confidential, I'll tell you we believe he was abducted. That's all I can say now."

"Abducted? What happened?"

"Sorry, I can't talk about that. I've given—"

"Lana," Dad said, "we don't want to put you in a difficult position, but considering your relationship with Dan, we deserve to have more information. I'll call my friend President Bernstein at QU and arrange a meeting with him. Maybe I can get some insight from him. Please take care of yourself."

"I will. Look, I'm tired. I'm going to bed. I'll keep in touch. Love you both."

Chapter 45

Saturday, September 28

When Chumbo called the Quincy Police headquarters the first thing the next morning and explained the urgency of his speaking with Inspector Bakewell, he was told the inspector would see him, but the earliest opening was at 1:30 p.m. At the appointed time, Chumbo and Stevie walked together into the headquarters of the Quincy Police Department. He was carrying a briefcase. They went to the window marked *Visitors Admission*.

A pleasant-looking, white-haired woman greeted them. "Good afternoon. Who are you here to see?"

"I'm Chumbo Porter, and this is Stevie Morgan. We have an appointment with Inspector Bakewell."

Looking down at the clipboard in front of her, she put her finger under one of the entries. "May I see your photo IDs? A driver's license is fine." They took them out and showed them to her.

"Thank you. He's in room 115 on this floor." She pointed to the side of the room. "Please go to door A. I'll buzz it open for you."

In a few moments, Chumbo knocked on the inspector's office door.

"Come in, please." A gray-haired man of medium build wearing black horn-rimmed eyeglasses motioned toward two chairs in front of his desk. "Mrs. Butler called and asked if I would see you. Sit down, sit down. What's on your mind?"

Chumbo took out his notes and gave the inspector a summary of what Omega Plus had found. Stevie added her thoughts for clarification and emphasis.

When Chumbo finished, the inspector's jaw dropped. "This is remarkable. Remarkable, indeed. I never would have thought a video analysis could produce so much information with such accuracy. I wonder what other ways we could use these techniques." He paused and slowly rubbed his hands together. "It looks like Mr. Butler was kidnapped and taken away in the van, and someone else—an accomplice no doubt—drove his car away. We were operating under the presumption Butler had driven away in his own car, and the van was uninvolved. I'm pleased we took the precaution to put out a search on the van."

"That was wise," Chumbo said solemnly.

"I've accumulated thirty-seven years of experience as a police officer, detective, and then an inspector. I thought I knew all there was to know in the collection of crime-related information. Looks like I was wrong. As close friends of Daniel Butler, you must exhibit extreme care in protecting information that could be detrimental to Dan's welfare if it were divulged improperly." Bakewell frowned. "Let's see. I'll use your last names. Agents Porter and Morgan, welcome to the unofficial Quincy Intelligence Service."

Stevie tightened her lips and brows. Chumbo glanced upward. Bakewell was the first to chuckle, and then everyone joined in. "I'm sorry. Police are supposed to be serious and deadpan, but I couldn't resist."

Stevie leaned forward. "Is there any chance we could look over the van if you recover it?"

The inspector raised his hand. "Let me call Sergeant Phillips. He's following up on the two vehicles. Normally I'd put you under one of my officers. But since you don't know anything about official procedures, things could blow up real fast. So, until further notice, I want you two to communicate directly with me. I'll handle Phillips. Understood?"

Chumbo and Stevie nodded.

The inspector placed the call. "Phillips, this is Bakewell. Anything new on the vehicles in the Butler case? . . . Last night, eh? . . . Landerville, eh? And you're with the owner now? . . . After they finish their inspection, ask the owner if he'd let two of Butler's friends have a look inside the van. . . . Yes, we're pretty sure Butler was kidnapped in that van. . . . Call me back when you have an appointment for them. You'll need to be there. . . . Yes. Porter and Morgan. Thanks."

Inspector Bakewell replaced the handset of his landline phone. "I have another appointment in five minutes, but why don't you write your names and phone numbers on this slip of paper, and I'll call you as soon as I hear from Phillips. Maybe he can get you into the van this afternoon."

Chumbo and Stevie provided the requested information.

"Thanks for your help. Here's my card. I've written my cell number on it. Don't abuse the privilege."

Chumbo drove Stevie back to the parking lot on campus where she'd left her car. As he pulled into a parking space, his phone chimed. "Hello. . . . Who? . . . Oh, Sergeant Phillips. . . . Yes, I know. . . . Definitely. How far is it? . . . Hang on a second, I'm putting you on speaker. Stevie, can you search for this address? OK, shoot."

Phillips said, "The van's at four twenty-one Elm Street. Landerville. You know where that is, right? About fifteen miles north of Quincy on route four twenty-two. The owner has to leave in an hour. When can you be here?"

Chumbo looked at Stevie. "In about twenty minutes." He reached over and grasped her hand.

Chapter 46

Stevie pointed at the dashboard of Chumbo's car. "Your car's clock says 'zero zero zero zero' and keeps flashing. Ever hear of auto maintenance?"

Chumbo puffed and looked at his watch. "It's twenty after three, and we're almost there. My phone's nav says two minutes to destination. The next right is Elm Street."

A squad car was parked by the curb near the mailbox bearing the number 421. On the driveway stood a familiar looking white van and two men.

Chumbo parked behind the police car, and the two of them walked up the driveway. "Hi, I'm Chumbo Porter, and this is my friend Stevie Morgan. We just left Inspector Bakewell's office. Are you Sergeant Phillips?"

"That's right, and this is Mr. Wyle, the owner of the vehicle."

Stevie shook Wyle's hand. Then she turned to Phillips. "How did you find the van?"

"It was found in East Tennessee. Can't be more specific."

"Anything different about the van, Mr. Wyle?"

"Different?" Wyle laughed. "All my tools and equipment are missing. And they installed two seats facing each other. To top it off, there's a stainless-steel compartment in the back corner of the van with a toilet but no latch on the door."

Stevie nodded at Chumbo and grinned. "Fits in perfectly with the Omega Plus analysis, which indicated movements toward and away from the right rear corner of the van."

"Our county crime scene unit finished its inspection," Phillips said to Chumbo. "We'll be moving the van to the police garage for inspection, and I expect the tow truck to get here in about twenty minutes. Bakewell said you can go inside and look around until then."

"Let's get to it." Chumbo opened the side door of the van, and Stevie climbed in.

"Carter was so sure Dan would have tried to leave a clue," Stevie said. "How about if you check around for bits of paper in the cracks, things like that, while I look for something in the toilet."

"Yes, ma'am!" He saluted her. "And congratulations on your promotion to agent-in-chief."

"Maybe you'd like to be the chief and work in the toilet?"

Ten minutes later Chumbo called out, "Horse apples! I can't find anything. What about you?"

"Uhh. Not sure. Come over here a second." When Chumbo reached the doorway of the stainless steel structure, Stevie was reaching around the right side of the white plastic toilet, sliding her hand along the back of the base of the bowl. "See if you feel anything back here."

Stevie got up and stepped out. Chumbo entered, dropped to one knee, and put his hand behind the toilet. He slowly ran his fingertips back and forth over the base. "Not really. Well, maybe. The compartment is too cramped to get my head back there. Let me try taking a photo." He held his phone three or four inches away from the back of the toilet and snapped several pictures. "Whaddaya think?" he asked, holding the phone up to Stevie.

She squinted. "I think I see a bunch of faint scratches. How about you?"

"I don't know," Chumbo responded. "I just know we only have ten more minutes in here."

"I'm calling Lana again. She saved us with the van motion problem." Stevie took her phone from her purse and brought up Lana's phone number. "Hi, brilliant one. This is Stevie. They found the van, and I'm in it with Chumbo. We only have a few minutes. I'm putting you on speaker."

"Go for it. Hi, Chumbo."

"Hi. Back to Stevie." He motioned for her to speak.

"Lana, we found some faint scratches on the back of a toilet in the van. Possibly a message scratched with his nail clipper. We took photos, but they are too faint to read. Any ideas?"

"Wow. You guys don't ask for much. Give me a minute."

Stevie and Chumbo stared at the time on her phone. They had about four minutes left in the van. Stevie began praying out loud.

"Hey, guys. Try this. Do you have any dark lipstick?"

"Fire red."

"OK. Smear it all over the scratch area. Then, wipe it all off with a tissue, shirtsleeve, whatever you have."

"Hang on, Lana." Stevie opened her handbag and pulled out a tube of lipstick and a tissue. After doing what Lana suggested, they took more photos.

Seconds later, they viewed the photos and gasped. The scratches, now filled with dark red lipstick, had become visible.

"A message. It says EOS DJB!" Stevie said. "Oh, thank God—Dan's initials!"

The door opened. "Time's up, folks," a voice called. The door clanged shut.

"It's from Dan all right. I'll handle Phillips," Chumbo said.

Stevie and Chumbo stepped down from the van, and he ambled over to Phillips. "Well, whatever might've been in there before, either your people found it or it's still in there." They turned and started for the car. After a few steps, Chumbo turned around and called back, "Good work on findin' the van."

After they'd returned to the car, Chumbo took his time making the U-turn and pulling away. "As soon as we're out of sight, I'll stop and call Bakewell."

"Haven't you just created a big problem between Phillips and Bakewell?"

"Why? Bakewell said we're reporting directly to him. Look, we know Dan was hauled away in somebody else's vehicle, and now we find a message from him that sounds like the name of an organization. Maybe a person. We need Bakewell to move on this."

Chumbo pulled over and stopped. He took out the inspector's card and called his office number. He got a recorded message. Then he called the emergency number on Bakewell's card and pushed the *speaker* icon.

"Hello, Inspector. Porter here. We just finished our inspection of the van and found something important. A few scratches on the back of the toilet base in the van. We enhanced them and took a photo. It says EOS and DJB. We're sure that's a message from Dan."

"Text the photo to the number you just called. Immediately. And congratulations on more good detective work. We might have to hire you two."

Chapter 47

Joe Stanley was the first person to arrive at Lana's place Saturday evening. He brought a lemon cake with chocolate frosting. "You've been providing snacks every night, so I thought this would be good for a meeting or two."

"How sweet of you, Joe."

He poured himself a cup of coffee from the thermal carafe. "How are you coping with all this?"

"Joe, I'm very worried. Dan and I had an argument, and the last, cold words I said to Dan were, 'Take me home.' I wanted to apologize but never got the chance. I'm trusting God and hoping for the best."

"That's too bad, but Dan's a decent person and probably has forgiven you already."

"Chumbo called a couple of hours ago," Lana said. "He and Stevie made another breakthrough. I hope it's the beginning of the end of this nightmare."

He started to pour some coffee into her cup, but she put her hand over it and shook her head. "Thanks. Maybe a little later."

By 7:00, the others arrived. After a few minutes of small talk, Lana expressed her appreciation to Joe for the dessert. She sliced half of the cake into four pieces and asked if Joe would like to offer the opening prayer. Then the meeting began.

"It's good to see everyone again, but I wish we didn't have a reason for these meetings. Excuse—" Lana swallowed hard, got up, and hurried out of the room.

Returning a few moments later, she went to the refrigerator and brought back a pitcher of water. "Sorry about that. They say it takes a while for a tragedy to sink in. Now I understand what that means. We need some optimism, and Chumbo told me that he and Stevie have some great news for us. Let's hear from the team's detectives."

Chumbo turned to his partner. "Stevie, you and Lana are the reason we made the breakthrough this afternoon—why don't you tell what happened?"

Stevie leaned forward. "I'd been thinking about our earlier discussion of Dan using the point of his steel nail clipper to scratch us a message in an obscure location. We know the car driver had Dan's car keys or remote, but Dan might still have had his nail clipper in his pocket since we know he kept them separate. A message written with a pen or pencil would have been too visible, but a lightly scratched message in an obscure place could have been overlooked.

"We met Inspector Bakewell at the police station, who told us the van had been found and returned to its owner in Landerville. Bakewell gave us permission to go there and inspect the vehicle. We did, and we found some scratches on the back of a toilet in a small compartment they had installed in the van, but the scratches were unreadable. We called Lana, and she suggested we could enhance the scratches by coating them with lipstick. When I wiped off the lipstick, it remained inside the scratches and made them visible. Chum, please pass around the photo."

"This is amazing," Joe said. "EOS—DJB. DJB is probably Daniel J. Butler, but what's the EOS? Got any ideas, Stevie?"

"Maybe it's a name or an abbreviation for an organization or even an acronym."

Lana perked up. "Could the E really be an S? If you move the bottom half of the vertical bar to the right side, you get SOS. Maybe Dan meant the situation was dire. Oh, good Lord!"

Chumbo put his hand on hers. "Don't get upset, Lana. It's probably not a squarish S. Look how different the second S is—a simple curved line. Easy to scratch, and faster too. There was no lock on the toilet door, so he had to move fast. No, it's EOS. What could that mean?"

"Whatever it is," Lana said, "you two are amazing. Let's give them a hand."

Joe held up his phone. "I got tons of hits on Google. No time to read them all, but here's a few interesting ones. Eos was the Greek Goddess of Dawn. It's also a family name. Lots of commercial uses too. It could be a code name for a spy or something, but how would Dan know that?"

"All plausible ideas." Lana smiled at Joe. "Good work. My guess is that scratching the message was the only way Dan had to leave a clue about his captors or their organization. Or where they were going. But they wouldn't have told him their destination. I vote for information about who or what his captors are."

"We called the inspector right after we made the discovery, and Chumbo texted him the photos." Stevie folded her hands and looked at Chumbo.

"That's right," her partner said. "And he texted back he was on it."

Chapter 48

Monday, September 30

Following Eos's early morning phone call, he and Dan were in the lab before 8:00. "Thanks for coming in early today, Dan. You'll be happy to know I sent the email to your parents this morning."

"Thanks."

Eos frowned and shook his head. "But time is passing fast, and we're not getting any good results. Let's do some deep brainstorming this morning."

"About new directions?"

"Let's start with what was different about the old experiment. After all, there are only so many ways something special could have occurred in Quincy. Let's list them all—at least all we can think of—and see if that gives us any clues."

"I've been doing that mentally ever since this cursed vibricity effect first appeared."

"I'll write our thoughts on the whiteboard. Obviously, the first point is something's different with the crystal." Eos wrote "CRYSTAL" on the board. "Now let's list every type and source of difference we can think of."

After they finished with that, Dan said, "The laser beam." Eos wrote the words, and they made another sub-list. The process continued throughout the morning.

"This is so frustrating." Dan paced the lab for a minute, then dropped hard onto his chair.

Chapter 49

Lana was excited and hopeful that morning. The day before, an FBI special agent from the Richmond field office had called her and said she'd like to interview Lana at home about the Butler case. She'd spoken about some of the areas they were interested in, and Lana had enthusiastically agreed to the interview. They'd scheduled it for 10:00 a.m.

Lana checked her watch. Almost 9:45. She sat on the sofa and reviewed again everything she could remember about Dan from the time he had the mysterious interview and job interview until he disappeared. She streamed some smooth vocal music from her phone at a barely audible volume to help keep her relaxed.

Her doorbell rang, and Lana went to the door and opened it. "Good morning, Ms. Madison, I'm Special Agent Kenisha Williams. FBI Richmond Field Office." She held out her identification. The woman wore a black, tailored business suit and a white open-collar shirt.

"Please come in and have a seat, Agent Williams. I've been anxious to meet you since we spoke yesterday."

"And I as well, Ms. Madison."

They both sat down. Agent Williams declined a drink, and the interview began.

Agent Williams took a small audio recorder from her briefcase and turned it on. "Ms. Madison, as I said yesterday, I'm working on the Daniel Butler case. I understand you're both Quincy U engineering students and very close friends. Is that right?"

"That's correct."

"I may have other questions for you later, but my purpose now is to focus on some things about Mr. Butler and what he may have told you about the three letters EOS that I believe you and the information gathering team you've put together have discovered."

"No problem," Lana replied.

Agent Williams took out a small notebook and pen. "Recorders are not perfect, and I want to be sure to get your information. Old fashioned, I guess. Did Mr. Butler ever say the EOS word to you, and if so, how did he pronounce it? Like E-O-S? Three separate letters like an abbreviation or like 'ee-yose,' two separate sounds, as if it were a name?"

"That's a very interesting question," Lana said. "No one has ever asked me that before, nor have I thought about it. I assume you are familiar with the on-campus interview Dan had with a supposed research lab recruiter a few days before his disappearance."

"I am."

"I believe Dan told me the name of the interviewer when he called me the night of the interview, but it was an excited and slightly crazy situation, and I forgot it. I remember it wasn't a name I'd ever heard before. It was short. It was male—I mean, he said 'mister.' And it certainly was not like 'Mr. E-O-S.' But it could very well have been the second way, like a name."

"Then it could have been a name, probably a last name, rather than an abbreviation or acronym?"

"Definitely."

"Did Mr. Butler ever say a word sounding anything like 'EOS' to you in any context *not* related to the job interview?"

"Not that I can recall. I doubt very much that he ever did. I would have asked him to explain it."

They talked for another half hour about anything Dan might have said about the recruiter's physical description, location, company, job description, salary, Dan's disposition and anxiety, and a few other things.

"Well, Ms. Madison. This interview has been very helpful. And if I may say something totally unofficial, I sure hope we can get your man back for you."

Chapter 50

After her teammates assembled in her apartment again that evening, Lana carried out a chocolate cake with three lit white candles. "This celebrates the three victories in our search for Dan. Omega Plus, the scratched message, and today Dan's parents got an email from him."

Everyone jumped up and cheered, clapped, and high-fived. Joe bumped into Lana, and she almost dropped the cake.

"How about if we blow out the candles together. Ready?"

After the cake was eaten, Lana opened the fifth team meeting by saying another prayer for Dan. "The only agenda item I'm aware of is Dan's email. Do any of you have updates?"

"Let's ride, cowpunchers." Chumbo, probably thinking a bit of celebratory levity was called for, spun an invisible lasso in the air.

"I'll pass out copies of the email Mrs. Butler forwarded to me this morning," Lana said. "Let's read the email, then discuss it."

Stevie raised her hand. "Do we know the source of the email?"

Lana nodded. "Mrs. Butler forwarded the email to the inspector and asked him that question. His staff thought it originated outside the US but said that didn't matter because it's so easy to bounce emails among one or more accomplices in different countries. It could have originated anywhere, even in Quincy."

Chumbo wanted to know if all the verifiable statements had been checked. Lana nodded. "Yes, I checked with Mrs. Butler, and she verified his nickname at home and the Irish stew, and I can verify the comments about me, Angel, and Mrs. Haynes. It's Dan, all right.

"But . . . Mrs. Butler noticed something strange in the message," Lana added. "She said that while she and her husband loved Irish stew, Dan wouldn't touch it."

"I think it's a fake," Joe said. "We know Dan moved inside the van in an almost empty parking lot seconds after he arrived. The only way his kidnappers could have gotten him into the van is at gunpoint or by knocking him out and dragging him in, and the second way isn't consistent with Omega Plus. Then a body double drove his car away and later dumped it at Dan's apartment to make it look like he drove home and then disappeared. And we know he was still in the van when it left. But his kidnappers don't know we know all that."

"Right, Joe," Carter said. "But at least we know he's probably OK."

"Very spooky." The normally laid-back Chumbo rose and paced. "Imagine. A PhD grad student with weird lab results receives a crazy internship offer, rejects it, and ends up getting kidnapped. Then ends up who knows where, at a company with a very thin internet trail. No communication for days. Then we get an email saying he accepted a one-month internship for five thou. His message suggests that he loves the whole idea, and please take care of his dog. Are we all in Loony Land?"

Lana frowned. "Hold on, Chumbo. Dan's smart. Clever enough to scratch a three-letter clue relating to his kidnapping, given that his abductors were probably watching him and had told him very little about what was going on. He must have known we'd worry about him, and I'm sure that explains a lot about the email. If he's cooperating with his captors, he must think that's the best, or only, option he has. Maybe these people aren't as evil as they appear to us, or maybe they're worse and threatened to hurt him or us if he didn't cooperate. Who knows? We aren't there. And . . ." She started to sniffle. "I'm sorry I'm getting so upset."

Carter, who'd been looking at the email while the discussion raged, looked up. "Stare at the email. It's right in front of your eyes!"

Chumbo sat on the couch and joined the others as they studied their copies of Dan's message.

"Don't *read* it. *Look* at it. Don't you see it?"

"I'm looking." Chumbo shook his sheet of paper like he was trying to make something fall out.

"Look at the first letter of every paragraph! I told you I know how his mind works."

"Yikes!" Stevie exclaimed. "E. O. S."

"Yes, EOS," Carter said. "Plus, he hates something but it's not the stew. He hates EOS, or EOS is bad. Something like that. EOS is probably his kidnapper's alias."

Lana nodded. "Very perceptive, Carter."

"I'm gonna call Bakewell." Chumbo stood and headed for the kitchen. "They need to focus on finding someone or something associated with the name EOS or StarWay Labs, which was also mentioned in the email."

Chapter 51

Eos put their findings in his briefcase. "We have an hour on the clock before dinner. How about if we look at some new directions?"

"Why not?" Dan almost moaned. "What we've been doing hasn't worked. That's for sure."

On the whiteboard, they wrote more suggestions, hypotheses, and even wild speculations but came up with no new ideas worthy of investigation.

"Where to go? What to do?" Dan threw his hands up.

"Not only are we unable to reproduce the big signal enhancements," Eos said, "but we can't get any significant enhancements, even using the AC coil. These crystals are supposed to be clones of the ones you had in your lab. Maybe there are some differences in the trace elements or in the crystal structure of the new rods. Maybe we should swap these rods for the ones back in your lab? I doubt anyone is using them right now anyway. What's your opinion?"

"Given what you folks have already done, only you can decide how much more theft you want to commit. Another thing, they'd be crazy not to have moved all that stuff into highly secure safekeeping."

Eos bit his lower lip. "You're probably right. I'll run it by the boss."

"The email we sent must've made some waves by now. If you were in Quincy, what would you be thinking?"

Eos narrowed his eyes. "I don't have to give you *my* opinion. I'll give it to you straight from the horse's mouth." He opened his briefcase and took out a sheet of paper. "Here's a copy of an article that ran in the *Quincy Daily Press* yesterday."

As Dan read it, he nodded. "This is amazing. They know it was an abduction in a van. My car was driven away by someone else. The police returned the van to the owner, meaning he must have reported it stolen. And then it talks about the email, which, of course, they already had by that time. But the first two things—how could they know about them?"

Eos squinted at Dan. "I was going to ask you that question."

"How could I possibly know anything? I was inside the van the whole time. After you gave somebody my keys and remote, I think I heard my car pull away. If so, maybe they got a good enough glimpse of him on their security camera to know it wasn't me. Maybe the time on the video from when I disappeared behind the van to when the car pulled out wasn't right. Maybe somebody on campus near the lot saw me get in the van. I don't know."

"No ideas about who might have leaked this information? Maybe your family or some of your friends?"

"How would they know anything? But maybe the authorities released the information in hopes that someone saw the van leave the city. Something like that."

Eos tapped the countertop. "Well, Shadow's been quiet, so I guess you're shooting straight. We had a spotter stationed there to intercept and distract any passersby. No one came. But your ideas on how they might have identified the fake car driver or the wrong time lapse are possible."

"Sending that email must have eased some of my parents' and friends' fears. Knowing that will help me sleep and work better. But even the personal information won't prove to them I'm OK. You could have forced all that stuff out of me."

"Why would we do that?" Eos raised his eyebrows in mock innocence. Then he lowered them and leaned toward Dan. "Did you tell anyone about the interview and job offer in Quincy?"

"My PhD advisor. I assume he's told the police." *No beep. So, Shadow only detects complete lies— It doesn't detect true but incomplete statements. I also told Lana about it. Hmm . . . that could be useful.*

Chapter 52

Stars glistened in a moonless sky by the time James Madison returned from his trip to Quincy to investigate the Butler disappearance. He found the house dark and his wife sleeping in the recliner in the den. On her lap was the family Bible. He heard her relaxed breathing and sighed. *She looks so much better than when I left this morning. It seems the sedative I gave her was effective.* As he tiptoed out of the room, the floor squeaked, and he stopped.

A soft voice called out to him. "Is that you, James? I must have . . . drifted off."

"Go back to sleep, sweetheart. You need the rest."

She pulled the recliner to the upright position. "My goodness, it's dark outside. I must have gotten another hour or two of sleep. I let Clara go home early, and I made some chicken vegetable soup for dinner. I'll heat it up. How did your day on campus go?"

He rubbed his lower lip. "On campus *and* in the city police headquarters. I spoke to several university people and also to Inspector Bakewell. We can discuss everything over a bowl of soup. In the meantime, a hot shower will do me good. I'm so sorry, dear. I forgot to ask how you're feeling."

"Much better. Reading the Psalms was a healing balm." She stood and gave him a kiss. "I'm sorry I let myself get so upset last night. I'm worried about Lana's involvement with Daniel Butler and this horrible kidnapping business. But go ahead and have your shower."

When James came back down in his robe and slippers, the powerful aroma from the dining room beckoned him. On the table was a large serving bowl and two steaming bowls of chicken vegetable soup.

He turned and walked into the kitchen. "I could smell your delicious soup upstairs."

She turned around and handed him a basket of hot dinner rolls and a dish of butter. "Here, dear, take these in. I'll be there in a second."

Moments later, Ann entered the dining room with a pitcher of iced tea and sat next to him. He laid his hand on her arm like he always did and said a blessing over their family and food.

"Well, dear, I'm on pins and needles. What did you find out today? Is Lana going to be safe?"

He smiled at her. "I'm sure she will be, and so are the people I spoke with. The president was out of town, but I talked to the dean of engineering as well as both Daniel's and Lana's thesis advisors. I also saw the campus police chief and drove downtown for a short meeting with Inspector Bakewell."

James took a big spoonful of the soup and sighed.

"Here's what I learned today. First, from the academics—and this is in strict confidence. Daniel Butler seems to be respected and well-liked by those who know him. He's about halfway through his PhD studies in mechanical engineering. The people I spoke with think he obtained some incorrect results about increasing the power of laser beams by passing them through what sounds like magic crystals. They've talked to experts who all say the effect is unheard of but not impossible. But I admit, Professor Kromer, Dan's advisor, who has seen the laser boost occur many times, was less adamant than the others. Kromer also said Dan told him he'd had an interview with a mysterious fellow from a private research organization, but he couldn't remember any names. They are also unanimous in their understanding of the kidnapping. They believe some group, domestic or foreign, believes the laser effect is real. Why they believe it is a mystery. And somehow they found out about Dan's results. So they've taken him somewhere to force him to work with them. Until they get what they want, Dan is safe. After that, all bets are off."

Ann tightened her lips. "It's terrible what happened to Dan Butler, but I'm most concerned about Lana. If the kidnappers don't get what they want, could Lana be in danger? Or others in his department, for that matter?"

James nodded. "Of course, it's possible, but everyone thinks it's unlikely. I asked Bakewell your question. His answer was the kidnappers know if Butler can't help them, it's much less likely anyone else, including Lana, could. Also, security measures on campus are being increased. More cameras, more officers, more awareness. And the city police are surveilling the five students on Lana's rescue team. Keeping them safe."

Ann breathed a sigh and ladled more soup into James's bowl.

"The police were in total agreement with everything the university people said. Then Bakewell gave me additional information, some of which has already been leaked to the media. He said two breakthroughs were made by Lana's team."

His wife's eyes widened. "Good heavens, what did she do?"

James explained what Lana and her team had found. "If nothing else, this indicates to me our daughter is behaving like the careful and intelligent adult she is. I hope you see it that way too."

"I do," Ann replied. "And I want you to know I've decided to go talk to our pastor about the situation between Lana and Dan."

"That's an excellent idea, dear. I'm anxious to hear how it goes."

Chapter 53

Tuesday, October 1

At 8:00 a.m., Eos entered the CEO's office, his heart thumping, his mouth dry and sticky. Sitting at his desk, Sirius glared at him.

"What's up, Si?"

"Don't 'what's up' me." He snarled, clenching his fists like an enraged tyrant sitting on his throne. "Nothing's up. Everything's down. The board is killing me! They wanna know what we're getting for the million shekels we spent on Operation Q. I keep stalling because *you* keep stalling. What's with this kid? He's been here two weeks with zero results."

"Keep your blood pressure down, Si. Doctor's orders, remember? Besides, it's only been a week, and this is only his fourth workday." Eos took the chair in front of the desk. He wiped his face and rubbed the back of his neck. "Butler's working as hard as he can. I know he's—"

"You *know*? Like when you told me in college you *knew* you could steal the chemistry final exam? But *you* didn't deliver. And *I* failed the stinkin' course." Sirius banged his desk. "Is that how you know?"

"Look," Eos replied, "Butler and I will make a new set of plans today. More creative plans. We'll go from ten to twelve hours a day."

"The board is worried about our balance sheet, J. J. The processor group didn't meet the delivery date on the hyper-computers, and the Russians are screaming bloody murder. The depleted-uranium tank penetrators failed their pre-acceptance tests in Iran. And worst of all, the sheiks are chomping at the bit waiting to get their hands on some of our Star Wars lasers. They beat the previous high bid we discussed."

"By how much?"

"They're offering us a hundred and ten million. Say they can get oil production and reserves way up if the lasers are as good as Halsey says they can be. Being able to blast deeper wells would uncover trillions of dollars of new oil wealth. I'm not at all convinced they want them just for drilling oil wells, but that's not our problem. We need the laser project to succeed. And I mean quick!"

"I'm convinced Butler doesn't know how to solve the problem."

"I'm convinced that he better figure it out soon. I'm just about out of patience with this kid. You know what happens when I get mad. I was hot-tempered even when we were young. Remember the frog at the Omega Beta Upsilon frat house?" Sirius pulled out his scissors and waved them.

"Yes. I'll never forget the frog. Hell week." Eos smiled because he remembered the story had a good ending. "We were both pledging OBU and rooming together at their frat house. They let us use one of the guest rooms because we were waiting tables for the brothers' breakfasts and dinners to earn a little cash. Remember? One of the sophomores—Dingle, I think—hid a frog in our room, and you woke up with the frog on your face." Eos sat back and grinned.

"You think this is funny?"

"Then you went crazy and cut the frog up with scissors. And you put the head sticking out of his rice. Dingle barfed on his plate, and the brothers voted to blackball you."

"Dingle was a dongle."

"Let's not forget the ending. I appealed your case to the president of the fraternity, who just happened to be my big brother at OBU. And he gave you a pardon."

"And what about when we were juniors.? They were having trouble finding a big brother for Crawley from Chicago because he was conceited and thought he knew everything. Remember him?"

"Of course, I do. I kind of liked him because he was tough—like me. So, I took him on as my little brother." Sirius nodded as though to say, "So what?"

"Until you overheard him at one of our frat parties telling some girls you were an obnoxious twitch. You were into one of the girls. You talked me into joining you two for a day on the ski slopes. You with me?"

"Yes."

"Crawley never skied before, but he thought he could learn in an hour or two. So we showed him how to snowplow, a beginner's technique. Then you told him we were taking him to a beginner's slope when it was actually an expert trail. What did he know? He came down alive but bloody from brushing several trees. Said he almost flew off a cliff. You could have killed him, you know."

"But he learned not to be so cocky and pay me more respect," Sirius responded. "He bombed out his freshman year anyway.

"But let's get back to the matter at hand—Butler."

Sirius grabbed the stress ball from his desk and gave it a vicious squeeze. "Can you give me one good reason Butler can't reproduce the results he got in Quincy other than he's stalling?"

"I think something's missing." Eos punctuated his words with a forefinger. "Something inconspicuous in the Quincy lab that's triggering this vibricity stuff. Our labs here have everything Dan had in Quincy. Give me another two weeks. We'll find it."

"Two weeks? . . . Against my better judgment, *two weeks*. Do . . . not . . . disappoint me. You need to know I'm strongly considering emergency action."

Chapter 54

He's never late. He hasn't called. What happened?" Staring at the clock, Dan muttered, took a deep breath, and blew it out. "I can't do any work until he comes." Eos had said no experimentation was permitted unless a second person was present.

At 8:30, the door buzzed and opened. Eos strode in. "Sorry, Dan. I got called up to the boss's office this morning. He has a . . . special job for me, and I've got to leave right away."

"But how can I work alone?"

"You won't be. I already assigned a couple of people from the mirror team to be ready to stand in, if necessary. You should be taking data within an hour or two. Work hard, Dan. Real hard." Eos squinted, and his mouth made a straight line across his face. "Like your life depended on it! When I get back, we're going to twelve-hour shifts." And with that, Eos departed.

Stand ins? Dan threw his hands up and his head back. After checking his computer and lab book records, Dan decided to do some system checks until Eos's substitute showed up. *Like my life depended on it?* A drop of sweat trickled down his forehead.

Shortly after 9:00, the buzzer sounded again, and the door glided open. Like a model featured in a photoshoot, a young woman in blue jeans, a long-sleeved tan blouse, and short leather boots appeared. Her flowing auburn hair and striking figure were framed artistically in the doorway.

"Hi, Dan," she said. "I'm Zoey Goodwin. J. J. says you need a partner for a few days."

"Please come in, Zoey." Dan rose from his desk and took a few steps in her direction. "I'm Dan Butler. Yes, Eos said he had someone lined up to work with me while he was away, but I didn't . . . uhh . . ."

She sashayed into the room. "You didn't expect someone like me. I'll make it easy for you and take that as a compliment. Fair enough?"

"Why don't we sit at the table and get acquainted?" Since it wasn't a date, Dan felt quite relaxed.

"OK." She grinned and glided over to a chair. "It's an honor to be the first person on the mirror team who meets the mystery man who tickled the dragon's tail. Since Eos set up shop in your lab, all we've seen are videos of you shot from the ceiling."

"Ugh."

"Not at all. I . . . enjoyed . . . it. But seeing you at ground level and in person is *much* better."

"Well, I'll take that as a compliment too," Dan said. "But tell me, what's the dragon's tail? I thought that term came from the Manhattan Project for the atomic bomb."

"I'm impressed, Dan. Yes, they used that procedure at Los Alamos to test the heart of the A-bomb. They had to check out the two pieces of solid uranium fuel the nuclear core was made of, which exploded when they were jammed together to create a so-called critical mass."

"Sounds painful." Dan tapped on the table. "I know a little about it. I'm working on a degree in engineering physics. It's a division of the mechanical engineering department."

"Marvelous. My MS was in nuclear physics."

"That's awesome, Zoey. But why did you say *I* tickled the dragon's tail?"

"Because we've had a team of eight people slaving away here for two years trying to coax the vibricity dragon to divulge her secret, but we didn't get anywhere. *You* play with it for a little while, and the dragon roars!"

"Maybe so," Dan said. "But whatever I did, it was intermittent, so I couldn't convince anybody."

"Well, you convinced Eos."

Dan motioned toward the lab table. "I guess we should get on with the show."

The pair continued with Dan's research until lunchtime. Since Dan hadn't received cafeteria privileges yet, Zoey offered to pick up sandwiches and sodas for both of them. She told Dan J. J. had given her a StarWay charge number to use for anything they wanted.

After lunch, they worked until 7:00 p.m., without making any progress. Zoey looked at the clock, then said, "Maybe we'll have better luck tomorrow. Time to quit?"

"I guess so. Your input today was insightful, especially the idea of mounting an ultrasound transducer on the crystal in the laser beam and seeing if high-frequency sound waves produce an increased light output. Let's see if we can borrow one tomorrow. I hope Eos stays away a few more days. I'll bet the two of us will make more progress than he and I did. Time to say good night. I enjoyed working with you."

"Dan"—she gave him a flirty smile and touched his arm—"what if we had dinner together tonight in your room? We could order through your dumbwaiter, get to know each other better. Talk about our backgrounds and career hopes. Eos told me you were having trouble sleeping. If you let me read something to you from my phone, I could put you to sleep pretty fast."

Dan knitted his eyebrows together. "I don't think it could . . . would . . . it's not a good idea."

"We've been together alone for ten hours, and I didn't bite you, did I? We can spend some enjoyable time together and help you forget the pressure of being here." She leaned forward until he could see flecks of gold in her brown eyes. "I'm positive I can help you relax. But it's your call. After all, maybe you don't . . . like me?"

"Don't like you?" Dan laughed and shook his head. "I'm *sure* you can relax me too. In fact, you're already doing it. OK. We'll have dinner. On condition that if either of us senses things are heading in the wrong direction, we part company immediately. Do you agree?"

"I do."

Dan returned to his room to take a shower and change clothes. *Come on. She's a work colleague. That's all. OK. A darn attractive one, but that's not her fault, is it?* He knew he was taking a big chance. But, heck, he needed a bit of relaxation. Besides, he could control the situation if it got out of hand.

After showering, Dan straightened the blanket on the bed and tossed his clothes in the laundry bin. Since he'd been feeling like a prison inmate, he'd been wearing shirts, trousers, and shoes of the same color. But tonight, he put on navy slacks, a tan shirt, and dark brown shoes.

He heard a knock on the door. He opened it, and there she stood. Her long hair down, she'd changed into a black skirt, cut above the knees, with black flats, and a blue, deep-V blouse. Silky. In her hand, she held a large tote bag.

Dan swallowed hard. "Come on in, Zoey. You look great."

"Thanks. You too."

They sat at the table, and Dan handed Zoey one of the two meal cards he held and a pencil. "Food must be ordered before 8:00 p.m. Let's get our cards in now. Then we can talk."

When the cards were on their way to the kitchen, Zoey rose. "Dan, let's sit in those recliners while we talk and wait for dinner."

"Sure." They relocated to the more comfortable setting. Trying to be subtle, he let his gaze sweep across Zoey.

"They gave us your bio when we started on the vibe project. But you don't know anything about me." Zoey grinned at him. "Interested?"

"Definitely."

"So where to start? I was born and raised on the Florida Gulf Coast. Clearwater. Plenty of sunshine and salt water. Played outside with my sister and neighborhood friends most of the time. Mom worked part-time in the local library. Dad had a joint faculty position at USF in the Departments of Electrical Engineering and Physics. No surprise where my career interest came from."

"So you got a leg up"—Dan swallowed—"early. My folks were blue-collar. We lived in a small town with good weather and beautiful scenery, which gave my brother and me a healthy and fun-filled childhood. On top of that, we learned boxing and weightlifting from Dad. Comes in handy sometimes. My folks gave us strong values and an old-fashioned church upbringing. Those things affected my life a lot."

"That's one area that was missing in my childhood," Zoey said as she switched the leg she was sitting on. "My parents were moral, ethical people but not churchgoers. Mom was a single parent by the time I hit double digits. Before Dad walked out on us, he always said the more he learned about science, the less he needed a father in the sky."

The conversation drifted to how they'd chosen their careers. As it wound down, the food arrived.

Dan put the plates, silverware, and napkins on the table while Zoey filled glasses with water. "Oh, I have a surprise." She went to her bag and retrieved a bottle of red wine and two plastic wine glasses.

"Very thoughtful. Unfortunately, I don't drink alcohol."

"Well, I do. Maybe you can just wet your lips. I'll pour some."

Dan said a blessing, and Zoey respectfully bowed her head.

Both diners commented on the excellence of the salmon they'd ordered. Zoey was especially talkative, undoubtedly stimulated by the wine she was drinking. Spending time in the company of an attractive woman put Dan in a good mood as well.

After dinner, Dan cleared the table and put out the dessert and coffee. Zoey said she had another surprise. Her large tote produced a game box—Upwords.

"How do you play it?" Dan asked and scratched his head.

"Simple. Kinda like Scrabble, but you can also put letter tiles on top of existing ones. Scoring is different. Each letter in a one-level-high word scores two points. If any words contain higher level letters, each tile in the word counts as one point. Wanna try it?"

"Why not? But I'm not the world's best speller."

They finished their desserts and put seven tiles on their racks. After several minutes of considering his choices, Dan blurted out, "I can't believe it. A seven-letter word!" and laid down all his tiles:
TUGGING.

Zoey wrote down his 14-point score and then, with a sly smile, put an H on the T:
HUGGING.

Dan looked at his seven fresh letters for several minutes and played three tiles:

```
    S
    A
HUGGING
    E
```

"That adds flavor to the game," Zoey observed.

"Yes, that's why you always find sage in sausage."

"Really? Well, how does this grab you?" she responded with a leer and added three more letters.

```
    M
    A
    S
    S
    A
HUGGING
    E
```

"I'll bet a little massage would be just what the doctor ordered." Zoey rose and walked behind him. She placed her hands on his shoulders and started squeezing.

"Wow. You feel like a weightlifter. If you want me to stop, one word will do it."

I should call it quits. But there's nothing improper here, and it feels so *good . . .*

"Dan, with this chair back in the way, I can't get below your shoulder blades. There's no sofa here, but would you mind lying on that bed?"

Lumbering like a person under hypnosis, Dan got up and went over to his bed.

Just a few more minutes, and then we stop.

Her hands moved from the tops of his shoulders to the small of his back. Up and down.

The time-out buzzer is going off!

"That felt wonderful," he said, pushing up into a sitting position. "But I think we better—"

"Dan, I need your restroom. My hands are getting tired. How about if we go back and sit on the easy chairs? I'll be right back." Zoey picked up her tote bag and turned the corner. On the way she dimmed the lights.

Moments later, as he sat back in his chair, breathing hard and awaiting her return, she came out in bare feet and glided toward him. "Those new flats hurt my feet."

He stared at her blouse. *She's not wearing everything she had on a minute ago. Buzzer going off again!*

Zoey sauntered to her chair and took her time as she turned around and sat. Her eyes were closed, as she slowly raised a leg and put the sole of her foot on the cushion.

Dan groaned and leaped up. Without a word, he rushed straight into his dressing room and closed the door. He dropped to his knees and then fell forward onto the carpeted floor and cried out, "Lord, please help me. My body is aching for hers. But it's a sin against You, and I feel like I'm betraying Lana. The Bible says we will never be tempted beyond our ability to resist. I beg You to fulfill that promise." He lay with the edges of both fists on the carpet.

"Dan, are you all right?" Zoey called from outside the door.

Chapter 55

Wednesday, October 2

J ames woke up at 5:30 a.m. in the den. *Looks like I fell asleep here last night after Ann came in troubled. Said she'd be in her studio until further notice. That must've been some meeting with the pastor. I hope this will pour oil on the troubled waters between Ann and Lana.*

Half an hour later, Ann came down to the den where James was reading. "Good morning, James. I want you to do something for me," she said.

"Anything."

"Please call Lana and tell her I want to have Dan over as soon as he gets back. And I believe he *will* return."

"It sounds like you and our pastor had a helpful meeting. Was it?"

"Very much so. We can talk later about that. And please tell Lana I had a long talk with Pastor Silverberg. I'd call her myself, except I'm not sure I could get the words out."

"Are you all right, darling? Did you get any sleep?"

"I'm fine. I spent nine hours talking with the Holy Spirit. I reviewed my life and my level of obedience to the Lord. Like King Belshazzar in the book of Daniel, I've been weighed in the balances and found wanting. My obsession with status and money has blinded me these past thirty years. Now I want to make amends."

"You're a good woman, and I love you. All of us can improve our relationship with God, and I'm glad you want to do that. When Dan returns home, we'll see how he responds to your change of heart. But your willingness to make amends will impact Lana immediately."

Chapter 56

When Dan arrived in his lab, Zoey was already there, slumped in her chair and staring at the floor.

He walked up to her and said, "Zoey, I'm very sor—"

"I asked George, the other sub, to fill in for me till Eos gets back. He can start this afternoon."

"I don't want to part company under these conditions. We were doing great, at least in the lab, until our emotions got involved. Besides, I'd love to explore the ultrasound idea with you. How about if we give it a try this morning?"

She looked up and said, "No man has ever responded to me the way you did. And I never had to *flaunt* myself either. Or steal away embarrassed and unfulfilled. Look, you need a safety partner. So I'll stay till noon and help you while I'm here. That's all I have to say."

Dan had requested the ultrasound transducer, clamps, and other items they needed to test Zoey's speculation, and everything was delivered before 8:30. They spent the entire morning trying to tickle the dragon's tail with sound waves. Zoey was his helpful but silent partner and only responded to comments or questions with head movements. Their efforts were fruitless, and Dan decided to quit at noon.

"I know I hurt your feelings, Zoey, and you're mad at me. I apologize that it turned out that way. But I wasn't rejecting you. If I hadn't been under two restraints, spiritual and relational, I'd have been all over you—all night long." He walked around the table and stood in front of her. "I want to restore our friendship, even though I don't share your lifestyle. And I still think you'd do the lab and me a favor by continuing to work as my partner until the . . . end. If J. J. agrees, will you do it?"

It seemed as though several minutes passed before Zoey replied. "Yes. For the lab and you."

"Thank you," Dan said. "Despite last night, I'd like to know you better. You—the person. Will you eat lunch with me outside today?"

"Maybe . . . well, OK." Looking down at the floor, she took a deep breath and exhaled loudly. After a moment, she looked up at him and smiled.

Zoey picked up the sandwiches and drinks from the cafeteria again while Dan got a blanket and a jar of stuffed olives from his room. They took the elevator to the forest and found a sunny place not far from the exit.

"This looks like a perfect spot for a mini-picnic in Shangri-La," Zoey said with a smirk. "Or maybe you haven't heard the nickname for StarWay Labs."

Nodding, Dan took a bite of his sandwich, then a swig of orangeade. He held up a finger, swallowed, and a moment later spoke. "Eos used that term on the first night of my . . . internship. May I say a few things that bear on our situation? Then maybe you'd like to give me your perspective."

"That might help explain an evening that ended very badly." Zoey put her sandwich down, folded her hands together, and waited for Dan to speak.

"I'll start by saying something that won't surprise you, Zoey. You're one of the smartest and best-looking women I've ever met. What happened last night was in spite of, not because of, your attributes. I really wanted you. But I'm a Christian, and that means I have deep religious beliefs based on the Bible. I believe the Bible is the word of God, and it prohibits sex between unmarried people. I'll tell you something no one but my brother knows. The only sexual experience I've ever had was relatively mild with a college freshman girl. I was guilt-stricken for months, until I did something Christians call repenting."

"Dan, you are one unbelievable guy. A hunk too."

"There's another reason. A very special young woman at Quincy University."

"Aha! A girlfriend. *Now* I understand."

"Not exactly. But before I tell you about her, please put your drink down. Otherwise, you're going to spill it. There you go. OK. She's my love coach."

Zoey burst out laughing. "Your what? I thought that's what I was trying to do!"

Dan gave Zoey his standard explanation for his problem with women. "So my coach has been giving me tips on how to approach and behave with women I'm interested in."

"But what does that have to with you running away from me? Shouldn't you have been using her tips to win me over? As if you needed any last night. And another thing. Is this person a professional dating counselor? Do you find her attractive?"

"One thing at a time, please." Dan thought while tapping his splayed fingertips together. "She and I have developed a deep but somewhat strange relationship. I didn't think we could become a couple because she is so far out of my league, but now I realize I have deep feelings for her. I think she may be the one for me." He sighed. "Last night I felt like I'd be cheating on her if you and I had continued any further. And regarding the other question, no, she's a grad student in biomedical engineering. She just took the coaching job because I asked her to."

Zoey shook her head. "Dan, I have news for you. This girl likes you . . . a lot!"

"You're not the first person to tell me that, although I can't make *myself* believe it. But let's talk about more recent matters. What was your take on last night, and why did you act the way you did? I'm more interested in the why than the what."

Zoey hesitated and then said, "J. J. asked me to be nice to you and then winked."

"He did, eh? So, tell me, Zoey, how much of last night was me and how much was J. J.?"

"Oh, it started at about seventy to thirty, I'd say. After you let me give you that rubdown, your score went to one hundred, and I kind of lost it. Everything clear?"

"Yep. Should we go back down to the lab and tickle the dragon some more?"

Chapter 57

Special Agent Jack Staunton, FBI Chelsea, MA Field Office, had just gotten home from work. He walked upstairs to his wife, Janet's, art studio. "Hi, honey. I'm a tiny bit late, so I brought some Chinese takeout for dinner tonight instead of going out. Is that OK?"

Janet laid her brush down on the oil paint pallet, got up, and they hugged. "Tiny bit late, ha! It's eight thirty. One of these days you'll remember to call me when you're going to be late. Let's go down and eat."

They sat at the kitchen table and made short work of the tasty moo goo gai pan along with a bottle of sparkling grape juice. One of their favorite meals.

"I'm reaching way back in my memory," Jack said, "but didn't you tell me you dated a guy named Eos in grad school?"

"I did. Why?"

"The office got a bulletin for information on somebody with that name. A very unusual one. What was your story?"

"It wasn't his name." Janet refilled both their glasses. "His real name was J. J. Puller. An unusual person. Got up every morning at daybreak and ran five miles. The guys in our group of friends jokingly referred to him as Eos, the goddess of dawn. He didn't mind it. In fact, he liked J. J. Eos better than J. J. Puller, so the name stuck. He told me the name was unbelievably rare. A diamond of a name, he used to joke."

"The bureau has been checking out all the Eoses it can find," Jack said.

"What'd he do?"

"Suspect in a graduate student kidnapping case. But since it's a nickname, looks like a dead end. Well, there are only—hold on." Jack pulled out his smartphone and started keying. "Forty thousand Pullers in the country . . . Could be worse . . . Let's see . . . Two million Smiths and Johnsons."

"Hey, Jack, I just remembered something. Even after he and I broke up after graduation, I still had a case for J. J., until I met you, of course." Janet held her glass up to her husband. "Wait a minute. I think J. J. sent me a greeting card a couple years before you and I started dating seventeen years ago. That would make it nineteen years ago. Maybe I saved it. Nah. But let me check my 'ancient history' folder upstairs. Be back in a minute."

Jack cleared the table and went into the den. He turned on a football game he had recorded. The game was just starting to heat up when Janet returned.

"Hey, look at this!" She handed him an age-discolored envelope.

"How about that? J. J. Eos. The state is smudged, but I can read the zip code. The date is also readable. Dum ditty dum ditty . . ." Jack did the arithmetic in his head. "Yep. Nineteen years ago. I think I'll call this in right away. You never know in our business. Thanks, hon."

Chapter 58

Monday, October 7

Lana was exhausted and frustrated. The team had met again several times, but there was little they could do since the FBI had taken over the investigation. She felt helpless. She ate a small cup of fruit cocktail and sat on the sofa to check her recent text messages when a new one popped up from Joe:

"Sorry to bother you, but I had to pick up something from the lab to read and noticed something on Dan's laser apparatus. Might affect his situation. Any chance you could come in for a minute? Thanks."

Yikes! I'm heading in . . . Mmm, better call first.

Lana placed the call. No answer. Before she left, she texted back she was on her way in.

She parked in the student lot and jogged to the Mechanical Engineering building. How many times had she worked late and covered this path at night? *Everyone's too jumpy these days.*

Inside her destination she approached Dan's lab and knocked.

The door opened. A man in a UPS uniform wearing a medical mask seized her arm, jerked her in, and covered her mouth. "One scream or false move will result in serious problems for you and Daniel Butler. Do you understand, Miss Madison?"

Lana, barely able to stay conscious for fear, nodded. From behind the door, another man wearing the same apparel and holding a gun stepped into view. He pointed to a crate on the floor with its lid open. The crate was about four feet long and its end about an 18-inch square.

"Get in!" he barked. "You're going for a short ride. If you cooperate and tell us what you know, you'll be released unharmed. Probably in under a couple hours. OK?"

Lana nodded again, and the first man released her.

"How can I fit in there?" she asked.

"This crate was custom made for you. Snug but manageable. The easiest way is to lie on your back and pull your knees to your chest while we close the lid. Or you can try lying on your side, if you prefer. I repeat. Get in."

Lana got in and pulled up her knees as instructed. "It's impossible to stay like this for more than a minute or two!" she pleaded.

"It's possible. We tested it with two women your size." The gunman laughed, and the lid was shut. She heard the boss say, "They figured her at a hundred and twenty pounds. The crate weighs twenty more. That's only seventy pounds each. Not bad."

"Let's have some fun with her. She's a real beauty, that one!" Lana tensed at the gunman's vicious suggestion. She couldn't make out the other's reply.

Lana knew this would be the worst day of her life, and she wanted to pray immediately. But she thought it important to listen and feel what she could about the trip to be able to report it to the police. If she survived.

The crate being lifted caused a sudden thrust and increased pain. Along the way, one of the kidnappers said, presumably to a late worker, "Yeah. A heavy crate of lab equipment for an overnight delivery. They probably need a quick repair." The travel time was consistent with the length of the hall to the back door of the ME building.

Lana felt them stop at the back door, go a few feet, and then turn left in the cold outside air that came through the air vents in the box. Then came a short walk to the transport vehicle, possibly a borrowed or stolen UPS truck, she thought. Then came the sound of doors opening. A sudden, agonizing, drop onto the vehicle's floor, which made the aching in her back and knees approach the unbearable for a few seconds.

Lana knew where the entrance to the lot was. By the directions of the turns she felt and the time between the points, she figured with some confidence that they had left the lot and turned north toward the industrial area of Quincy.

Lana reduced the excruciating pain in her back and legs to one of merely extreme discomfort by making some moves like a contortionist. She moved her hips to the far right, painfully compressing her hip flesh. Then she rotated her left knee into the upper left corner and pushed it with both hands until it went into the foot half of the box. She tried to muffle her scream from the knee pain she suffered. Then she moved far left and successfully repeated the process with her right knee. She ended up with her left foot against the right wall and vice versa. It was not comfortable, but was much less painful. Her captors must have known this, but they put her in the wrong way to cause more suffering. "Thank You, Dear Lord." She put her hands to her mouth and blew kisses to God.

Finally, the vehicle and engine sound stopped.

The lid opened, and the man in charge slipped a blindfold over Lana's eyes. "You may get up now. I see you passed the intelligence test. That's good." He stood her up with his hands on her shoulder to guide her around. Lana had no opportunity to see the building they were entering, but the metallic sound of the door opening, the squeaky hinges, and the dank, musty smell reminded her of an abandoned warehouse or large garage. She heard a wooden door open and close as they entered what was apparently a room in the building. He moved a chair against the back of her legs and pressed down on her shoulders. She sat and heard other chairs move.

"OK, Lana, are you ready to begin?"

"Y-yes," was her reply.

"Before we start, I want to explain the small crate. I doubt anybody we might have passed in that building, and we did pass someone, would think there could be an adult of normal size inside a crate that small. But the reason we kept you in the crate the whole time was we knew from the testing we did how uncomfortable that is. That would have been useful in case you refused to give us honest answers.

"Oh, and I want you to wear this watch during the questioning." He put it on her wrist and latched the leather band. "If it beeps, you may have to go back into the crate for a few hours. Now let's begin.

"Lana, are you and Mr. Butler good friends? Are you dating?"

"The best answer would be we are somewhere between the two. Except we had an argument just before he disappeared."

"I see. Do you and he discuss his laser work?"

"Yes. But it's not my field of expertise. So I don't understand everything."

"Do you know what material he has been studying?"

"Yes. Transparent yttrium oxide."

"Is anything else in the material, Lana?"

"Yes. Two dopants. Earlier, I think one was a Lanthanide group element and one wasn't. Later, I believe both were Lanthanide elements."

"And which Lanthanide elements?"

"I don't remember that. There are so many atomic elements. I think one was always Lanthanum. I remember that one because it's the same as the group name. And excuse me, but could I have a drink of water?"

Lana heard footsteps leaving the room. A moment later, the footsteps returned and she was given the water. She took a drink. "Thank you very much."

"Shall we continue? Did Mr. Butler ever mention using more than two dopants?"

"Not to my recollection. I'm fairly sure about that."

"Good enough. Now I have a series of questions about another topic. Activities outside the lab. Ready?"

Lana nodded.

"Is Mr. Butler professionally active outside the laboratory? Has he ever talked about research conferences he's attended? Meetings he's had related to his laser work? Things like that?"

"When you say meetings, are you thinking of large group meetings or one-on-one meetings?"

"Both types."

"Dan's never spoken to me about large conferences. He attends departmental research seminars. He even presented one himself not too long ago. He has meetings with his PhD advisor, Professor Kromer. And he had a meeting with a business recruiter recently who offered him a two-week internship."

"What was that all about?"

"He said it was a nice offer, but the recruiter wouldn't give him enough time to think about it."

"Any other details about the meeting?"

"No. Nothing I can think of. We both thought the offer was a bit strange. I remember something about their headquarters being in North Carolina and the internet address of the company webpage."

"No other information related to the meeting?"

"Nothing definite that I can remember."

"Well, Lana, I'll take the watch back now. We'll take you to your car. Or at least near enough for you to walk the rest of the way. Now listen carefully to my final warning, Lana. If you go to the police or talk to anybody about this, you will never see Daniel Butler again. We have eyes and ears everywhere. The same thing is true if anything happens to us. We report in several times a day, and you better not do anything that might interrupt those reports. Do you understand?"

Lana nodded emphatically.

He turned to his accomplice. "Time to close up shop."

"Now, what's the hurry. I thought I could spend a few minutes talking to Lana myself. In private."

"I said we were leaving. Now. And this time Lana will be sitting beside the crate."

Chapter 59

Tuesday, October 15

Dan and Eos had spent the morning trying desperate ideas. After lunch, they began to review their results at StarWay Labs. Dan pointed at the clear rod mounted in his duplicated research apparatus. "We've got all this data on my best crystal from the QU collection. But no significant increase in laser power. Vibricity, or whatever you call it, is dead here."

"Dan, our time is up. I can't restrain Sirius much longer."

Eos's phone chimed. He answered it and walked over to the far corner of the lab. Dan watched Eos shake his head the whole time. Finally, Eos put the phone in his pocket and came back. He spoke in a flat monotone. "It looks like I can't restrain him at all. I'm sorry, Dan."

The door locks clicked open and two blue-suited guards entered. They sandwiched Dan and dragged him out of the lab. *This is the end, Lord. I'm Yours.*

The guards marched Dan down a long, empty hallway. They palmed the door open at the end of the hall, and he entered a large office. Behind a massive desk sat a large-framed man wearing a gray mask. *The same kind they used for the Mask and Meet.* Cold chills raced up and down Dan's spine.

The masked man remained motionless. Dan wondered if he was real, but then he pointed to a plain black chair facing the desk. Dan walked forward and sat in it.

"Good afternoon, Mr. Butler. My name is Sirius," he said, as he opened a desk drawer and withdrew a pistol, which he laid on the desktop. "And so is my disposition. The cost of the operation to bring you here, to create and equip two identical copies of your laboratory, and to make all the custom crystal rods, as well as the personnel salaries, amounts to over one million dollars. But you have produced nothing for us. So, Mr. Butler, the directors of the StarWay organization are displeased. Mr. Eos has been gentle with you, against my recommendations, but that has not been fruitful. We have no choice but to bring matters to a head. You may not enjoy the next few hours very much. But remember, this is your last chance to convince me you should live."

Sirius pressed a button on his desk. His office door opened, and the two guards reentered the room and took Dan away. They went down the hall where they palmed open an unmarked door leading to a dimly lit staircase. The three men descended to a small landing, and one guard opened a metal door leading to a small metal cell, illuminated only by a blue overhead light. At the back was a metal chair anchored to the floor and facing away from the door. A small metal shelf was mounted on the right wall. The guards thrust Dan into the room, then turned and left. The door clanged shut.

For the first time in his life, Dan felt unmitigated terror. He backed into a corner of the room. Tremors engulfed his whole body, and he clasped his arms around his shoulders in an effort to stay warm. As his legs gave way, he slid to the floor.

"Oh my God and Savior, can You hear me? Will You help me?" He wailed and stammered out the two prayers that had comforted him in the park when Angel first appeared. As the minutes passed, he took control of his emotions but continued the prayers. Later, he began a silent conversation with his Maker and begged Him for guidance and rescue.

Then his thoughts shifted.

"They're going to kill me," Dan muttered in tears. "I'll never go home again . . . never see Lana again. I have . . . to see her one more time before I . . . die. To hold her. . . and tell her how much . . . I . . . love her."

After what seemed like an eternity, Dan heard the door open again. One of the guards entered with his pistol drawn, followed by a man a foot shorter than Dan. He wore black attire and a black mask of the same design as the one Sirius had worn. In the man's hand was a small black suitcase, which he placed on the shelf and unlatched. He removed a metal box and other parts and laid them on the shelf next to the case.

"It seems, Mr. Butler, that you are not cooperating with our organization," he said in a thick Eastern European accent. "Perhaps after our little session together, you will try harder. Please stand when I talk to you!"

"I'm sorry. I meant no disrespect." Dan rose from the floor.

"Sit on the chair! Roll up your right sleeve and pantleg!"

The short man bent over and plugged an electric cord into an outlet.

The short man walked over, holding two coiled electric cords stretching from the box on the shelf. At the end of each cord was an open metal cuff.

"If you do anything inappropriate, Mr. Butler, the lights will go off in your head. Put one of these on your wrist and one on your ankle, and snap them shut tightly. That's right. Now we try the low-power mode. It's low voltage and current. Only a two-percent chance your heart will . . . stop."

He threw a switch handle, and a buzzing sound came on. Dan's arms shook, and he groaned.

"How did that feel? Good?"

"No. It felt terrible. Please, I will try to work—"

"Now comes the medium-power mode. The odds are still in your favor, Dan. In this case the fatalities run about twenty percent. I love this little machine. It makes all our visitors so much more cooperative. They stop . . . trying . . . and start telling us what we want to know. Maybe you are beginning to remember how to generate vibricity? You did it in Quincy, Mr. Butler."

"I think the lab was colder there. Let's try—"

"Wrong answer. Bye-bye." The torturer slammed the handle down. A much louder buzz reverberated.

Dan spasmed and screamed.

The noise stopped after a few seconds, but Dan remained in physical and mental shock. His heart began to beat irregularly.

"Now I think you remember how you made vibricity work in your lab. Am I correct, Daniel Butler?"

"Oh, God, I would tell you if I knew the answer."

"Now comes the fun—full-power mode. Ready, Dan?" He sneered. Even through the mask he wore, the miscreant sounded delighted.

The cell door opened, and the second guard put his head in. "The CEO wants Butler in his office."

"He's just had a small taste of how our electrical equipment at StarWay works, haven't you?"

Dan took a deep breath and said a silent prayer of thanksgiving.

The guards raised Dan from the chair and dragged him back to Sirius. After he was seated, the CEO stood and picked up his gun.

"Mr. Butler," he said, "I hope your hour of meditation with a bit of education in electrical engineering was enlightening." He chuckled. "The electrician says he only had time to use the medium-voltage mode. What a shame."

As Sirius spoke, he flipped the gun's safety switch on and off.

"We didn't want to hurt you, Dan." Sirius pressed the magazine catch. The bullet-filled magazine dropped a couple inches into his waiting palm, after which he shoved it back up with a loud click.

He laughed. "Back to the lab, back to the cell? Or maybe"—he patted his gun—"we should settle the problem right here. You have five minutes to help me decide." Sirius took off his wristwatch and placed it on the desk.

Instead of terror, a wave of peace poured over Dan, and he looked up and smiled. "I'm afraid I can't help you, Sirius. That decision is between you and God, even if you don't believe in Him. But weigh your decision carefully because it will have eternal consequences for you."

Chapter 60

Dan's grip on the arms of the chair relaxed, and he stared unblinking at the CEO of StarWay.

"You little piece of . . ." Sirius's phone alarm interrupted his diatribe.

Dan saw a red light on the wall begin to blink, and a bell rang. Sirius grabbed his phone. "Yes, Chief . . . FBI SWAT? Are you sure? . . . Patch me into the PA system." Sirius trained his gun on Dan.

"Attention, all personnel," Sirius shouted into the phone. "This is the CEO. We are in an emergency situation. Details will follow. I am executing Emergency Plan Alpha immediately. If everyone stays calm and does what you've been trained to do, we'll all be fine. Carry on."

After a moment's pause, Sirius spoke again. "Listen, Chief, I want you to go to the top-management circuit, oh, and patch in Eos and Powers. Yes. Keep them all informed. Now, assemble the security force in the armory immediately. You have to keep the feds busy for at least fifteen minutes. Got that?"

Sirius jammed the phone into his pocket and waved his gun at Dan. "Saved by the church bell, eh? Now you're going to save *me*. Let's go, Mr. Evangelist!"

Still wearing his mask, Sirius pointed at the right side of the large wooden bookcase behind his desk. Having recovered somewhat from his ordeal, Dan walked to that location, then stopped. Sirius slapped the left side of the bookcase twice, and the whirr of a motor was audible. The bookcase slid to the right, exposing a dark shoulder-width tunnel.

"You first, and keep moving," Sirius barked.

Sirius entered behind Dan. He pounded the wall four times in rapid succession, and a long line of overhead lights turned on. The whirr started again, and the bookcase returned to its original position. "Run," Sirius snapped. "Faster!"

"I'm doing the best I can after you almost killed me," Dan yelled, as he jerked and stumbled along. He thanked God his recovery was proceeding quicker than he expected.

"Maybe a bullet in your back will speed you up. Move it!"

As they passed under each light, it turned off. The underground tunnel veered back and forth every fifty feet or so to reduce any assailants' visibility and shooting distance.

When they reached the last light, it remained on. To their left was a metal door somewhat smaller than the bookcase. "Wait there." Sirius kept his gun pointed at Dan. He motioned toward the side of the door and repeated the original procedure. They entered a twenty- by twenty-foot metal hangar on a concrete slab where a helicopter stood on a large hydraulic lift.

Dan felt his heart skip a beat. *I've flown the helicopter flight simulator on my computer!*

They both got in the aircraft, Dan in the left seat and Sirius in the helicopter pilot's seat on the right. He kept his gun trained on Dan's chest. "Before we start," Sirius said, "buckle your seat belt. Now, open that compartment and take out the cuffs. Slip one of the cuffs under your seat belt, and click the cuffs on your wrists. OK. Now remember, once this thing lifts off the ground, any aggressive moves on your part, and you die or we crash."

When Sirius had started, Dan kept listening while he mentally compared the main flying controls to the ones on his flight simulator. It wasn't easy, but his life and escape depended on his listening while surveying the controls. Everything was the same or very similar, but he hadn't 'flown' the simulator for several months and never a real helicopter, so he quickly reviewed the action of the controls using his pet mnemonic names. *Horizontal stick between seats is the 'up-or-*

downer'. Pull up—go up. Push down—go down. The vertical column up front is the "tilter" stick. Tilter forward—nose drops, go forward. Tilter right. Right side drops, go right. Works for all directions.

While Sirius did the control checks, Dan developed his action plan. He also said a silent prayer.

When Sirius pressed a button, the two halves of the building's roof slid apart horizontally, and the lift rose until they were at ground level in a clearing 100 feet across in the compact forest. It wasn't circular or square but amoeba-shaped. *Smart. From above it would look less suspicious, more like a natural clearing.* Sirius buckled his seatbelt, started the engine, and the rotors began to revolve.

As the engine revved up, a voice boomed from behind the aircraft, "FBI! Stop or we shoot!"

Sirius's hand went to the up-or-downer and pulled it up hard. The aircraft lurched up from the hangar deck. Dan, who was almost fully recovered now, flipped up his belt latch, whipped around to the right, and dove for the gun. Sirius twisted his right hand, which was on top of the tilter, toward Dan and fired. Dan felt a shooting pain in his upper ear and the scalp behind it as his hands grasped his captor's wrist.

They grappled wildly for control while the helicopter soared upward. Sirius's upper body was now in front and Dan's against the pilot's seat looking forward. Sirius still held the gun. Dan wrestled the other man's hand, and the gun went off again, firing toward the back of the ship. It missed Dan's head completely this time.

Dan now rammed his assailant's hand with all his might down onto a nearby bare metal object, the tilter. Sirius shrieked, and the gun dropped to the floor. He wrapped his left arm around Dan's neck. Dan turned and broke loose and brought his handcuffs powerfully down on Sirius's nose. A loud crack sounded. Sirius screamed again and turned his head away from Dan. The boxer, now turned streetfighter, wrapped his handcuffs over his dazed opponent's head and pulled the chain tightly into his throat. Sirius reached back and grabbed Dan's wrists. He gurgled and squirmed and flailed his arms and legs madly.

After a minute or so had passed, Dan whispered into Sirius's ear, "Want to give me more shocks and shoot me again, you . . . !" Seconds later, the CEO of StarWay Labs went limp.

Dan centered the tilter and moved it forward to maintain horizontal airspeed. The ship leveled out, and its nose dipped down. He pushed the up-or-downer, which was still in the full up position, down to the central position to stop the climb and noticed the altimeter reading indicated they were almost at 3,000 feet above the ground. Then he fished the handcuff key out of the compartment and moved the cuffs to his unconscious opponent's wrists behind his back.

Finally, Dan had some time to think and tend to his injuries. He took his handkerchief from his pocket and compressed his ear and scalp wounds. Dan felt missing tissue at both sites, and both the handkerchief and his shirt were covered with blood. He groaned and mumbled, *I'll bet this is going to look good when I get home. If I get home.* He huffed, and then looked over at the holes in the door he'd entered through and above the right seatback and gasped. "Either shot could've killed me," he said audibly. "Thank you, Lord."

There were duplicate sets of foot pedals in front of both seats, and Dan depressed his right pedal to begin a right turn while he searched for the irregular clearing above the underground hangar where he would try to land. The only place he could land, considering the dense forest everywhere else. After about halfway around the turn, he caught sight of the clearing four or five miles ahead. Dan centered his pedals and pushed the tilter all the way forward. The nose dipped, but the engine began to cough and fade intermittently.

Dan could feel the copter losing altitude during the fades and saw his flight path dropping lower. The altimeter confirmed the loss of altitude. He tried increasing the up on the up-or-downer, but that only made the noise and fading problem worse. *Am I going to reach the hangar or hit the trees along the way? Don't panic!*

Then he remembered a trick his dad's glider pilot friend, whose planes didn't have engines, used to estimate whether you could reach a certain point. *He told me you keep watching the place you want to get to. If it seems to be slowly dropping on your windshield, you're golden. If it keeps rising, you're not going to reach it. Think of the runway when you land in a plane. It goes under the plane, not above. Up is bad.* Dan daubed his fingertip on his bloody ear and made a little red smear on the windshield where the hangar clearing was. He held the controls steady and could only watch and wait. The engine fading issue didn't improve. If anything, it seemed to be getting slowly worse and louder. And when they were about two miles away, he saw the field had moved up a little above the spot on the windshield. *I'm not going to make it.*

He put another red smear on the windshield and tried to toy with the up-or-downer. He repeated the test with the tilter, which gave a better result. This time the field stayed right on the red mark. *Maybe we can make it. Maybe.* Dan squeezed the tilter he was holding, and his knuckles turned white.

The noise from the engine increased, and the fades got deeper. With around 500 yards to go, they were about 100 feet above the trees. At 200 yards, the trees were 30 feet below, and the airport clearance kept moving higher on the windshield. "100 yards. Five feet! We're gonna crash! God help us!" he yelled.

They plunged into the trees with a resounding din. Dan bent forward, watching to dodge whatever might come in. A head-width limb approached like a spear. He lowered and covered his head. The limb tore through the front of the cockpit. The copter smashed into the trunk of the tree and stopped.

Dan opened his eyes and saw they were halfway up the tree, lodged in its branches. Dan felt intense pain on the side of his head and in his side. Before he had time to think about moving, a deafening crack split the air as the weight of the aircraft broke the limb off, and the ship fell to the ground right-side up.

Dan felt himself losing consciousness. The last thing he saw was the pool of blood forming on the floor in front of Sirius.

Then nothing.

Exactly three minutes after Sirius hung up, the ninth member of Chief Carroll's security force ran through the open door of the armory. The chief used his remote to close and lock the door. "OK, ladies and gentlemen, we are now in DEFCON Alpha. Our above-ground cameras picked up maybe a dozen FBI tactical agents, probably Hostage Rescue Team, swarming the forest looking for the access ports to the lab. Thank God, they all got fake grass on them. Listen, I only have . . . a minute and a half to finish this— and no time for questions. I need team Bravo to create a diversion. Defense Port Two seems clear now, but there are three agents about a hundred yards away. The three of you grab your heavy weapons. Leave the port open and stay inside, heads below ground level. The rest of you take your assigned Alpha stations down here."

Everybody got up and hustled to the weapons cache. Stubbs, the Bravo leader, asked, "What are we diverting?"

"Stubbs, I want you to take Johnson and Cooper to Defense Port Two. Make a commotion, and draw them toward the port. Just start shootin' in the air from the platform under the port. But for cryin' out loud, don't hit anybody, and don't get hit yourselves. Pop-shoot-duck. At fifteen forty hours, stop shootin', lock the port, and go to your station. Listen to your radio for further instructions. Now move!"

Team Bravo hightailed it to Port Two. Stubbs took his weapon and shield up the shallow ramp to a landing about four feet beneath the large port. Crouching, he reached up and pushed the spring-loaded lever that unlocked and opened the port. Johnson followed him up and held the shield in front of Stubbs. "Don't see anything. You?" Johnson asked.

"Nah. I'll just shoot a ways up into the trees."

The ack-ack of the automatic weapon was deafening. "Hang on a sec, I want to make a quick three sixty." Johnson rotated his head and body in a complete circle. "Nothing out there."

Stubbs fired intermittently for another couple minutes. Then they switched roles, with Johnson firing and Stubbs shielding. Stubbs thought something moved, but Johnson didn't see it.

"Hey," a voice from below cried. "It's fifteen thirty-eight. We got two minutes left on this diversion. I'm comin' up."

"Affirmative, Cooper. We're low on rounds."

Stubbs descended the stairs. Johnson picked up the shield, and Cooper aimed her weapon.

Suddenly, a burst of gunfire ripped the air from behind them. Both Stubbs and Cooper dropped from the landing, making two horrible whomps.

Stubbs moved to aid the fallen man and woman when a teargas missile arched down through the open port and exploded on the main floor.

Meanwhile, the elites, approved for special treatment by the CEO, had assembled in the small library at the end of the hall. Eos stood at the rear bookcase, and facing him were the directors of operations, finance, information technology, research, and Dr. Powers.

"Welcome to Salvation Station," Eos said. "Among my roles as our leader's right-hand man, I'm also station chief. No time for questions. I just received a report that the invaders are now on the main floor."

An automatic gunfire salvo in the distance provided a punctuation mark to Eos's warning. He slapped the rear bookcase three times, and it opened. "Everybody shuffle your shoes on the carpet to get any dirt off."

"Why?" Powers asked.

"It's a surprise, Halsey. When the others get inside and the lights are on, would you mind pressing the light switch and lock the door behind you? Then join us. Follow me close, everybody."

When they were all inside the dark, narrow tunnel, Eos repositioned the bookcase and turned on the lights. "I doubt they'll get here quickly, but let's keep moving. This is going to be a sci-fi adventure."

Eos led the group down another zig-zagging tunnel, and the overhead lights switched off as they passed under each one. After passing turn five, he raised an arm and stopped.

"See the dead end ahead and the steps and port above it? That leads to a wooden walkway, so no tracks will be left. The walkway goes to a narrow stream in the forest. They can't quickly tell how far we went or even if we left from here because our shoes will leave no tracks or dirt on the floor in the tunnel or on the walkway. Does that answer your question, Dr. Powers? And we aren't even going that way. We're going back."

"Are you insane?" the director of research shouted.

Eos huffed and walked back to a place between turns five and four. The overhead light came back on, and he touched a pen to the wall. "See any cracks here?"

Several people made negative responses.

Eos slapped the wall four times and a door swung open away from them. He turned on the lights and said, "As I said before, ladies and gentlemen, welcome to Salvation Station. By the way, the overhead lights in these last two legs are on a five-minute timer. If our pursuers make it this far, they'll go out the port and never find this door."

Eos closed the door. They were looking into another narrow tunnel, and its lights only extended a few hundred feet. Right before them lay an eight-car minitram. The tiny one-seat open cars had rubber wheels running in grooves in the concrete.

"This is unbelievable. Sheer madness." The director of operations rocked her head.

"That's what I told Si after he showed me the design when the lab was being planned twenty years ago. So here we go. All aboard!" Eos took the driver's seat in car one.

"We'll be going about thirty miles an hour, so be careful. It'll take about forty minutes to go twenty miles. All in the dark in a four-foot-wide straight tunnel. But don't worry. This baby has bright headlights and good brakes. Keep your arms inside the car." The tram lurched forward.

The group arrived at the end of the tunnel thirty seconds early. On the side wall was another stairway and port.

"Don't leave anything on the tram," Eos cautioned.

After everyone assembled above ground, Eos closed the self-locking port hatch, also covered with fake grass. "Now, a short hike to our final transportation leg."

In minutes, they arrived at their destination. Before them was a large object on a low platform, covered with a green and brown tarpaulin just inside the edge of a small, flat clearing in the trees.

"Let's uncover our next ride." Eos pointed a finger. "First, we unhook the cover straps from the O-rings. . . . Next, we gently pull it away . . . easy, easy." He nodded toward the two men standing next to him. "Connor, you and Jim fold it up and put it in its bag." Eos opened the luggage compartment and removed the bag from the six-seat helicopter they'd uncovered. "OK, Tony, pull the chocks, disconnect the winch cable, and let it roll down the ramp into the clearing."

BOOK THREE

Chapter 61

Saturday, October 19

With the left side of his head and his hip bandaged, Dan sat up in his old bed in his folks' house. His first morning back in Quincy, he felt at peace, except for the dull ache on the side of his face.

On his nightstand was a stack of Dad's *Boot and Trail* magazines. *Reminds me of all the great hikes Dad and I used to go on.*

He heard a light rap, and Mom pushed the door open enough to poke her head in. "Get any sleep after breakfast, Danny?"

"A little. Hard to sleep with these gashes all over me. I know you can see the bandages on my ear and head where Sirius's bullet grazed me. And the bigger bandage here on my cheek, where a branch lacerated it when a limb came in and nailed Sirius." Dan flipped the covers off to the side to expose the left side of his hip with a large bandage on it. "But I don't know if you've seen the main event where a half-inch-thick branch punctured through my hip tissue and then broke off. I look kind of weather-beaten, but this is nothing compared to what happened to chief executive officer and monster-in-charge, Sirius."

"What was that?"

"Besides the job I did on him in our fight for his gun, the big limb that came in smashed right into the unconscious evil one and severed his lower leg halfway across. They had to amputate it below the knee to save his life."

"It looks like he got what he deserved." Dan's mom patted his shoulder gently. "Well, after that horrible story, I have something to tell you that will cheer your heart, Danny. Lana called. She wants to come over after lunch if you're up to it. I told her that would be fine, OK?"

"Excellent, Mom. Thanks." *And thank You, Lord!*

"Try to go back to sleep. I'll make you something soft to eat after Lana leaves."

Dan nodded and soon fell back asleep on his right cheek with visions of a love coach dancing in his head.

Lana ran up the stairs to the porch and pressed the doorbell. On one arm hung a shopping bag, and in the other, little Angel wearing the blue and white doggie sweater Dan's mother had made. Mrs. Butler opened the door. "Oh, Lana, you look so nice. I'm sure Danny will be thrilled to see you. I'll see if he's awake."

Mrs. Butler returned and motioned for Lana to follow her. She took her to Dan's room, and after the young woman entered, she closed the door gently.

As soon as Angel saw Dan, she jumped out of Lana's arms and onto the bed, yipping and wagging her tail in a wide arc. She climbed on his stomach and licked his right cheek, which he'd turned to her in self-defense.

Lana placed her bag on a chair, then walked over to Dan and put Angel on the floor. She sat on the bed and put her arms around him. Lana held him without words, the way he'd held her hand in the dark silence of her apartment weeks ago. After she'd flicked away her tears, she released him and pulled away, unable to speak. He must have understood. He took her hand and gently pressed it to his lips. Then he spoke, his eyes glistening. "I missed you so much, Lana. That was the hardest part."

"Oh, Dan, I didn't know . . . if I'd ever see you again."

They held each other with their eyes.

A double tap sounded from the door. "May I come in?"

"Sure, Mom."

Lana stood, and Angel jumped back on the bed.

Mrs. Butler came in holding a tray with two glasses of Coke. "I thought you might like these."

"Thank you, Mrs. Butler," Lana said, taking the glasses. Mrs. Butler smiled and left.

Dan got out of bed and put on a robe. "Let's go to the den. It'll be more comfortable. Even though I'll get more sympathy, and maybe some more hugs, if I lie in bed and moan."

After they'd taken the two easy chairs, with Angel settled in under the coffee table, Lana spoke. "From what Inspector Bakewell told us, you got that battle decoration on your face when you disarmed StarWay's CEO. He also said you had a puncture wound in your side."

"Yeah, I was in his office getting last rites when he learned an FBI SWAT team had arrived. He took me hostage at gunpoint to a two-seat helicopter." Dan filled Lana in on the helicopter crash. "Do you know where the lab is? They wouldn't tell me."

"Bakewell said the feds were vague. Somewhere in the Northwest. Do you know what happened to the StarWay personnel?"

"A little," Dan answered. "Three security people fired above the rescuers to create a diversion so Sirius could escape with me. It didn't quite work, and two of them were killed. One wounded. The managers and staff were taken away for questioning and possible prosecution. Sirius, the CEO, the guy who took me hostage, was badly injured when the helicopter crashed and had his leg amputated. Some of the other administrators may have gotten away. Based on what I told the feds about the CEO and Eos, his henchman, I imagine their futures aren't looking too good. Sirius was captured. Not sure about Eos."

"Yes, Bakewell told me that's how they found you," Lana said, "via the EOS clue you left. He said they put out a systemwide alert for information on someone or something named Eos. A senior FBI agent reported his wife dated somebody in college with that nickname. Somehow they found enough information to track down the area where StarWay was located."

"Oh," Dan said. "They also made me wear a watchdog wristwatch. That's been removed and taken for evidence. They're going to close down the lab, pending the investigation and trials."

Should I tell him about my kidnapping? What good would it do? It'd just make him miserable that his situation led to my fright and suffering. Better kept buried on this side of eternity.

"Well, I know you can't be feeling too well—"

"I started feeling better the minute you walked in."

"That's so sweet, but you need to rest, so I'll say goodbye. I left a shopping bag in your room with your favorite cookies."

"Thanks a lot, and thanks for taking care of Angel."

"I enjoyed her. Maybe we should plan an outing to Beaver Lake with our friends, as soon as you feel up to it. I need to fill you in on how we discovered you were taken in the van. You'll love it."

"Can't wait to hear about that. Did you tell the gang I'm home yet?"

"Bakewell told Chumbo and Stevie. I let the others know. They were all ecstatic. Chumbo said he'd come over as soon as he could. The others said after you'd recovered."

"Hey." Dan's face brightened. "Why don't you come here for dinner tonight? My dad will love meeting you."

"I'd like that, if your mom is comfortable having a dinner guest on such short notice."

"Hang on," Dan said. "I'll check."

Dan returned a minute later with his thumb up. "Before you go, I have something to say."

"Uh-oh. This sounds serious."

"It's all good, Lana. I worried a lot during my StarWay detention because of how I treated you after your family dinner. If Sirius had killed me, I'd never have had a chance to apologize. That's why I phoned you from the QU lab the day I was kidnapped. Will you forgive me?"

Tears inched down Lana's cheeks. "Forgive . . . you? I was the one shouting."

"We can forgive each other and start new." Dan smiled down at her, but then his face turned serious. "But I want to tell you something else."

"What?"

Dan held her at arm's length by her shoulders. "Lana, you mean more to me than being my coach. Much more. I want us to be together as a couple. I don't want to see anyone else." His eyes scanned her face. "If you don't want that, I understand."

She leaned into him with her head on his shoulder. "Oh, Dan. You don't know how much I've dreamed that someday you'd say that."

They embraced while Angel bounced around the room.

"As soon as I come back down to earth I have to tell you something else." Lana stepped back and took a deep breath. "Mom wants you over for dinner as soon as you're ready. Think you can manage that?"

"Sure," Dan replied. "Would you do the scheduling for me?"

Lana nodded. She walked over and gave Angel a little scratch. Then Dan accompanied her to the front door.

"I can't wait to meet your dad tonight," Lana said as she stepped out onto the landing.

"I'm sure he'll feel the same way. You know, Lana, if someone with your long list of exceptional qualities can find me attractive, I'll never have to worry about my self-confidence again. Especially because I know your appraisal of men is not just based on physical appearance. And I feel the same about you."

She looked up at the sky, took a deep breath of the brisk air, and walked to her car on cloud nine.

By 9:00 that evening, Dan, Lana, and the senior Butlers had finished dinner and were having dessert and hot beverages in the den. During the meal, while Dan had a mouth full of his mushy food, he'd remarked, "Thish isn't as bad as it looksh."

Angel lay under the coffee table while Lana summarized her team's triumphs.

"That's amazing, Lana," Arnold Butler said. "After what Inspector Bakewell told us you and your team did for Dan, I thought *This girl has to be a genius*. And I was right."

Lana smiled and blushed. "Most of it was done by the rest of the team."

"Maybe so, but now I know who formed and managed the team. The brains behind it. My son owes you his life."

"If the SWAT team hadn't shown up exactly when it did, I'd probably never have left the office of the CEO alive." Dan reached over and squeezed Lana's hand. "Well, coach, I think you deserve a toast. In fact, you deserve a raise."

Everyone laughed, and Dad saluted her. Dan led the Butlers in a round of "For She's a Jolly Good Lady." Lana blushed again, and then excused herself from the room.

Dad turned to Dan. "You know what you've got there? The Queen of Diamonds. And probably the Queen of Hearts, as well."

"It's like this, Dad. Lana and I had an unbelievably affectionate friendship, but we had a talk this afternoon, and now it's going to be a lot more than that."

Mom beamed, and Dad smiled and slowly nodded.

A moment later, Lana returned to her chair. Dan said, "Why don't you tell my parents about your research at QU?"

"Oh, Dan, they wouldn't be interested in that."

"Of course, we would," said Mom. "I'm sure it's *very* interesting."

Lana brightened up. "I'm studying artificial skin materials and promoting wound healing. I've just started animal studies on immersing the specimens in different gases."

"Sounds like a worthwhile endeavor," Dad said. "Please keep us updated."

"I will. And thank you all for the lovely evening and dinner. It was a pleasure to meet you, Mr. Butler. However, I have a big day on campus tomorrow." *Advanced Engineering Math exam!*

"I sure hate to say good night, Lana." Mr. Butler's eyes drooped with sincerity. "But there's one bright spot here. I recorded the

Suarez-Williams boxing match, and now I might watch it. If I'm not knackered out."

"Oh, knackered, is it?" Mrs. Butler cleared her throat. "That'll be the day when Mr. Butler is too tired to watch a boxing match. Wild horses couldn't drag him away from that TV."

~

Sunday, October 20

Early the next evening, Dan hugged his parents goodbye and moved himself and Angel back to his apartment. She licked Chumbo's face and seemed happy Dan was home again, but she also lingered near the door and whimpered over Lana's absence.

"Sounds like you're gonna have to invite Lana here more often to keep my second roommate happy," Chumbo joked, as Dan and he sat together in the den.

"Yeah, and your first roommate too. To put it in your lingo, Chum, Lana and I are now full-time dating!"

Chapter 62

Monday, October 21

The next morning, Dan drove to campus for a recently requested meeting.

He parked in the grad student lot. Chills ran down his back when he passed the spot where his car had been the night he was kidnapped. He walked straight to the administration building.

"Good morning, Dan." Dr. Kromer was waiting for him by the entrance. "You look pretty good, except for those bandages on your head. I can't wait to hear what happened. Thanks for coming back to campus on such short notice for this meeting."

"No problem. Do you know what it's about?"

Kromer shrugged. "Your ray gun research? Ha." He motioned for Dan to follow him. "President Bernstein has a PhD in inorganic chemistry. Maybe he knows something about what's going on."

They entered the anteroom to the president's office and approached an unoccupied desk with a nameplate that read *Nora Westland*.

A matronly, middle-aged woman came from the adjacent office and said, "Good morning, Dr. Kromer. This must be Mr. Butler, the most famous person in Quincy, and maybe Virginia, this past month. President Bernstein would like you to go in, please."

"Yes, yes, by all means. Come in, gentlemen." The president walked toward them with his hand out. "I'm Sam Bernstein. Dr. Kromer I know, and you, young man, must be the recently liberated Daniel Butler. Shall we sit here at my conference table? Please have some pastries and coffee."

Kromer demurred, but Dan reached for an apple strudel and a cup of coffee. *Ahh. Joy.*

"Daniel, I hope you're feeling better."

"Yes, I am. Thank you."

"From what the investigators learned from the interrogations," Bernstein continued, "the people at StarWay had developed a theory they called vibricity that predicted the existence of the phenomenon you'd been observing in our lab here. But triggering vibricity required something that wasn't present during their earlier experiments. So they didn't get any increase in the power of their lasers. And that's why they needed you there."

"Correct," Dan said. "But I couldn't make it work there the way it did here, and they were preparing to eliminate me when the SWAT team arrived."

"The hand of God. That's unbelievable. What could've been in our lab that they didn't have?"

"I have no idea. They built an exact duplicate of our lab and equipment."

"That's what I want you and your advisor to find out. Suspend your original thesis research topic for a few months and work full-time on laser power-enhancement research. Here's my proposal." He handed them each a copy.

PROJECT DELTA

1. Larger and more secure laboratory space in another building.
2. Research budget of $60,000 for the first six months.
3. Additional funds for a second science/engineering graduate assistant, working under Dr. Kromer and Mr. Butler.

4. Ability to replace current equipment with new equipment, if necessary, to reduce possibility of erroneous results.
5. Other needs (including further financing) negotiable.

Dan and Kromer read the sheet, and Bernstein continued. "We'll need total confidentiality to protect any patent rights. The university would own any patentable inventions. However, university-based inventors receive fifty percent of all net patent income."

Bernstein looked at Kromer and then Dan. "What do you say, gentlemen?"

Kromer looked at Dan. "What do *you* say?"

"I'm in," Dan answered. "Everything I've seen so far tells me we have a puzzle with a critical missing piece, and I want to find it."

"One other matter, gentlemen," Bernstein added. "I'm going to tell Ms. Young that you two have carte blanche communication privileges. Whenever either of you calls about anything related to Delta, she'll put you through to me as soon as possible."

Two hours after the meeting, Lana and Dan sat together near the campus fountain. "I won't be able to eat my sandwich until you tell me what Dr. Bernstein said."

"But you can only tell your parents, if you accept the offer I have for you."

"Another offer?" They both chuckled.

"Bernstein wants to give me a special assignment for up to six months to track down the laser anomaly. A new lab, new equipment, and sixty kiloclams too!"

"Sixty thousand dollars? Good heavens."

"And here's the best part." He took out a piece of paper from his shirt pocket and read it to her. "'Additional funds for a second science/engineering graduate assistant working under Dr. Kromer and Mr. Butler.' Got any ideas who might want to fill that spot?"

"Hmm," Lana answered. "Sounds like you're offering *me* this wonderful opportunity. But what about my PhD? What about my advisor's permission?"

"Look, Lana, everything's in God's hands, but taking off a few months from your research won't matter that much in the long run, especially if we strike oil. We'll both be able to get any job we want after graduation, hopefully at the same place. There'll be royalties from any patents we receive, and we'll split them fifty-fifty."

Dan handed Lana the paper. "As far as your advisor, Dr. Wilson, is concerned, listen to this. The president said Kromer and I were getting special privileges to contact him at any time. He's really excited about this project. If necessary, I'm sure he'll"— Dan coughed—"*talk* Dr. Wilson into letting you go on a special assignment for a few months. Wanna give it a try?"

"After all we've been through? Absolutely! Plus, we get to spend more time together."

They jumped up, holding hands, and spun around like kids under a sprinkler.

Is it possible? Be with him all day? Thank You, Lord.

When Dan returned to his lab, he called his advisor and told him about Lana. Dr. Kromer said he'd check with Dr. Wilson and let Dan know the results.

Before Kromer left for the day, he called Dan back. Wilson had confirmed Lana's transfer for up to six months.

Chapter 63

Tuesday, October 22

New partner. New lab. The paperwork was being completed for Lana's transfer. And the two grad students dove into their joint research with joy.

"I had to reload my lab notes into my laptop from my backup flash drives," Dan confessed. "I can easily afford a new laptop computer now, but the old one still works." *I better let the IT people check it for StarWay malware.*

"Funny." Lana had a little smirk on her face. "I'm your old love boss and you're my new lab boss."

"Finally, I get to be in charge." Dan grinned as he gave Lana a tour of the brand-new lab and its equipment. She asked lots of questions.

"Well, partner, are you ready to start researching?" Dan asked.

"I'm raring to go." Lana gave him one of her heart-stopping smiles.

They worked all morning and half of the afternoon without a trace of an increase in the laser output.

"Let's take a walk around the old lab," Lana suggested. "Maybe something you left there was influencing the results."

When they arrived at Dan's old lab, Joe was busy at work.

"Hey, pal, how's it goin'?" Dan asked. "Getting lonely here?"

"Definitely. But I see you're not. Hey, Lana."

Dan turned to his new lab mate. "Lana's been kind enough to accept a temporary assignment in Kromer's lab to help unravel this laser business. We needed a break. We decided to walk through my old hangout and see if we could dig up any clues."

"Sure. But you'd better hurry. Ron Steinberg's movin' in tomorrow."

"Ron?" Dan's voice cracked. "What's that all about?"

"I needed a safety partner, and Ron's research is mostly based on computer simulations, which he can do anywhere. And that opens up his old space for other students."

"Ron's a good guy," Dan said. "I was feeling guilty about getting a new lab and leaving you high and dry. We'll just look around for a few minutes."

After they'd finished their inspection, Lana walked over to Joe. "What kind of gases are in those bottles against the wall?"

"I use a bunch of different gases in my research. Why?"

"Lana also uses gases in her research," Dan interjected. "Maybe you two should compare notes."

"Will you give me a list of what you've been studying?" Lana asked.

"You can have my entire gas usage history. I always keep these two flash drives plugged into my laptop to back up all my data and inventory files. My software keeps track of everything." Joe pointed toward the computer on his desk. "Lemme eject one of them for you.

"By the way, Lana, Carter Edwards and I went roller skating together—kind of like a date."

"Glad to hear it, Joe."

He made a few keystrokes and pulled out one of the flash drives. "Here. Copy this into your computer. Just search for the file named 'gas inventory.' Let me know if you see any similarities with your thesis work."

When Lana and Dan got back to their lab, she plugged the flash drive into her laptop and tapped away at the keyboard.

"Checking those gases, eh?" Dan put his hands behind his head and leaned back in his chair.

"Here's the file he mentioned. Let's see what he's got. Hmm. Gas name. List of start and finish times for every run. Dan, can we compare his runs with your signal boosts?"

"OK. But I don't see how any gases got from Joe's bottles into my crystals. But since I also have my data runs logged in my computer, let's move our laptops to the big table and compare notes."

They set up their computers, and Dan read out Joe's data. First, he read the dates and times of Joe's calibration runs using air while Lana checked for laser signal increases. No enhancements.

Then they went on to Joe's runs with pure nitrogen gas. Nothing.

"Dang it, Lana, I've been running around so long chasing after the cause of the power boost in the laser beam. Running, and yet I feel like we're standing still. We're . . . uh—"

"Moving yet still . . . kinetic but static . . . kine-static!" Lana exclaimed.

"Kinestatic! Like running on a treadmill. What an interesting word." Dan beamed. "Oh well, back to work."

Next Dan read out the runs where the first small signal increases had been seen.

"This is interesting," Lana said. "Every one of the runs with the smaller signal boosts came when Joe was using argon gas. But argon is a noble gas. It doesn't make any chemical reactions. Weird."

"OK, partner. Here are the runs where the signal increases are getting larger."

As he read out the day and time of each run, Lana checked the gas in use. "They all had neon gas. That's a lighter noble gas than argon. Still no chemistry. Wow. I see where this is going." Her voice became melodic.

After the largest signal increases were vetted, Lana jumped up. "It's helium! The lightest noble gas. Hooray!"

They gave each other high fives. "The largest signals," Dan crowed, "were *all* taken when helium gas was in Joe's system!"

Since there wasn't enough room for dancing, they stood and hugged.

"Now hang on," Dan said. "How could that helium gas get from Joe's system into my crystals? There must be a leak in his apparatus. I'm gonna call him right now."

"Wait a minute." Lana frowned and put her fingers on her cheek. "Any leak had to have been slow or Joe would have noticed it by the gas pressure drop. But that means there's not much of it going into the air. And even less makes it to your apparatus and gets absorbed by the crystal. Can that work?"

"I don't know, and we don't know how much is needed to trigger the phenomenon. But the laser boosts correlate perfectly with Joe's gases, so let's find out what he did."

Dan took out his phone and called Joe. "Quick question—and Lana's here so I'm putting you on speaker. You notice any leaks in your gas lines?"

"No. Why?"

"Because we have strong evidence your gases got into my apparatus and triggered the laser boosts," Dan said, breathing fast and hard. "Do you know how that might have happened?"

"Sure. From my gas dumps when I changed the pressure for my various runs. To avoid turning the gas pump on and off, I always went to the highest pressure first. After that run was finished, usually twenty or thirty minutes, I'd bleed off some gas until the pressure dropped to the next lower value needed. Take more data. Bleed off more gas, and so on."

"Where did you bleed it to?" Lana called out excitedly.

"The gases I've been using have been nontoxic and nonflammable, so they went right into the air. I installed a small fume hood to dump toxic or flammable gases into for future runs. I'll do that for gases like ammonia, hydrogen, oxygen."

"What direction did the vented gasses go in?" Dan asked.

"Let me think." There was a slight pause. "Wow. You're not going to believe this."

"What?" Dan felt his heart beating.

"It goes right toward your apparatus."

"Unbelievable! That's it! Thanks. Gotta run, Joe." Dan punched the end call icon on his phone.

"Wow," Lana said. "Dumping those odorless gases into the air here would have released *thousands* of times more gas than a slow leak would!"

With his heart pounding, Dan called Dr. Kromer and explained their breakthrough. From the other end of the line came a "yahoo" followed by "I'll be there in five minutes."

When Kromer entered the lab, Dan said, "Behold the genius!" and held his hand out toward Lana.

"You are amazing, Lana. And on your first day? Your story, young woman, will be told for years to come."

Lana gulped and grabbed the table.

They sat down before the two computers and reviewed the findings. "I'm convinced," Kromer said. "What a discovery! Dumping noble gases into the air, eh? No wonder nobody got anywhere at StarWay. The reason there's a tiny signal increase even with no helium dumps is because there's a tiny amount of noble gases, including helium, already in the atmosphere. Right?"

"Yeah, and the reason it drops after Joe stops running is the helium slowly bleeds back out of the rod. Amazing." Dan looked up at the ceiling and raised his hands.

"Well, helium doesn't react chemically, so it must be physics!" Kromer added. "Shall we borrow some helium from Joe Stanley?"

"There's some in the storage room," Dan said.

Within half an hour, they'd wrapped a garbage bag around Dan's apparatus and filled it with helium. They waited thirty minutes to allow absorption into the YO crystal and then fired up the laser. The laser sensor read 7508.

Kromer slapped his forehead. "What? The laser power jumped *seventy-five times higher*. Unbelievable! Let's wait and give the rod time to absorb more helium. Anyone for coffee?"

In the second run, the sensor shot up past 30,000. Kromer dropped onto a chair with his legs straight out and his hands on his forehead. He could barely talk. "*Three hundred* times higher!"

There was a loud zapping sound, and the system shut down.

Dan looked at his advisor. "What happened?"

Kromer shrugged. "Let's have a look. I can't wait to let Dr. Bernstein hear about this."

There was a burning smell, and a thin trail of smoke rose from the left end of the setup.

"It's the laser light sensor. Look at this." Dan removed the sensor, holding it with a pair of needle-nose pliers. "We fried it!" Smoke drifted from a black hole in the center of the sensor.

Kromer touched it lightly and jerked his finger back. "You did it, team! A lab laser powerful enough to burn a hole through a light sensor should be enough to convince anyone that vibricity is real. Let me take a photo of that with my phone. I'll send it to Dr. Bernstein tonight. On second thought, let me have the sensor itself. I'll take it over to his office tomorrow, instead of emailing a photo. You never know who might be watching. I can't wait until Dr. Bernstein sees this thing. He's going to go ballistic."

The two students turned and caught each other's eyes.

Chapter 64

Wednesday, October 23

Lana met Dan at 7:00 a.m. at the park near her apartment.

"Good morning, Dan. Thanks for suggesting this," Lana said, sitting on a bench as he approached. "Glad you brought Angel along. Come here, sweetie."

"I assume you're talking to the dog," Dan said.

Lana chuckled and took Angel into her lap.

"This time of year is perfect for brisk morning walks." Dan took a deep breath. "Just point the way you wanna go."

A few single runners passed them. Some had dogs, too, and Angel barked at them all.

"I guess she doesn't want any of them to feel left out," Dan said, grinning at his pup.

"Are we still on for dinner tonight at Mom and Dad's?" Lana asked.

"Of course. Your call yesterday was the third best thing that happened this past week."

"What were the other two?"

"First was seeing you again, followed by being rescued before Sirius killed me."

Lana took his arm as they continued their stroll. She wasn't sure her feet were touching the ground.

"I've got good news for you, partner," Dan said. "Tentative and confidential but very promising."

"What's that?"

"Bernstein told Kromer he has some plans for us."

"Really?"

"Yep. Kromer said I could share this with you but no one else. He said if things continue to go well, he may recommend us both for faculty appointments when we graduate. He may even start a laser-power program and put us in charge. Of course, it's up to the department chairs and deans and a bunch of faculty committees to handle the official details. How about that? They never give out faculty appointments at graduation."

Lana held her arms out and did a ballerina turn. "Sandcastles in the air. But that's very kind of Dr. Bernstein to think so highly of us. Have you thought about what you want to do after you graduate? You're several years ahead of me."

"That's about all I've been doing. When I'm not thinking about you—or lasers."

"I'm glad I have *light* competition." Lana gave him an elbow.

"Seriously," Dan said. "I think we have a future together in laser power research, even though neither of us are trained in that area. Kromer said we'd be a shoo-in for big research grants. We could hire faculty and post-doctoral students working in that area, and we could brainstorm and manage things. Of course, that depends on what you think about this."

"Thanks a lot. I'm glad you think we should work together in the future. I've been thinking the same thing.

"And there's something else I want to tell you," Lana said. "It happened when we first met."

"In The High Note?"

"No, before that. It happened on Campus Awareness Day. Do you remember it, Mr. T?"

"Are you serious? That was you?"

"Why didn't you contact me, Dan?"

"I couldn't. Like an idiot, I handed *your* ID card, instead of mine, to one of the other women and didn't discover the mistake until after you'd left. I was miserable over that."

"That makes me feel much better."

"How'd you know it was me?"

"I had several clues. Your voice. Hair. Build. Aftershave. But I couldn't be sure, not having seen your face."

"I felt a vague familiarity about you, too, Lana, the night of The High Note. Same factors except the voice—darned laryngitis— and aftershave, of course. I should have realized it was you. But why didn't *you* say anything before now?"

"I wanted to wait until I was ready to tell you something else. And I'm almost there."

She took a deep breath and exhaled a silent sigh. *So he did want to contact me but couldn't. I could have but didn't. Oh, all the could haves and should haves of life. But it's all coming to a beautiful conclusion.*

Chapter 65

At 7:00 that evening, Lana and Dan were back in Cedarwood Falls at the door of her parents' home. Lana's heartbeat picked up when she pressed the bell.

Her mom opened the door, looked at Dan, and began crying. She hugged Dan so hard he almost dropped the vase of red roses he was trying to hand her. Then Lana teared up. Even Dad and Dan got a little misty-eyed. *I can't believe this. I wonder what Pastor Silverberg told Mom.*

Her mother took the roses and swapped them with her purple asters on the dining room table. She came back and hugged Lana.

After everyone else had seated themselves in the den, Ann stood in the center of the room. "Before I say anything else—oh, Lord, let me keep speaking—I want to tell Dan—" With that she broke down, but she gripped her hands together and burbled on, barely intelligible. "Thank you for giving a foolish . . . old . . . woman a second chance."

"Don't worry, Mrs. Madison, I'll give you and Dr. Madison all the chances you need, as long as you'll extend the same courtesy to Lana and me when we need it." Dan walked over and took her mom's hand, which he held for a long moment and then pressed to his cheek. Warmth rose in Lana's face and exhilaration in her heart.

"Do you mind if I take Dan on a tour of our flower and rock gardens?" Lana asked. "Maybe we'll catch something still in bloom."

Lana's mother nodded. "Take the flashlight. Some of the sedum still have bronze flowerheads. Clara is off today, so you'll have to bear with my cooking."

The dinner conversation glowed with warmth and fellowship. Everyone complimented Mom on her scrumptious beef tenderloin. They also admired her beautiful table centerpiece, which caused a lot of grinning. The dinner proceeded as though Dan were part of the family already.

After dinner, they all settled back in the den for dessert. Dan got up. "Before we eat this wonderful homemade pie, Lana and I have an announcement to make. Lana, will you stand with me?"

Dad smiled and touched his chin, but Mom's expression tightened a bit.

"Actually, two announcements. First, the important one. Lana and I are now, as my roommate would say, a full-time dating couple."

Both parents came and hugged them. "My heartiest congratulations," Dad said, and Mom added, "You two deserve all the Lord's blessings, and mine too."

"Thank you both from the bottom of our hearts. And now, before I divulge it, I have to ask you both to give us your solemn promise you won't breathe a word about this to anyone outside these four walls."

Her parents nodded.

"Last night, Lana, my thesis advisor, and I checked out an idea together that Lana came up with about the laser power enhancement we've been working on. Her idea worked better than we dreamed possible. We made the laser power three hundred times bigger. The university should be able to patent this invention, and we, as coinventors, will get fifty percent of the net income. My advisor, Dr. Kromer, might be awarded part of that amount, and I'd fully support that. He's the world's best advisor."

"Patents require nondisclosure—that's why we need confidentiality. If this all materializes, I may not have to worry much about money anymore. We'll both want to devote a lot of any windfall we receive to humanitarian efforts. And to make our priorities clear, Mrs. M, your expression of love means more to us than any patent royalties we might receive."

"That's very sweet, Dan. I like the nickname you gave me, but please feel free to call me Ann, if you like."

Chapter 66

Saturday, October 26

Azure skies and mild temperatures framed the autumn weekend. Lana and Dan had invited their four friends to the Beaver Lake outing she'd planned. They came in three cars. Dan and Lana. Joe and Carter. Chumbo and Stevie.

After everyone had chatted for a while, Lana stood and rapped the picnic table.

"Since it's already eleven, how about if we have a Frisbee competition and then have lunch? Afternoon events are recitations of the poems or limericks you were all invited to write and a long walk around the lake trail. OK?"

"How about we wait until dark for the walk in the woods?" Joe kidded.

"Very funny," Carter answered. "Actually, that might not be such a bad idea." Everyone chuckled.

"Listen up, please, for the Frisbee toss," Lana said. "Dan'll explain the rules."

"All right. That trash can I put out there's the target. Five points for hitting it. Three for ending up closest. One point for second closest. Ten points wins. Ready?"

After several rounds, Joe led with eight points, Dan had six, Carter, five. The others all had four points. When Carter, last in the rotation, came up, Dan stood to earn three points and Stevie one. Carter swung her arm way back and grunted as she let go. It landed far to the right and rolled. Everybody cheered. It kept rolling and ended up leaning against the can. The group cheered even louder. She won with thirteen points. Carter took a mock bow and got five hugs. Joe's lasted the longest.

Into the friendly chatter over lunch, Chumbo threw out a wisecrack. "Hey, roomie. The word on the street is you're giving your love coach a new title. You're dropping the word *coach*.'"

Everyone applauded, and Dan got up and took a bow. Lana was radiant.

"We got six people here," Joe said, not to be outdone. "Paired as three couples. Anybody wanna venture a guess as to who will still be together two years from now?"

Utter silence prevailed until Chumbo piped up. "Yeah, Dan and me." Everybody cracked up.

Next came the love fest. They drew lots and did it by couples. First, the guy would declare his feelings, then the girl.

Joe removed his baseball cap and held it toward Carter. "Here's my poem:

Under the wide and starry sky
I'll take her, for a kiss to try.
After I know my Carter more.
She'll get that kiss, now that's for sure."

After some polite applause, Dan asked, "Hey, Joe, what was your grade in English composition?" This was followed by a burst of laughter.

Then Carter jotted off a mixed-form poetic response:

"So, we'll go on a hill one dark night.
Just to look at the heavens' starlight.
But even if I don't resist,
He'll leave me there without a kiss.
And I'll tell him to go fly a kite!"

She added, "Keep dreamin', Joe." Everyone bellowed.
Next Chumbo stood and recited his masterpiece.

> "This ain't no mumbo-jumbo.
> I love you, Stevie!
> Chumbo."

There were laughs and guffaws. Joe yelled, "Way to go, Dante!"
Stevie's was next:

> "Oh, my heart's in the hands of my Chum,
> Since he's given up beer, wine, and rum.
> I never am blue,
> 'Cause to me he is true,
> If I keep him right under my thumb."

Her limerick got a big round of applause.
Dan hesitated before reading his poem. But he chuckled the whole way through it.

> "Does Lana love me? Maybe not.
> She keeps me in a guessing spot.
> And teaches me the way to woo,
> But never tells me 'I love you.'"

This brought the house down.
Lana responded with a limerick admonishing her student.

> "I once met a guy in a lab,
> So smart and so cute; he was fab.
> Till he got in a van,
> And away went our Dan,
> Now I let him take only a cab."

Lana received a standing ovation. She stood looking at him, and he filled her heart. *Today I tell him the whole story.*

Finally, the group split into couples to take the wooded, two-mile trail around the lake.

Words came into Lana's heart and mind as their friends walked away.

It is the summer of our youth that only comes once.

Since the other couples had gone off hand in hand, Lana took Dan's. "This will be a lovely stroll in the shade. Dan, I feel so close to you."

"Me too. Gorgeous day, a gorgeous girl, and a forest bursting with fall color. Who could ask for more?"

"Let's walk in silence for a while, Dan. I want to inhale all this. Then I'll tell you the final chapter of my story." Finally, she would reveal her heart. Over two months after they'd met face-to-face at The High Note and ten weeks from the Mask and Meet. Two days she would never forget.

They moved through the woods, and the only sounds were their footfalls, bird calls, and rustling leaves.

Lana broke the silence first. "May I tell you my story about The High Note?"

"I'd love to hear it."

"I asked Tom Highland, my long-time buddy, who moved away recently, to be my escort that night and help *me* find someone desirable. We'd visit restaurants, cafés, wherever, to look around. I thought being with a man would make me less conspicuous, and I'd feel less like a lioness-hunter. Then we'd settle near the person I'd selected. After a few minutes, Tom would leave, opening the door for the gentleman of interest to approach me.

"Tom was reluctant because he's shy, too, but he agreed to try. We went into The High Note, listened to the music for a while, and then he followed me across the room while I looked around to check out the men. I was getting ready to leave and try another café. But I saw someone, and I stopped and sat at a table."

"Who'd you see?"

"I saw you."

"What?" Dan halted. "You two stopped near me and acted out that scene to catch my attention?"

She smiled at him but shook her head. "We didn't act anything out. We just talked until we got tired and frustrated. He wanted me to encourage you, but that's not my style. So he gave up and left. I glanced at you a couple of times, but you didn't do anything. Then that horrible man came over, and you know the rest."

"And the whole time before my vacation at StarWay," Dan stared at her and grasped his head, "I thought you liked me but not in a romantic way. Lana, ever since I met you, I've been in love with you. But I couldn't admit it to myself and suffer the heartbreak of rejection. I didn't dare let you know, either, because I thought it might scare you away. But when they put me in the torture cell at StarWay, I realized how much you meant to me. Only after our decision to see only each other did I realize you felt the same as I do."

Lana looked up at him, took a deep breath and smiled. "Well, Daniel Butler, it looks like I'm going to be your *permanent* love coach—but only if you let me give you the personal attention you deserve."

Dan drew Lana close. She raised her lips to him for the first time. Like sugar in a frying pan, she melted in his arms. He kissed her and then whispered in her ear.

"I waited a long time for this lesson."

Taking her hand, he slowly guided her off the trail and into the woods. They stopped in a clearing where clouds of magenta flora glimmered above a knee-deep field of grass in the soft breeze of the late afternoon sun.

"This is perfect, darling," Lana whispered.

Dan tilted Lana back and eased her into the tall grass. Then he dropped to his knees, bent over her, and their lips met again.

They lay side by side for a long time, interspersing kisses with sweet words of love.

The sun had set, and a mulberry sky layered the darkening western horizon when the couple rose again.

"Do you know what we've been immersed in all this time, princess?"

"Not really. Tell me, my Hercules."

"Purple love grass."

Epilogue

"Sunrise on Christmas morning at the high end of Greenacres Park. What a wonderful way to spend our first Christmas together." Lana's heart was bursting with love, joy, and thankfulness, and Dan's smile, expressive, drawn-in eyes, and slowly nodding head showed he understood her sentiments and felt the same.

I'm so glad you suggested we open our presents to each other this way, Dan. And the three-inch snowfall a few days ago put an exclamation point on your idea!

"We're just high enough to see over the trees," she said. "Look at that beautiful view of the snow-covered homes and landscaping in the Quincy suburbs. And the downtown in the distance."

"Couldn't agree more." Dan had a look like he was getting ready to say something clever. "But I'm very familiar with being just high enough to see over the trees."

They both had a good chuckle, although Lana wished she had used better wording. He turned to her for one of their long embraces, with sweet words and a kiss at the end. "You know, princess of my heart, I think I must have been killed in that helicopter crash, because I know I'm in heaven right now."

She turned and kissed his cheek. "OK, Dan, I now *officially* resign from my job. You certainly don't need any more love coaching."

They walked hand in hand back to the car, parked a few hundred feet away. He picked up his present for her and the snow

311

coverings. She took the small, insulated carrier with their breakfasts and cinnamon-spiced hot cider and her presents.

When they reached their spot again, marked by their tracks in the snow, Dan spread out his large rubber exercise pad and carefully centered the thick blanket on it. They put the rest of their belongings on the blanket and sat.

"You look fantastic since Dad eliminated the scars on your head. Just a touch of discoloration remaining, which we'll soon take care of."

"Really?" Dan kissed her cheek three times.

"Lana, I wish I could tell you how much I love you. But it would take too long."

"How long might that be, gallant sir?"

He thought for a moment. "The time is best expressed as one divided by zero."

"Eternity!" Lana's eye's opened wide as she took Dan by the shoulders and kissed him. He kissed her hands back and forth and gave her the present, a beautifully wrapped package, with glossy green paper and a red ribbon.

"Ooh, I'm too excited to open it." She opened the present carefully, like a surgeon entering a king. A maroon leather-bound book with gold foil lettering and scrim caressed her heart. Raised bands decorated the spine of the book. The title was *My Search for Lana* and below it, Daniel J. Butler. As Lana perused the pages, warm tears ran down her cold cheeks.

"Oh, Dan, it's the most precious gift I've ever received. It even starts at the Mask and Meet. My gifts will seem so paltry in comparison."

"How can a gift from my eternal love be paltry? If you gave me a rusty nail, I would frame and treasure it all my life."

She sighed softly and handed him her first gift. Red paper with a green ribbon and bow. He pointed to the decorating materials lying untorn by her side, and they both chuckled.

While he was unwrapping his gift, Lana mused out loud, "You know, maybe I'll write a book and call it *My Search for Dan*." That got a snicker out of him as he opened the unwrapped box and took out a dinner plate–sized wooden heart. The wood had a rich, natural grain ranging from dark brown to light tan tones. On it was carved *DB and LM.*

"It's gorgeous, Lana. Tell me about it."

"I made it myself. It's acacia wood. Like the wood God commanded His people in the Bible to use to make holy objects. My first woodcarving project."

Dan stood and helped Lana up. "I will treasure your heart all my life," he said. They kissed and swayed.

"And this other gift is just something I hope will come in handy for you."

Dan said, "I'm not quite sure what it is, darling."

He opened the second package and touched the shadow of a scar still slightly visible on his face. "A large bottle of my favorite concealer!"